PRAISE FOR THE PEYTON COTE NOVELS

Fallen Sparrow

"This edgy and emotional thrill ride will captivate readers."

—*RT Book Reviews* (4 stars)

"[Keeley's] tough but compassionate heroine triumphs against the odds."

—*Kirkus Reviews*

Bitter Crossing

"The author paints a striking portrait of the northern Maine landscape ... Peyton's strong personality and her unfailing courage should make for some intriguing future adventures."

—*Mystery Scene*

"A solid bet for Nevada Barr and Tricia Fields fans."

—*Library Journal*

"Packed with thrills and high-octane action, *Bitter Crossing* is an impressive debut with a fearless heroine you'll want to follow for many adventures to come."

—Tess Gerritsen, *New York Times* bestselling author of the Rizzoli & Isles series

"*Bitter Crossing* is my favorite kind of page-turner, enlivened by a compelling heroine—U.S. Border Patrol Agent Peyton Cote—and set in a place so strongly described it is almost a character itself: the remote no-man's-land between northern Maine and Canada."

—Paul Doiron, author of *Massacre Pond*

For Linda –

I hope you enjoy
the Book!

destiny's
PAWN

Best,

D. A. Keeley

destiny's
PAWN

A PEYTON COTE NOVEL

D.A. KEELEY

MIDNIGHT INK
WOODBURY, MINNESOTA

FIRST EDITION
First Printing, 2016

Book format by Teresa Pojar
Cover design by Kevin R. Brown
Cover Illustration by Dominick Finelle/The July Group
Editing by Nicole Nugent

Midnight Ink, an imprint of Llewellyn Worldwide Ltd.

This is a work of fiction. Names, characters, places, and incidents are either the product of the author's imagination or are used fictitiously, and any resemblance to actual persons living or dead, business establishments, events, or locales is entirely coincidental.

Library of Congress Cataloging-in-Publication Data

Names: Keeley, D. A., 1970– author.
Title: Destiny's pawn : a Peyton Cote novel / D.A. Keeley.
Description: First edition. | Woodbury, Minnesota : Midnight Ink, [2016]
Identifiers: LCCN 2016003094 (print) | LCCN 2016006725 (ebook) | ISBN
    —9780738742250 (paperback) | ISBN 9780738748856 (ebook)
Subjects: LCSH: Border patrol agents—Fiction. | GSAFD: Mystery fiction
Classification: LCC PS3603.O773 D47 2016 (print) | LCC PS3603.O773 (ebook) |
    —DDC 813/.6—dc23
LC record available at http://lccn.loc.gov/2016003094

Midnight Ink
Llewellyn Worldwide Ltd.
2143 Wooddale Drive
Woodbury, MN 55125-2989
www.midnightinkbooks.com
Printed in the United States of America

This book is for my mother, Connie Corrigan.

ACKNOWLEDGMENTS

Thanks, as usual, to Kevin Stevens, deputy chief of the US Border Patrol (Ret.), for his insights and feedback. The generosity he offers me by sharing his knowledge and time is greatly appreciated and always makes books in this series better.

Thanks also to attorney Marcus Jaynes of Landis Arn & Jaynes for answering a year's worth of questions on immigration and political asylum applications; to Adam Stoutamyer of the Maine State Police for insights into Maine marijuana laws; to commercial fisherman Mike Link for information regarding shipping routes and some history into stowaway travel from Eastern Europe to Nova Scotia; to Kim Sprankle for serving as my undaunted advanced reader; to my agents Ginger Curwen and Julia Lord for being everything to me from advanced readers to cheerleaders, advisors, and friends; to Nicole Nugent (editor), Beth Hanson and Katie Mickschl (publicists), and Terri Bischoff (publisher) at Midnight Ink, for your wisdom, support, and belief, respectively; and, of course, a sincere thank you to Lisa, Delaney, Audrey, and Keeley for your laughter and love.

Power is only vouchsafed to the man who dares to stoop and pick it up.

—Fyodor Dostoyevsky, *Crime and Punishment*

PROLOGUE

The first time Michael saw it, the doll intervened.

Six years old, he followed his uncle Ted, who'd offered to watch him while his parents were at dinner. Ted tucked him in, read him a story, and closed Michael's bedroom door when he left.

Then Michael heard the stairs to the third-floor apartment creak. And he panicked.

Was Uncle Ted leaving him alone?

In the dark?

This night, as a nor'easter blew into Aroostook County from Canada, Michael wouldn't be left behind. Not in the dark house. He was out of bed and following. The narrow, panelled stairway to the upstairs apartment was outdated and dark, lit by a single hanging lightbulb.

The floorboards creaked again.

"Uncle Ted?" Michael's voice was a whisper in the dark. His bare feet padded up the stairs.

His uncle never allowed him up there. "My personal things are up here." He'd always closed the door behind him quickly. Even his father concurred: "It's your uncle's space. Leave him be."

But this time, aware of his in loco parentis *responsibilities, Ted left his apartment door open, unaware his young nephew crept behind.*

Three steps from the top, Michael crouched, peering over the top step, seeing his uncle's flashlight pointing beneath the sofa. Michael could hear windswept snow like sand against the windows. His uncle held the flashlight between his teeth as he tugged a wooden box out from under the couch.

First Michael saw the thick plastic, then red felt. Then he saw something else. His eyes widened and narrowed as he struggled to comprehend the beauty.

Absently his hand brushed something in the dark stairwell. He turned, still crouching, his eyes falling upon the porcelain doll. The figurine beside him had a disfigured face, years ago having melted in the summer heat and frozen during winter before the attic was converted to Uncle Ted's temperature-controlled apartment.

To six-year-old Michael, she looked like the face in the trick mirror at a circus—elongated and frightening. He gasped and recoiled, accidentally knocking her down the stairs.

He bounded down them behind her, the sound of his footfalls drowning in the wake of the doll's crash. He was in his bed, feigning sleep, by the time his uncle descended, picked up the pieces of the doll, and checked on him.

As Michael lay in bed, he heard his uncle reclimb the stairs to his apartment, the place Uncle Ted had lived since March of 1990.

"Stay out of Uncle Ted's apartment," his mother would reiterate many times over the years.

And so the apartment door remained locked.

But in the ensuing years, Michael had learned where the spare key was. It's like visiting a secret place, *he wrote in his diary.* Feels like I'm time-traveling when I go up there. Feels like I'm meeting a deity.

And as he grew older, the wooden box spawned his fascination with history. And with art.

ONE

Monday, March 3, 2:35 p.m., near the Canadian border

BY THE TIME SHE heard him behind her, he'd gotten so close that she instinctively reached for her Smith & Wesson .40 as she turned to face him.

They stood at the tailgate of Border Patrol Agent Peyton Cote's Ford F-150 service vehicle. She'd been loading water bottles into the pockets of her backpack, preparing for a three-mile hike, a routine border sweep, when she'd heard his feet scuff the frozen chunks of dirt and snow behind her.

Now, facing him, she felt nearly embarrassed to be holding her weapon—the boy wasn't much older than her eleven-year-old, Tommy.

So why did she have that feeling, the one that had befallen her hundreds of times before, the one that told her something wasn't right? She didn't immediately reholster her .40. Her sister called it Mother's Intuition; agents called it Field Instinct.

She shuffled her L.L.Bean leather hiking boots, her snowshoes on the ground near her feet. Behind the boy, to the northeast, was a dense, commercially owned forest of eastern pines and Norway spruces.

Peyton knew the boy had emerged from the tree line.

She also knew the woods behind him ran to the Canadian border.

It was a warm morning, one of those glorious late-winter days residents of Aroostook County, Maine, felt they'd *earned* on the heels of a winter that saw temperatures plunge to forty below twice this year and the snowfall total top ninety-one inches (and counting).

"What's your name?" she asked.

Was that a shiver? Or a flinch?

She couldn't tell, but his blond bangs swayed. His face was dirty, his pant leg torn at the knee. Red-cheeked, he'd obviously been outside for an extended period.

A wind gust hit them, and somewhere overhead, a large crow sounded. She took a different approach.

"Like to snowshoe?"

He shrugged, so she kept going.

"I love it, especially on days like this." She pointed to a nearby tree. Sunlight turned ice-covered branches to refractive chandeliers. "It's beautiful out here."

He shook his head and looked down. "Very cold."

Her first reaction was as an agent: she heard the accent. Russian? Her second reaction was as a mother: the boy wore only a hoodie, and beneath it his T-shirt collar was frayed. Where were his hat and mittens? She wouldn't allow Tommy outside dressed like that during winter.

She left her backpack where it was and tossed the snowshoes into the truck's bed.

"Come sit in my truck," she said and moved to the passenger's-side door. She opened it for him.

He looked at her. She nodded reassuringly, and he climbed in. She rounded the hood, got behind the wheel, started the engine, and set the internal temperature to seventy-two.

"Are you lost?"

"No," he said. The skin near his eyes was pale. Dehydration? His bare hands were raw, the red skin cracked and bleeding. He rubbed them on his thighs, seeking friction to warm them. "Waiting for you," he said.

She'd been reaching for her phone but paused. "You've been waiting for me?"

He looked down at his fingertip. It was split, a white half-moon open where a tiny drop of blood emerged. "For Border Patrol," he said.

She watched him closely. He didn't appear nervous.

"Is that a Russian accent?" she asked.

He nodded.

"Where do you live?"

He shrugged.

"You don't know?" she asked.

"Not anymore."

His cheeks were red, but he wasn't out of breath—he'd been exposed to the elements of the harsh winter for too long.

"You might have frostbite. Tell me your name."

"Aleksei Vann," he said. "I wait to surrender."

Stone Gibson entered Peyton's kitchen wearing a sweat-drenched T-shirt and sweatpants, toting a gym bag.

"You're late," she said, "and you stink."

"Thanks for noticing," he said and kissed the back of her neck, "on both fronts. And I'm sorry. I'm not usually late for a meal. Can I use your shower?"

"You left your razor in there," she said. "Don't dilly daddle. Steak tips are just about ready, and I have salad, bread for Tommy and me, and a six-pack of gluten-free Omission IPA for you."

"Christ," he said over his shoulder, "I'm moving in."

She turned but just caught a glimpse of his wide shoulders rounding the corner as he headed up the stairs. She'd hoped to see his face, wanted to read his expression.

Had he read her mind?

It was nearly dark at dinnertime on this March evening. And that was an improvement: Garrett, Maine, in Aroostook County, was north of Montreal, which meant during December and January each year nightfall came early. Peyton often left the house in early-morning moonlight and returned after the 3:45 p.m. sunset.

She lit a cinnamon-scented candle left over from the holidays. The aroma mixed with the scent of garlic she crushed and put in the pan with the steak. She liked being at home, liked typical domestic activities like cooking dinner. And she liked Stone Gibson, maybe more than she wished. They'd been dating for six months. He was a state trooper, one of four assigned to Aroostook County. They'd met—Peyton was loathe to admit—when her mother's millionth attempt to set her up with a man actually worked. Now he was a large part of her already complicated life: work and Tommy seemed all she could handle. But somehow Stone overturned her emotional apple cart. And she hadn't minded one bit.

She called Tommy in from the living room. He entered the kitchen, cell phone before him, thumbs dancing. "Hey, Mom, can we have *ployes*?"

"Your grandmother makes those so well that I'm not competing with her," Peyton said. "Don't text and walk. You'll hit a wall. And, hey, I thought we discussed what the phone was to be used for."

"Only to call you in an emergency."

"So I assume you're texting *me*. What's the emergency in the living room?" She heard water running in the shower upstairs.

Tommy smiled and shook his head. "Sorry."

"If you weren't so cute . . ." She squeezed his shoulder and kissed his forehead.

"Mom, don't do that in front of Stone."

"If you're bored, don't text. Read a book."

"I will."

"Now, please put the salad on the table."

He slid the cell phone in his pocket and went to the fridge. "Stone said we have a karate competition this weekend, Mom."

"Great," she said. "Can't wait."

Tommy carried the salad to the dining room table.

Peyton returned to the stove and pushed the steak around with a wooden spoon. It was done, so she took the pan off the burner, added a little more garlic, gave one last stir, then scooped the steak tips onto a serving platter to rest.

She hadn't been the only one who benefitted from Stone's return to Aroostook County. School had never come easy to Tommy. And the previous summer, before his dyslexia diagnosis, Tommy had begun karate lessons. Stone Gibson was the instructor. So as Peyton journeyed down fate's odd path, attending a blind date set up by Lois of all people, Tommy had also met and was befriended by Stone.

The water in the upstairs shower stopped. Peyton carried the steak to the dining room table. In less than three minutes, Stone bounded down the stairs and took an end chair.

"Quick shower," Peyton said. "You must be hungry."

"I was going to slide down the banister."

"Glad you didn't."

"Can you teach me how to do that?" Tommy said.

Stone winked at him. "Here's to my favorite Aroostook County people." He raised a chilled glass of Omission IPA.

"You must be forgetting your mother and sister," Tommy said.

"No," Stone said. "You guys are my favorites. You're not crazy."

"Are they *really* crazy?" Tommy leaned forward, eager to hear more.

"Foot in mouth." Stone grinned at Peyton.

She drank her wine. "Everyone has crazy relatives."

"We don't have crazy relatives," Tommy said. "We only have Gram and Aunt Ellie."

Peyton looked across the table at Stone.

"Care to add anything to Tommy's remark?" he asked.

She liked his boyish smirk. "We watched the Celtics game last night," she said.

"You're fast on your feet, agent," he said, smiling. He ate a piece of steak and groaned in obvious appreciation. "How was your day?"

"A thirteen-year-old Ukrainian boy surrendered at the border."

"To you?"

"Yeah. I was near the woods behind McCluskey's Potato Processing Plant, getting ready to sweep the border, and he stepped out from the tree line and walked over to me."

"How did he get here?"

"Long story," she said.

Tommy rolled his eyes. "May I be excused?"

Peyton examined his plate. "Yeah. But I want you to read. No phone."

Reluctantly, Tommy nodded and slid out from the table.

"I'm all ears," Stone said.

"After I did a preliminary interview with the boy, I spent a couple hours on the Internet seeing what I could learn about Ukraine and what's going on there. Then I called a professor from U-Maine at Reeds." She sipped her red wine. "Vladimir Putin's annexation of the Ukraine was particularly harsh in a town called Donetsk, where this boy is from. The airport was demolished. I mean, it's rubble. Still finding bodies a year after the battle there ended."

"I hadn't heard the fighting was that bad."

"Some Ukrainian cities have been turned into third-world countries. Pro-Russian separatists bombed this boy's house. Might've been an accident. You remember Malaysian Air MH17?"

"Of course."

"Well, that was a Buk missile. One hit the boy's house, and his mother was badly injured. A few days later, his father put him on a boat to Nova Scotia, trying to get him to his aunt in Garrett. He's only two years older than Tommy."

"Did he come through the Black Sea?" Stone asked. "Wouldn't that take forever?"

"Not sure about all the travel specifics yet. But, apparently, the father feared for his son's life. I brought the boy—his name is Aleksei Vann—back to the station. His English isn't bad, but his aunt lives in Garrett, so we're hoping to have her help us interview him in the morning."

"Where is he tonight?"

"In DHHS care."

"It must've taken weeks for him to get here. And then Halifax is several hours' drive from Garrett."

She nodded. "This looks carefully planned."

"And well executed." Stone sipped his beer. "Being gluten-free isn't easy," he sighed.

"If anyone can do it"—it was her turn to smirk—"I'm sure it's you, big guy. We're hoping for answers tomorrow. The boy already asked for political asylum."

"He sounds well aware of the immigration mess in Texas and wants a piece of the pie."

"This is different," she said. "He's not asking for amnesty. Political asylum has been granted to people for a long time. The policy exists for cases like this one. Aleksei's mother needs constant care. According to the boy—who, by the way, cried when he told us the story—his father fears for his son, sent him here to live with his aunt in Garrett."

"Sounds like the boy's father thought this through," Stone said.

TWO

THIS OFFICE HAD PROBABLY begun life as a child's room when the building was a three-bedroom ranch. Sunlight shone into Patrol Agent in Charge Mike Hewitt's small office. The office was packed. Susan Perry, from the Maine Department of Health and Human Services; Peyton; and Bill Hillsdale, from the US Citizenship and Immigration Services office in Portland, all sat in metal folding chairs across the desk from Hewitt.

Peyton was surprised by Hillsdale's demeanor. The top USCIS official in the region had come to Garrett on routine visits and usually couldn't go two minutes without adding a dry one-liner to any conversation. Now he looked like he was facing a root canal.

"Good to see you again, Susan," Hewitt began.

She smiled. "You don't mean that, Mike."

"You're right. The last time I saw you we were looking for the mother of an abandoned baby."

"This isn't that bad," she said.

"Not yet," Hillsdale added.

"You're cheery," Susan said to Hillsdale, who shrugged.

"Susan, a woman from the State Department called here today," Hewitt said. "She says Washington is worried that this might set a precedent."

Hillsdale cleared his throat. "We just want to make sure this is handled correctly."

Susan said, "Do you mean *ethically*?"

"Not necessarily." Hillsdale shook his head. "I mean *correctly*."

Hewitt shifted in his leather chair.

"The USCIS people have had lots on their minds over the past couple years," Hewitt said. "We can all understand why they would be jumpy, given what they've been dealing with on the southern line."

"Bill," Peyton said, "Washington sent you to this meeting to make sure the northern border doesn't turn into south Texas in 2014?"

"Ukraine is bad, getting worse, and this kid took a boat from Hamburg, Germany, to Halifax. Stowaways have been doing that for years. But we've never had a thirteen-year-old show up here before. We think this could happen again and possibly escalate."

"The northern border will never become what we saw in Texas. We're not going to see fifty thousand kids walk across the border up here." Peyton shifted in her seat several times, then finally reached to her service belt, unclipped the pepper spray canister digging into her lower back, and dropped it into her pocket. "This is isolated. The kid wants—and qualifies for—political asylum."

"The United States Citizenship and Immigration Services, in conjunction with the State Department, will determine if he qualifies for it," Hillsdale said.

Bill Hillsdale was all of 150 pounds, ran 5Ks, and did a lot of hiking—a makeup typical of many Border Patrol agents. But Peyton got the feeling Hillsdale didn't mind pushing paper as much as he did confrontation. So, she figured, given the choice between Border Patrol and immigration work, he'd made the right career choice.

Hewitt smoothed his shirt front. The silver oak leaf pinned to his lapel designated him PAIC, patrol agent in charge. He wrote something on his legal pad.

"Are those UGGs?" Peyton asked Susan.

Susan smiled. "You always notice my shoes."

Peyton raised a black, ankle-length trail boot. "See why?"

"Ouch," Susan said.

"My boots are Timberland," Hewitt said and grinned, "if anyone cares."

"Can we move on?" Hillsdale was staring at the floor.

"Lighten up, Bill," Hewitt said.

Susan flipped through some notes. "The boy will speak to you this morning. His English is not great. Russian is his native language. Most people in Donetsk speak it. The foster parents should have him here by nine. They told me Aleksei woke in the middle of the night screaming about the explosion that injured his mother. And I've asked his aunt to come as well, to provide emotional support for him and to translate, if needed. Then he'll go home with her afterward."

"I haven't approved that," Hillsdale said.

"You don't need to," Susan said. "The boy is a minor, he has relatives here, and, as far as we know, his father consents to having the boy with his sister, the boy's aunt."

"What his father wants might not be relevant."

"I see," Susan said. "I can rationalize this situation another way for you: His aunt is the only person in this region who speaks the boy's native language. We feel he should be with her."

"Cute," Hillsdale said.

"I can see that you want to make this difficult for the boy," Susan said. "But the fact is, putting him with his aunt is pretty standard."

Peyton shook her head. "If Washington honestly thinks this kid, who you say took a boat from Germany to Halifax, is going to set a precedent, then Washington is even more out-of-touch than I thought. I mean, Ukraine is landlocked, Bill. The kid made two long land journeys as well—first to Germany, then from Halifax to here. This isn't going to happen often, if ever again."

"Don't shoot the messenger. I'm just doing what I'm told, Peyton."

"Well, someone has an agenda," Peyton said. "For God's sake, I've had friends I worked with, agents who dedicated their lives to doing what we do, get shot and killed in the line of duty, so I'm also against letting thousands of illegals walk into the country. But this is an isolated situation. The boy's mother requires constant care, which the father is providing."

"And when she's well?" Hillsdale asked. "Will they follow him here then?"

"Given the severity of her injuries," Susan said, "that could be years, Bill."

"Have some compassion," Peyton said.

Hillsdale looked at her. "You sound more like a mother than an agent."

"Don't insult my agent," Hewitt said.

But it was too late. Peyton had turned to face Hillsdale.

"First off, Bill, I *am* a mother, a single mother, and proud to be a *working* mother. But I was speaking as an agent. And as such, I know what the hell I'm talking about. Don't ever accuse me of getting my two roles mixed up, because you have no idea what it's like to be in the field or, for that matter, to raise a child alone."

Hillsdale sat looking at her. Hewitt centered his legal pad. Susan was staring at the floor.

Hillsdale finally shook his head. "This is going to take months to iron out. There'll be lawyers and Washington officials involved, I'm sure." He stood. "Tell the boy he can go with his aunt temporarily. But be clear that this isn't permanent." He looked at Hewitt and nodded, then walked out.

Hewitt looked at the two women across from him. "Peyton, you're the first person Aleksei Vann met. I'd like you to interview him this morning."

She nodded.

"Obviously," Hewitt continued, "Bill's report will most likely recommend the boy return to the Ukraine. If I were you two, I'd anticipate Washington sending a bigger gun the next time we meet about this."

Both women stood.

Peyton said, "You think the comparison to Texas is crazy, too, don't you, Mike?"

"I don't get paid to express opinions on political situations, Peyton." He shifted his legal pad again. "And, frankly, neither do you."

With that, the meeting was over.

Aleksei Vann didn't look thirteen. Not up close.

Up close, he looked even younger than Tommy. He was in clean clothes, his blond hair had been washed, his blue eyes were clear now, his cheeks were no longer red, and his hands weren't grimy. For all its flaws, the foster care system, Peyton thought, at least in this case, had done its job—the boy looked rested, clean, and even well fed.

Peyton was sitting across the breakroom table from him, her bag at her feet. This wasn't her typical interview. No jingling handcuffs, no lawyers. Her iPhone lay between them on the table, ready to record the conversation. Next to it stood three bottles of orange juice, two apples, and two jelly donuts. Susan Perry was to meet with the boy afterward, and, eventually, Hillsdale would return. Or, based on what Hewitt said at the end of their meeting, Washington would send someone else to meet with Aleksei.

"Aleksei, do you remember me?"

He nodded and looked at the orange juice. "Coca-Cola today?"

She smiled. "Maybe later. It's only nine in the morning. I'm Agent Cote. You can call me Peyton."

"Peyton?" he said, his accent drawing her name out in two long syllables—*Pee-tone*. His eyes fell to the iPhone, its red recording button glaring.

"Yes. That's my first name."

"Are you record what I say?"

"Not if you don't want me to."

He looked from the iPhone, to her, and back to the phone, his tongue licking his chapped lips.

Casually, she reached forward and picked the phone off the table and slid it into her pocket. "You've taken quite a trip. Want to tell me about it?"

He shrugged, his smile vanishing. He turned to stare at the floor and picked at the cuticle of his thumb, his hands dancing as if independent from his body.

Clearly the question made him uncomfortable. Had he been told not to tell anyone how he'd gotten here? If so, by whom? His father? She hadn't asked Bill Hillsdale where he'd learned the boy took a ship from Germany, but she assumed Hillsdale had questioned Aleksei Vann himself. And if that was the case, and the boy had spoken freely to Hillsdale, why was he balking now? She'd long existed in a male-dominated and militaristic professional world. Meeting men who saw her as weak and who were less cooperative because she was female was nothing new. But she'd never had that reaction from a thirteen-year-old before.

"Aleksei, you are thirteen?"

"Yes." He bit into a jelly donut. She'd asked Miguel Jimenez to prepare the room. Leave it to Jimenez, who played the same games on his phone that Tommy did, to consider donuts an appropriate breakfast for a teenager.

"I have a son a little younger than you. I couldn't imagine him making the trip you made. Were you alone?"

"Yes."

"How did you get from the Ukraine to Germany?"

He shrugged.

"Has anyone asked you that?"

"No."

"Did you meet with a man yesterday?" She described Hillsdale to him.

"Yes. I tell him."

"Did you tell him how you got from Ukraine to Germany?"

"No."

"Why not?"

"He did not ask," he said, turning *did* to *deed*.

She had the iPad on her lap and had been typing notes on the virtual keyboard, but stopped. Had Hillsdale been so quick to have his theory proven—that the boy had made it from Eastern Europe to the northern US border (and, thus, it could happen again)—that he failed to learn any details of Aleksei's trip? She wanted to give Hillsdale more credit than that.

"Well, I'm asking," she said. "How did you get from the Ukraine to Germany? That's a long way."

Aleksei pushed away from the table and looked down at the floor.

She would try something else. Asking a specific question based on his recent experience meant he'd be more likely to confirm or deny, and thus less likely to shut down.

"Did you fly to Hamburg, Aleksei?"

"Fly?" he asked.

"Yes. Did you take a plane?"

He shook his head. "Car. Then walk a long time."

"To Hamburg, Germany?"

He nodded.

She'd done her homework: it took nearly thirty hours to drive (or seven to fly) from Donetsk to Hamburg.

"Tell me about it. When did you leave?"

"February third, my mother birthday."

"Your mother's birthday?"

"Yes. My father say sending me was promise to her. And he keep it."

"He promised to send you here, so he did so on her birthday?"

He nodded and finished his orange juice. "Coca-Cola now?"

She smiled. "Soon. Your mother—"

"She was hurt by the fucking bastards."

Peyton was taken aback by his anger. Thirteen. Looked even younger. His words came from someplace deep inside him, from a place only someone with his life experiences knew. He'd seen death and destruction up close at a young age. Tommy would never know that anger. Neither would she. They were lucky, and she knew it.

"The 'bastards' are the pro-Russians?"

"Yes. Putin want take back all the land." A smile formed on his face then—not one of humor, but one of pride. "But Father will not let that. He staying to fight."

"Your home is in Donetsk?"

"Yes."

"Tell me about driving and walking to Hamburg."

The boy picked up the second donut and stared at it, holding it without taking a bite.

"You don't want to talk about it?"

"My father leave me at boat." Overcome with sudden emotion, his pale face flushed quickly. "He go back..."

"You thought he was making the trip with you?"

He nodded. "But then say he stay to fight."

"And you were on the ship a long time?"

"Yes, long time."

"Who knew you were on the boat?"

He looked at her, puzzled.

She realized he wasn't a stowaway. And she thought briefly of Bill Hillsdale, of his concerns.

"Your father paid someone to take you to Halifax?"

He nodded. "He not nice. Not like this." The boy pointed to the door, indicating the agents beyond it who had immediately cooked a meal for him and found fresh clothes for him when he arrived.

"What was his name?"

He shook his head then.

"You won't tell me?"

"Cannot."

"He told you not to say?"

"He kill my father if I say."

"If you tell me who he is, I can work to be sure that doesn't happen."

He made no reply, but his expression told her he simply would not say.

"Okay. That's fine. Did you stay with him on the ship?"

"No. I was alone, locked in room with"—he searched for the word —"bed. Very sick."

"Seasick?"

He shrugged, then nodded.

"What was the ship carrying?"

He looked at her, uncomprehending.

"Were there cars on the ship, or fish, or …?"

He looked down, embarrassed by questions he couldn't answer. "It dark when I got on, and I come out of room only at night."

"Were you locked in the room?"

Again, he nodded. "I taken out for air, like ... like dog. Then, when we land, took me in car. Drove all night. Then stop. Tell me to walk, then wait. Then I see you."

"Was the man who transported you Ukrainian?"

Aleksei looked at her but didn't answer.

He wasn't going to jeopardize his father's well-being, but she'd learned one thing: Whoever had taken Aleksei Vann from Hamburg to the Canadian border knew what he was doing. He'd known an agent would be patrolling the land near McCluskey's Processing. The drop of the boy, on the heels of a month-long journey, had been timed and executed perfectly. Whoever had gotten Aleksei into the US was every bit a professional and not unlike the coyotes on the southern border.

She knew why the kid made Hillsdale nervous.

11:35 a.m., McCluskey's Potato Processing Plant

McCluskey's Processing was Garrett's largest employer, the region's lone potato-processing plant. And it was owned by Kyle McCluskey, who, ten years earlier, inherited the facility from his father.

The guy wearing a dark knit cap and gloves in the gatehouse waved Peyton through the entrance.

As she crossed the lot, dirt and melting chunks of snow and ice beneath her feet, she thought of a poem she'd read years earlier at the University of Maine. "April is the cruelest month," it began. T.S. Eliot had never lived in Aroostook County. Up here, March was the month that could never be trusted: it was forty-two degrees this day, and sunlight felt warm on the back of her wool field jacket, but the next day's forecast called for eight inches of snow, which would push the season's total near one hundred inches.

She entered the sprawling facility, told one receptionist she was there to see the plant president, was pointed to another receptionist, and walked a long corridor to the administrative offices, which, given the decor and ambiance, seemed a very long way from the plant's floor where men sweat and hustled.

"You look familiar," McCluskey's personal assistant said. "Did you attend Garrett High?"

Peyton told her when she graduated and introduced herself.

"I was a year behind you. I'm Barb Michaud. I played JV basketball and remember when they put your banner up."

Barb Michaud clearly had either just returned from a southern vacation or she spent time in an indoor tanning facility.

"That was a long time ago," was all Peyton, now thirty-seven, said. She'd been the school's first (and only) one-thousand-point scorer. The feat enabled her to attend the University of Maine and to graduate debt-free.

"You can have a seat," Michaud said. "I'll squeeze you in."

Peyton thanked her and sat down. She took her iPhone from a pant leg cargo pocket and checked her email. Susan Perry wanted her to do a home visit, checking on Aleksei Vann's move to his aunt's home.

"You can go in now," Michaud said, and Peyton did.

———

It was good to be Kyle McCluskey. Peyton knew it. So did anyone who drove past his five-thousand-square-foot home or saw his "camp" on Portage Lake. So did the men and women earning ten bucks an hour at the processing plant—and showering to scrub the smell away after every shift.

Peyton had spoken to the man twice since college, both at school events; McCluskey's son, Peter, was Tommy's age. Each time, she'd felt as if he considered himself to be the leader of the region's First Family.

"What can I do for you?"

McCluskey came around his desk and motioned to the sofa along the far wall. His office was larger than the bullpen in Garrett Station and offered a glass wall overlooking part of the plant floor. Peyton recognized men and a few women from the diner, their faces covered with sweat and dirt or oil.

She sat on the sofa. McCluskey took the red leather chair across the glass coffee table from her. He was balding and had a deep voice, and only in his forties, he looked much older; he had a full, fleshy face and looked soft beneath his starched and ironed white shirt. The skin near his chin pooled and spilled over his tie.

It was not a comfortable look.

"You've done a few PTO things, right? This some PTO fund-raiser? You need money?"

"No," she said. "When I'm in uniform, I'm working. I don't dress this way when I'm doing PTO stuff."

"Yeah, I remember you from the book sale last summer. You wore pale-blue shorts and a white T-shirt."

If someone had asked her what she'd worn that day, she couldn't have told them. His memory—and the way he narrowed his eyes while looking at her now—creeped her out. He was thinking of something.

And the sudden redness in his cheeks told her what.

She wanted to slap him, but settled for, "You own quite a lot of land along the border."

"It's a large facility, yes."

"Do you have surveillance cameras along the perimeter?"

He leaned back in his chair and folded his arms across his chest.

She'd seen that posture hundreds of times. Either bracing for bad news or preparing ways to avoid it.

"This isn't going to be good," he said, "is it?"

She smiled. "Well, I said it's not a PTO visit."

"We talking about another drug bust back there?" He motioned his chin toward New Brunswick. The skin hanging over his tie waddled.

"No," she said, "but it appears someone illegally entered the US from Canada behind your plant."

"What does that mean? He smuggling something?"

"No."

"I'm not following you. If it's not smuggling, why wouldn't the asshole just cross at Customs?"

"I don't know if that's important, Mr. McCluskey. I'd just like to see any surveillance footage you might be able to provide."

"Call me Kyle," he said. Then, "Hey, I just realized something. You went to Orono."

She nodded.

"You were a basketball player, right? I gave you a ride somewhere once, right? You grew up here."

"You were a senior when I was a freshman both here and at Orono, and you gave me a ride home from U-Maine one weekend. You had a Corvette in college," she said.

"Yeah. Great car." He looked through the glass wall, recalling those days.

She didn't like to. Those hadn't been great days for her or her family. Her father had lost the farm. Without basketball, college wouldn't have been an option. And even now, a Corvette *still* wasn't an option. Her Jeep Wrangler had 110,000 miles on it.

"Where'd you go after college?" he asked.

"Texas. All agents start on the southern border."

"And you wanted to come home?"

She nodded, not wanting to go into the details of how, after being shot at, she'd put in for a transfer. "The southern border was a great place for an agent, not for a single mom."

He looked her over, appraisingly. "I bet you can hold your own."

"I can. I'd like to see surveillance footage," she said again.

"Are we talking about an illegal alien?" he asked.

"Do you have video cameras?"

"In the woods? No. It's about five miles to the border."

"Your land runs all the way to New Brunswick. It's one of the only places that's not separated from Canada by the Crystal View River."

"Yeah," he said. "A few years ago I got wind of a marijuana-smuggling operation behind the plant. I called Maine State Police, then I hired my own guys. I have one private security guy on at all times. When did you find this person?"

"Mid-afternoon, yesterday."

He shook his head. "Hard to see how my guys missed him. One is a former state trooper. Did the asshole say how he got here? I don't want any assholes using my land to come here and steal public services from our people."

"You running for office?" She kicked herself for slipping into an informal tone.

"As a matter of fact," he said, "I will be soon. I'd like to be mayor of Garrett."

"Is Marty stepping down?" Marty Bartlett had been mayor for more than a decade.

"When I beat his ass, he will. I'd like to be able to count on the federal employees' votes. I'm looking for someone to help me reach those members of the constituency. Interested?"

"I'm really busy with the PTO, as you know. Could I interview the security officer who was on duty yesterday?"

"Interview him?"

She nodded.

"He in trouble?"

"No, I just like to be thorough."

"I like that in a girl."

Girl, she thought.

"He's got the day off today," McCluskey continued. "I'll tell him to call you. You guys still in that old house?"

She took out a business card and slid it to him. "Thank you." She stood.

"I like people who are thorough," he said. "I like you."

"I'm not looking for validation."

"I can tell. You're a confident girl. I like that."

"I think you meant to say I'm a confident *agent*."

"Was I being patronizing?"

"Yeah, but you probably can't help it," she said and walked out.

3:15 p.m., 7 Drummond Lane

Bohana Donovan had a Ukrainian forename and an Irish surname and looked as puzzling as the combination suggested. Her narrow face was pale but, Peyton thought, striking—large jade eyes dancing like gas flames when they recognized Peyton; a long smooth jaw line; and somehow, as if her complexion was determined to live up to her married name, freckles dotting her nose.

The temperature had risen to thirty-seven, and the snow was melting.

"Oh, when they told me someone would be dropping by, I guess I didn't expect *you*," Bohana said. "I always forget what you do for a living."

"Not working for the PTO today," Peyton smiled and said for the second time in two hours as she entered the foyer. The house had an in-ground pool and was in a cul-de-sac. Peyton smelled onions. "What are you making?" she asked.

"Beef stew, for dinner. Michael loves it, and Steven will eat anything with onions in it." She had an accent that reminded Peyton of the former Baltic states; clearly she was the boy's aunt.

"That's what I smell," Peyton said. "How long have you been in the US?"

"Oh, about twenty-five years now. Nearly half my life. I never lost the accent, though."

Peyton knew that while Kyle McCluskey owned the region's largest company, Steven Donovan owned Donovan Ford, the largest—by far—auto dealership in Aroostook County.

Peyton had witnessed his success firsthand. When no dealer could find a used Jeep Wrangler that met her specifications, it had been Steven Donovan who called to say there was one in Virginia, and he was in the midst of a dealer-to-dealer swap to acquire it for her. And he'd not charged a penny above what Peyton's research told her she should pay.

Success seemed to run in the family. Bohana was president of the PTO and their son, Michael, now a senior at Garrett High School, was ranked second in his class, according to an article in the *Star Herald*.

"Sorry to come at this time," Peyton said. "I know school is over and the bus will be arriving."

"Michael doesn't take the bus. Steven gives him the worst used car on the lot in exchange for changing oil on weekends. Actually, he works on a lot of cars—that boy can fix anything. His father says he should become an engineer."

Peyton smiled politely.

"And have you seen the new high school schedule? Seniors can leave at one every afternoon, if they have no classes. I'm pushing for some sort of in-service program. We have two hundred teenagers with nothing to do every afternoon."

"That's why I voted for you," Peyton said. "You're on top of things. Can we talk about Aleksei?"

"Of course. Come in. Coffee?"

"Black. Thanks."

"I wouldn't recognize you in that outfit—the gun, the baton—based on how you dress at PTO meetings."

"I wear jeans to those."

"And no hat," Bohana said. "If I had auburn hair, I'd grow it to my knees."

Government regulations dictated that Peyton wear her hair short, in a bun, or beneath her hat. This was still—and would always be—a major concession.

Bohana handed Peyton a coffee cup and led her through a stainless-steel kitchen to a living room with a stone fireplace. The fire was roaring.

Peyton sat on the hearth and held the cup in both hands.

"I love to have a fire," Bohana said. "Even after all these years away, and even when I don't need one in order to heat my house. We burn oil, too, of course, and Steven complains about the dry air from the wood. But, to me, there's nothing like a fire."

Peyton liked this woman, had liked her the first time they'd met at Garrett High School. Bohana Donovan, who sat in a leather chair beside the hearth, knew who she was and was comfortable in her own skin.

Peyton took her iPad from her bag. "I know you spoke to Mike Hewitt this morning, and I apologize for asking more questions, but I couldn't be there."

"It's okay. I'm happy to help. I just want to be sure my nephew is allowed to stay in the US. He has nowhere to go back there."

"I should tell you that the decision is not mine to make," Peyton said.

Bohana looked at the floor.

"Did you know he was coming?"

"Not until my brother wrote telling me Aleksei was en route. Then I got a call from the woman at DHHS after he arrived."

"Why did the boy land here?"

"I assume Dariya thought Aleksei would be sent to me, if he arrived here."

Which was, Peyton thought, exactly what had happened. "How is Aleksei adjusting?"

Bohana thought about it. "Overall, well, I'd say. He struggles with verb tenses when he speaks, sometimes using them correctly, other times forgetting the verb altogether. But that's minor, given what he's gone through."

"Have you heard from your brother?"

"Yes." Bohana looked up. "He wrote me for the first time several weeks ago."

"For the first time?"

"In almost three years."

"That's a long time."

"Yes. He said he was glad to finally reach me."

"Had he tried before?"

Bohana shrugged. "You know how it is. I was here, he was there. We each got caught up in our own lives. We fell out of touch."

"I see," Peyton said and continued typing notes.

"Dariya and I came here together, to study in Boston. Neither of us graduated. My father had worked to get us visas and saved for years to send us. I still feel badly about it. But I was in love. I met Steven— through a friend of Dariya's, ironically—married, and moved here. Dariya went back to Ukraine. He never completed his degree."

"When was that?"

"March of 1990. I'll never forget it. I was sad for him, you know? He came here to achieve something, to get a journalism degree from Emerson College, but then he just up and left during his second year. I know he was finding the coursework very difficult—the language barrier, you know, made it so hard for him. I was sad to see him give up."

"How did things go once he got back?"

"For us, on a personal level, not well. He never called and rarely wrote."

"That's too bad," Peyton said.

"Yeah, but professionally things went well for him. Not immediately. It took him a few years. He traveled a lot for a while. But then he settled down and landed a TV job. After a time, though, he started to be viewed as pro-Western, which hurt his career. And he lost his network position."

"What did he do then?"

"According to the letter I got last month, that was just two or three years ago. He was freelancing when Liliya was hurt. I think his house was targeted."

"Targeted?"

"Yes. Aleksei woke up screaming last night. A nightmare. The missile took off one side of the house while they slept. Aleksei said Liliya was awake reading in the living room when it hit."

"What's wrong with her?"

"A host of things. I don't know all of the medical details, but she needs twenty-four-hour care. Dariya is with her, providing that."

Aleksei went to bed with one life, Peyton thought, and woke with another. "And the letter told you all of this?" Peyton asked.

Bohana looked at her, then crossed the room, opened a coffee-table drawer, and retrieved a handwritten letter. She brought it back and handed it to Peyton.

"This is in Russian?" Peyton pointed to the text.

Bohana smiled apologetically. "Yes."

Peyton counted twelve pages. "May I take it with me? I'll return it tomorrow."

"Oh. Can you read Russian?" Bohana said.

"We have a translator."

"Oh, um, I guess you can take it."

Peyton found her reaction odd. Had Bohana offered the letter only when she was sure Peyton couldn't read it? "How's your brother coping since his wife was injured?" Peyton asked.

Bohana looked at her and pursed her lips, thinking. Finally, she shook her head. "None of them are okay."

"What do you mean?"

"I think he'll end up dead, is what I'm trying to say. I try not to think about it. He's my brother."

"I see. Aleksei told me his father was staying to fight the pro-Russian separatists. That's what you're talking about."

Bohana nodded.

"But his father is a journalist?"

She shrugged. "He wrote that he was staying to fight in his note to me as well. I wrote back, trying to convince him to leave too. But he never answered my reply."

Peyton didn't respond immediately. There was no way she would encourage Bohana to request her brother enter the country illegally. Overtaking the aroma of the fireplace was the aroma of onions and meat.

"So Dariya, your brother, wrote—his first contact with you in years—to explain that his son was on the way here?"

Bohana nodded. "And to tell me about Liliya, who I never met."

"How did Aleksei get here, Bohana?" It was the question she'd come to ask.

"His father hired a man, someone he knew, to take him to Germany. There, Aleksei got on a ship with the man—I don't know who, and it's probably not important . . ."

It might be, Peyton thought, if it turns out to be a human-trafficking ring.

"… and he led Aleksei all the way to Youngsville, New Brunswick."

"And to the woods behind McCluskey's?"

"Yes."

"This is a family friend?"

Bohana considered the question.

"Do you know the man's name, Bohana?"

She immediately shook her head, the denial coming too fast. There was something there. Peyton had seen it many times before. "Bohana, I know your first priority is to keep your nephew here. With that in mind, it's in your best interest to offer all the details you have. Aleksei has asked for political asylum. His situation is different than the kids who enter the US along the southern border."

"Yes, that's pretty clear, Peyton. Why do you feel the need to tell me that? He's *not* going back."

Peyton heard the agitation in her voice, saw it on her face. "Let me be more specific," Peyton said. "We're all trying to do right by this boy. However, given what has happened in Texas over the past couple years, the federal government is very leery of allowing that situation to arise again."

"Up here?"

Peyton nodded.

"The man who brought Aleksei here," Bohana said, "is no threat to do it again. In fact, I am surprised he succeeded at all."

"Why?"

"He'd never done it before."

"Is that in the letter?"

"Yes. And judging from what Dariya wrote, I'm not even certain the man can make it back."

"Your nephew said he didn't know whoever brought him here. But from what everyone has told me, I'm led to believe this entire trip was well organized and well executed."

Bohana shook her head.

"Why do you deny it?"

"Is…"

"You know the man who brought your nephew here, don't you?"

"No, Peyton," she said. "I do not."

And for the first time, Peyton heard something in Bohana's voice that indicated a fierceness—the inner strength necessary to leave everything behind and start anew, and the determination necessary to help a loved one do it as well.

Peyton stood. It was time to go. Bohana was the person to whom Aleksei was closest. If she hadn't done so already, Peyton couldn't risk alienating Bohana because she needed to know who had brought the boy to the US.

"Thanks for your time, Bohana. I know you have lots to do."

"I'm sorry I couldn't be more helpful."

Peyton thanked her again and showed herself out, knowing she'd soon return, because she needed the coyote's name.

6:45 p.m., Reeds Inn and Convention Center

Stone Gibson, seated at a window table, looked up from his menu and smiled broadly when she entered the restaurant.

Peyton could remember when the monstrous hotel had been called Keddy's. Gram Russo's, the facility's restaurant, was still serving up the best Italian this side of Bangor. But Peyton wasn't thinking about the ziti when she crossed the room toward Stone. She wasn't even thinking about how Stone looked, wearing his blue sports jacket and clean shaven for the first time since he'd finished investigating a child-molestation case. The case had gotten to him, and she'd worried about him.

But even that wasn't on her mind now.

She thought of her late father. Couldn't step foot in Gram Russo's without thinking of him. Charlie Cote, despite dying young, had taught her most of the lessons she needed to know. And she'd figured the rest out on her own.

When she thought of her father, she didn't think of him at the end of his life. She rejected those final hours in the hospital, following his heart attack. She thought of him in the potato fields, on the tractor, or in the potato house—wearing his dark-blue Dickies work shirt and pants, his hands dirty, dust and sweat dry on his face, and always wearing the big crooked-toothed smile that hard work seemed to give him. Or she recalled him in the woods, toting his .30-06, hunting deer.

The thought of him dressed in green, mopping floors in her high school after the bank had taken their farm and left them with one acre, was too much. As was the thought of him dying in a white room with the tubes and the drip bags. If she *had* to think of that time—of him seated across the kitchen table from the men in suits, of him looking around the kitchen at his daughters and wife, the sense of failure she saw in his eyes—if her evil mind ran to those days, she recalled her father declining the trailer and instead building a thousand-square-foot home with his own hands. The bank be damned.

That thought always put a smile on her face.

"You looked sad for a moment," Stone said when she reached the table, "but then you smiled again."

She could smell his musky cologne.

"Just thinking," she said.

"Don't take that the wrong way," he said and stood. "You look stunning. I was just concerned. Are you okay?"

She nodded. She was wearing a black dress with a cotton mesh bodice top and a V back that she'd gotten online from Nordstrom.

"I'm fine. And you're a gentleman." She patted his cheek. "Pulling out my chair. I should be asking you the same thing. How are you, now that the asshole is in custody?"

"I love a woman who can wear a black dress like that and still say *asshole*. I'll be better when he goes to Warren."

The Maine State Prison was in Warren.

He retook his seat, his eyes shifting away from Peyton's. "The little girl, Sara, started therapy today. I brought her an Amazon gift card because she loves to read. It's probably been her escape for years."

"Nice of you."

"Have to focus on the victim. If I think too much about the per-petrator, I'll break the uncle's legs."

"He deserves it," she said.

"And some."

The waitress came to the table. "Hi, you two." It was Marsha Camp-bell. She'd gone to high school with Peyton. "What can I bring you?"

Peyton asked for a glass of chardonnay; Stone asked for Omis-sion IPA. They didn't carry it, so he went with a martini.

"I haven't been here in a long time," Peyton said, when Marsha left. "The place always makes me think of my father." She could smell garlic bread and meat sauce. A tiny white candle burned brightly between them.

"Sorry," he said. "I guess I shouldn't have suggested this place."

"No, I'm glad you did."

"Is it hard constantly running into people you grew up with?"

"Depends on the situation. When I run into them as part of an investigation, it can be."

"They expect you to cut them a break. *You're one of us.* All that bullshit?"

"Yeah. But when it's not that, I like it. This is my home."

They were quiet as they watched Marsha cross the room, carrying their drinks.

When she left again, Stone said, "How's your Ukrainian boy?"

"Aleksei? I interviewed his aunt, trying to figure out who brought him here."

"She helpful?"

"Partially. She gave me a twelve-page letter from her brother. It's written in Russian, so I was at the U-Maine branch at Reeds this afternoon having Russian Professor Mark Rogers read it to me. There's nothing in the letter that's very helpful. Mark read it to me twice. Just a bunch of *I miss you* and *take care of my son* comments."

"Nothing to indicate who brought the boy?"

"No. The letter is vague and describes the guy as incompetent."

"No name?"

She shook her head. "And Bohana denies knowing whoever it is. Says only that there's no need to worry about him trafficking anyone else because, based on the letter, she doubts he can even get home."

"Is that meant to be reassuring?"

"I think so."

"What does that even mean?"

"To me, it means we're going to keep an eye on her to see if she meets up with the guy."

"Whoever it is," Stone said, "they sound lost or stuck."

She nodded and sipped her wine and looked around. "Speak of the devil." She nodded to a table across the room.

Steven and Bohana Donovan were eating with Kyle McCluskey and a blonde who looked far too young to be at the table. The blonde looked bored too. Peyton saw McCluskey touch the girl's hand to get her attention. As Steven and Bohana spoke, he whispered something to her. She grinned as if they'd just shared an inside joke.

"Who are they with?"

Peyton said, "The big guy is Kyle McCluskey."

"That his daughter?"

"Hardly."

"Let's talk about something else," Stone said, and Peyton heard a note of nervousness.

"Okay."

"You know, these past six months, getting to know and spend time with you and Tommy, have been really great, Peyton. Best half year of my life."

She could feel her face flush. The last time a man started a conversation on this note, she'd ended up married. Then she'd watched her ex, Jeff McComb, walk out on Tommy and her six years later.

She reached for her wine again.

"Maybe this isn't a good time to have this conversation," Stone said.

She was no longer sipping and set the wineglass down. "I need to use the ladies' room," she said and stood.

———

If she hadn't been wearing mascara, she'd have splashed water on her face.

What was she doing? She'd nearly *run* across the room. She'd handled Bill Hillsdale, a federal hotshot, not twelve hours ago. But the thought of a serious commitment sent her jogging across the dining room in a black cocktail dress?

Tommy.

If Stone Gibson was about to propose, what could she say? She could not make such a commitment without consulting Tommy first. Was *consulting* the right word? She didn't need an eleven-year-old's permission to allow herself to be happy. Did she?

She wasn't sure. She'd spent so much time since Jeff had left them focused solely on Tommy and his needs that maybe she'd forgotten her own.

Was that why she was hiding in the bathroom?

————

"Are you okay?" Stone said, when she returned.

"Just slightly neurotic," she said, "but you've probably figured that out by now."

It made him chuckle. "I love you," he said. "I've told you that for four months. Do you believe it?"

"I do."

"And you've said it back each time I've told you," he said.

She nodded. "I have. And I told you I wish I had met you years ago."

"Our lives would be very different, if we'd met then."

"Yes."

"I'd like to take the next step."

"How big is the step?" she asked.

"Not a leap," he said, "just a step."

7:30 p.m., 7 Drummond Lane

His younger cousin was weird.

Michael Donovan could tell that right off. How many thirteen-year-olds, after all, don't like to watch ESPN?

Michael's parents had gone out to dinner, and he was home "watching his cousin"—his mother's description for babysitting. He'd only met this cousin a day or so earlier. And his mother kept telling him to be nice to the middle-schooler.

"Being nice" to his cousin, so far, had consisted of taking him to a basketball game and sitting with him in the bleachers and trying to explain to Jenny why he had a middle-schooler with him. (It was hard to convince Jenny to go under the bleachers to make out since he couldn't leave Aleksei alone.)

And, Michael sensed, this was just the beginning. His mother said he'd be driving Aleksei to and from the middle school each day. Taking him to school wouldn't be bad, but sometimes he and Jenny liked to stop on the way home. Each told their parents they stayed late for extra help, but Michael kept a blanket in the trunk of the used Pontiac. They'd been warm on even the coldest days.

Across the room, Aleksei sat up straight on the loveseat, his eyes leaving the TV to look out the dark window.

Michael wondered what Aleksei was thinking. For years, he'd heard his mother make occasional references to the uncle he'd never met, the one on his mother's side in the Ukraine. His other uncle, the one on his father's side, Ted, lived alone in the upstairs apartment.

"What you doing?" Aleksei asked, clearly bored by the NBA half-time show.

"Reading."

They were in the great room, as his mother called it. He'd always thought that sounded arrogant, and it embarrassed him when she said it to guests. But he knew the house had been designed around the room with its vaulted ceilings, stone fireplace, bar, big-screen with surround sound, and its leather furniture on which Uncle Ted fell asleep at least one afternoon each week.

"What you reading?" Aleksei asked.

"You're supposed to say *are*. 'What *are* you reading?'"

Aleksei nodded. "What are you reading?"

"A book about art. It's my homework. I'm taking a class at the community college."

"College?"

"Yeah. I'm a senior. You can do that—take a community-college class to count next year at U-Maine."

Michael could tell his cousin understood none of it. He would never say it to his mother, but he wondered how long Aleksei was staying with them. He wondered, too, about his friend Davey Bolstridge, wondered how the chemo had been on this day. His mind had wandered to Davey often recently. And he was glad he'd finally discovered a way to help him.

"You are lucky for college," Aleksei said. "Very lucky."

"You want to go to college?"

"Oh, yes. My dream. My father went to college here. He wants me to go college here also."

His mother kept saying the situation was "complicated," and Michael knew it was. Did this latest information mean Aleksei was staying with them until he was old enough for college? That was five years away. His mother told him about what happened to Aleksei's mother and that his father was staying to fight the pro-Russian separatists, which seemed just plain crazy. They would never defeat the separatists, not with Putin funding them.

"I hear you're starting school tomorrow."

"I cannot wait," Aleksei said.

"Really?"

"Yes."

"Look, Aleksei, don't say that at school."

"Why?"

"The tough kids will push you around."

"No," Aleksei said, "they will not."

Michael set his book down on the arm of the chair. He'd heard a tone in his cousin's voice he hadn't heard previously in the voice of a contemporary. Impressive. And a little scary. Aleksei was thirteen, four years younger than him, but he seemed much older than that.

"You aren't afraid?"

"Of who?"

"I don't know ... the bullies."

"See this?"

Aleksei pushed back the hair above his ear. Michael got off his chair and moved closer. The scar was only two inches but jagged.

"That from one of Putin's 'bullies.' He tell me move out of way. When I"—he shook his head, searching for the word, failing, growing frustrated—"not fast enough, he do this. He do not kill me. Your bullies will not either."

"I'm just saying there are a few dickheads in school. And some teachers are jerks too."

"My mother say education is a gift. I have not gone school since war started. Putin take school away."

Michael hadn't read anything about that, about Putin closing schools. Did he mean that literally? What was that all about?

"And he take my mother. I want to learn. It important."

Michael looked at his cousin—pale, skinny, with dark rings under his eyes, but with a seriousness in his voice, to his words, that middle-school kids didn't have.

"Are you homesick?"

"I miss Father. I think of him. . ." His voice trailed off. He turned back to the TV. The halftime show was over. The Celtics game was on.

Michael could tell Aleksei understood nothing of basketball. "I'm sure your father is okay," Michael said. "Want something to eat? I'll get it for you."

Aleksei shook his head. "Thank you."

"You like to read?"

Aleksei nodded.

"Like to play video games?"

Aleksei shrugged.

"I'll show you," Michael said.

Michael went to the TV and got the Xbox controllers. For the next half hour, they played *Destiny*.

THREE

Wednesday, March 5, 6:35 a.m., 12 Higgins Drive

PEYTON ROSE EARLY AND was at the stove cooking cheesy scrambled eggs, just the way Tommy liked them, when he entered the kitchen. He went to the table and sat, took his four gummy vitamins—two were fish oil (Peyton had read somewhere that they helped kids focus)—chewed them, and drank some orange juice.

The kitchen smelled like strong coffee. She'd bought the house because of this room, had seen the potential for renovations. It paled in comparison to Bohana Donovan's kitchen. Bohana could hold an entire New Year's Eve party around her center island. But the thought of installing granite counters and stainless-steel appliances had sold Peyton on this house.

She brought Tommy's eggs and her coffee to the table and sat across from him. When it was just the two of them, this was where they ate, not the dining room.

"What's going on today?"

Tommy was looking out the window and turned back to her. "What do you mean?"

"Have a test or anything today?"

He shrugged. "Can we go snowmobiling again?"

She'd taken him on the station's Arctic Cat, which was against regs, but Mike Hewitt had okayed it for one afternoon.

"That's a long shot, pal. My boss let me take you that one time because he knew how much it meant to you."

"Can we buy our own snowmobile?" He was wearing his Tom Brady Patriots jersey and blue jeans.

"I don't think so."

"Why not?"

"Snowmobiles cost a lot of money, sweetie."

He nodded, understanding, and ate some eggs.

"Do you have extra mittens packed," she said, "in case one pair gets wet during recess?"

"Mom, it's not cool to change your mittens."

"I change my gloves all the time when I'm outdoors."

He shook his head, smiling. "Not cool."

"Hey, pal, can we talk seriously for a minute?"

"About what?" His eyes narrowed; he put down his fork. "The last time you asked that, I had to get a math tutor."

"Keep eating," she said, "and the math tutor has worked out well, hasn't it?"

"She's mean."

"Mrs. Watson isn't mean. She was my sixth-grade math teacher. I told her that if she could teach me, teaching you would be a breeze. We're lucky to have her working with you."

"The other kids play soccer after school. I come home and do school all over again."

"You play soccer too." She drank some coffee. "Sweetie, how do you feel about Stone?"

"He's cool. You know that."

She did know that, but this wasn't about her. "You know he thinks the world of you, right?"

Tommy leaned back in his seat, arms folded across his chest. "Yeah. So does Dad. He just has to work a lot."

"I know that, Tommy."

Jeff McComb—her ex, the man who, at least partially, she'd moved back for, hoping he'd play a larger role in Tommy's life—hadn't seen Tommy in eight weeks. Hadn't called him in six. Yet Tommy held out hope, which broke her heart. She wanted to lean over and kiss him. At the same time, she wanted to kick Jeff McComb in the kneecap for hurting her son.

"Sweetie, how would you feel about Stone moving in with us?"

"What about Dad? What about if he wants to move in?" Tommy stood. "Do you ever think about his feelings, Mom?"

"Tommy, please sit down. Let's talk about this."

But he was gone before she'd finished saying the words. She heard the cacophony of a zipper and the stomping of feet into boots. Then the front door slammed. And he was gone—to the end of the driveway, twenty minutes before the bus would arrive.

She went to the window next to the front door. Tommy's back was to the house. She considered going to him but knew this wasn't the time. She'd upset him enough before school. His dyslexia provided enough fodder for classmates who teased him. She didn't want him getting on the bus in tears.

Where would this leave things with Stone?

It wouldn't be fair to Stone, or her, to allow him to move in if Tommy was going to fight the arrangement. That situation would be destined to fail.

Twenty minutes later, she watched the yellow school bus stop at the end of the driveway. The doors opened and Tommy climbed the stairs. The loud gears shifted. And Tommy, sitting near a window, ignored the house, stared straight ahead.

Then the bus was out of sight.

8:44 a.m., McCluskey's Potato Processing Plant
She didn't go in the building.

The courteous maneuver was to go inside and let Kyle McCluskey know she was about to search the woods behind his processing plant. But she didn't have much use for Kyle. Thought he was a chauvinistic jerk, actually. So she parked behind the building, grabbed her backpack and snowshoes, and started through the woods, heading northeast.

The morning Aleksei Vann surrendered she'd parked near the Canadian border, planning to walk these woods from the other direction, traveling several miles *toward* the plant. This day, she would backtrack, maneuvering around the balsam firs and northern white cedars, toward Canada.

The sun was bright overhead, and she wore sunglasses, her Border Patrol cap, and fleece-lined Gore-Tex pants over her uniform greens. It was thirty-one degrees, but the sunshine felt warm—one of those March days that offer a tempting hint of spring, one you want desperately to believe, like a kiss on the cheek that never leads to the real thing.

Hers was the only vehicle parked behind the plant. The others—maybe fifty trucks and cars—were out front in the enormous parking lot. She had her snowshoes attached to her pack. She wouldn't need them at the start. Ten feet from her tailgate in the west corner of the lot lay the mouth of a narrow, hard-packed trail at the side of the windowless building. She wondered what it led to, since everything an employee of McCluskey's Processing needed was inside. But she was glad for the helpful egress: the longer she could avoid using snowshoes, the more energy she'd have at the end of her shift.

As she started down the trail, leather hiking boots crunching loudly on the frozen, hard-packed snow, and zigzagging through the green sea of fir trees, she began to develop a theory regarding the packed trail. Had Kyle McCluskey given employees the green light to cut Christmas trees from the forest of balsam firs? Most of the trees back here were too large to be six-foot Christmas trees, but if cut accordingly, the top would serve nicely.

She'd walked for longer than an hour and was more than a mile into her hike when she heard the generator. She walked another half mile before spotting the shack.

———

The wood used to construct the outside of the structure wasn't clapboard; it looked more like plywood, although she didn't think it was. The hut had been painted forest green and was the size of the ice shacks she and her father sat in on winter nights on Madawaska Lake.

She pushed fallen (or carefully placed) pine branches out of the way to get to the structure's door. Locked? She couldn't see a handle or any way to open it. She circled the outbuilding once, feet sinking through the crusty top layer of snow, and spotted a rope running through a small hole near the roofline and coming from somewhere inside. It hung against the back of the shack.

Peyton's father had told her about structures built by hunters, places where one could sleep and store food, usually a halfway point to a hunting spot deep in the woods. Bear hunters, especially, found these places useful. Her father's description seemed fitting. Except for the generator. It hummed loudly inside the shack. She thought of the unnamed man who led Aleksei to Garrett, of Bohana's strange description of him: *I'm not even certain he can make it back.*

If anyone was living as a troll in the woods between Garrett and the Canadian border, the coyote fit the description. She unclipped the safety strap on her service weapon and knocked on the door.

No answer. No sound above the rumbling generator.

"Anyone in there?" she called.

No answer. No audible movement.

She went to the back of the cabin again, gave the rope a pull, and felt something release on the other end of the rope. Apparently, the crude pulley system allowed whoever was using the shed to lock and unlock it from the back. She returned to the front and found the door ajar.

She knew where her rights began and ended. There was no need, legally, to ask Kyle McCluskey's permission to walk his land. Section 287 of the Immigration and Nationality Act authorized her to enter private lands without a landowner's consent within twenty-five miles of the border when she was on patrol. The Act didn't, however, grant her entry into a structure on the property.

But the door was cracked.

And the coyote who led Aleksei had yet to be captured.

11:25 a.m., Tim Hortons

"It's Kyle McCluskey's land, right?" Stone Gibson said when he, Peyton, and Mike Hewitt had gathered in Reeds, fifteen minutes south of Garrett.

"That's right," Peyton said.

They'd taken a window booth. Traffic moved slowly on this stretch of Route 1. The cars were covered in white residue left by the salt and calcium used to treat icy roads.

"And you just searched the land and the inside of the structure?" Stone said. "No warrant?"

"None needed for the land," she said.

Hewitt explained section 287 to Stone, who, listening, sat shaking his head.

"Border Patrol always seems to have a loophole that allows them to do what they want," Stone said.

Hewitt ignored him and scribbled in his notebook.

She liked Stone's outfit: jeans, a button-down shirt, and a navy blue sports jacket. When he leaned forward, she saw his 9mm Glock in a shoulder holster.

Hewitt turned to Peyton. "You obviously entered the shack, in order to know what was inside."

She said, "The door was ajar."

"When you arrived?"

Across from them, two women sat, drinking what looked like smoothies. One had a baby stroller beside her. Both looked relaxed, their conversation rolling easily. Peyton looked at Hewitt, saw his narrowed eyes, and suddenly wanted to join the two women. She knew an illegal search wouldn't be permissible in court. Knew also that if an illegal search was proven, her action would compromise the investigation.

"There was a rope hanging off the back of the structure. When I pulled it, the door opened. It's a pulley system. The latch can be set and released from the outside."

"And you pulled the rope?" Hewitt said.

"Not intending to open the door."

"A warrant to enter the shack would've been nice."

"Five miles separate the processing plant from the Canadian border. A, for lack of a better word, *refugee* just entered the US through those woods, and we haven't located the coyote who led him here. For all we know, Aleksei and the coyote spent the night in that shack before Aleksei got to me. I heard the generator, saw a small structure that someone could be hiding in . . ." She spread her hands.

"And you thought of the coyote?"

She nodded. "That's probable cause, Mike."

"Probable cause to get a warrant, Peyton."

"I could see inside from where I stood and saw something that looked suspicious. The door was ajar, so I entered and found six marijuana plants in two aquariums. The shack has been insulated— nothing very professional, but insulated nonetheless. And the generator keeps it very warm. There are heat lamps and fans and tinfoil lining the aquariums. Some chairs, blankets, a portable heater, even a storage closet, which was empty."

"How big is the inside?" Stone asked.

"About the size of a storage shed, but taller. It's framed and half the ceiling's finished, like a little loft, maybe six and a half feet high. I assume there's insulation above it."

"Pot's being grown in the fish tanks?" Stone asked.

"Yeah. And there was a small amount hung up to dry."

"Then I'm glad you went inside," Stone said.

"I'm sure you are," Hewitt said. "She's done the dirty work for you."

Stone didn't respond. He looked tired, having come from Houlton, where he'd conducted more interviews for the molestation case. Peyton saw the stress on his face. Whatever had been said earlier that morning had taken its toll. The dark half-moons under his eyes reminded her that for him, this was a case that would linger long after retirement. She was glad she wasn't a state cop in Aroostook County; they were vastly undermanned and overworked.

Her mind ran to her breakfast with Tommy. Stone would surely ask about Tommy's reaction. What would she say?

Stone poured a tiny bit of cream into his tea. "I haven't used one, but I've heard about these shelters. Someone, usually a hunter, builds one, uses it, and it just stays there. Maybe the hunter comes back to it the next year. Maybe another hunter uses it. They serve as a communal base camp of sorts, so you don't have to walk all the way out to the road."

"I want to put a camera out there," she said. "McCluskey told me all about his all-star security team. Hard to believe they missed it."

"It's a long way from the plant," Hewitt said.

Peyton nodded and recrossed her legs. "I called Stone because he can work the drug aspect of this."

"Not the Maine DEA?" Hewitt said.

"For six pot plants?"

"Why are you in this at all?" Stone said.

"I'm interested in the area," she said. "Aleksei Vann came through that path, and Bohana Donovan says the guy who brought him here might still be around."

Hewitt wrote something on his notepad, then looked at Stone. "So here's where we stand: You always like a drug bust, Stone, and we're looking for a coyote. You need cameras to catch whoever is growing dope with heat lamps out there. And we have cameras and don't need permission to mount them ..."

Stone smiled. "Sounds like we might make a good team."

1 p.m., 7 Drummond Lane

"How are things?"

Michael Donovan looked across the table at his father. He knew the game; they'd played it on and off since the fall. He'd come home from school in the early afternoon, following his final class, and knew that was why his father arrived home for a late lunch.

He bit into his BLT. "Fine, Dad." He straightened a crease along the arm of his black T-shirt. The shirt had the words *NERDY BY NATURE* across the front.

"Just fine?"

"*Great.* Is that what you want to hear?"

"How's Davey?"

"Chemo is kicking his ass. He looks awful. The cancer spread to his kidney."

"Oh God. I didn't know that."

"Not many people do. He only told a few of us."

"How are you doing with all of that?"

"I'm okay," Michael said. "He'll be fine."

His father looked at the floor. "So the prognosis is good?"

"Davey says he'll be fine."

His father thought about that, then said, "Let's talk about *us*. I feel like something changed between you and me a while ago. And I'm trying to figure out what it is, Mikey. Have I done something?"

"No. Nothing's changed."

"You say that quickly, like you've been waiting for me to bring it up." Michael didn't respond.

"I offered to take you hunting all fall. You never wanted to go. We haven't gone to camp together all year."

"I'm busy."

Steven sat staring at him, then finally stood and went to the counter. His back to Michael, waiting on the Keurig, he said, "Learning anything interesting in that art-appreciation class at the community college?"

Michael couldn't believe his father asked the question. He set his sandwich down on the paper plate and pushed it away. "Actually, we're talking a lot about Rembrandt's *The Storm on the Sea of Galilee*."

"Really?" his father said.

"Did you spill your coffee, Dad?"

"Yeah, most of it. I need to be more careful. If I make a mess, your mother will kill me."

"You know that painting was done in 1633? It's the most beautiful thing I've ever seen."

"You really appreciate art. I respect that about you. Maybe you could see it for real sometime. It's probably in a museum somewhere."

"Not likely. It's been missing for a quarter century."

"Really?" Finished wiping the counter, his father returned to sit across from him. "You talk about that in your community college class?"

"Yeah. We talk about how you can't sell stolen artwork."

"Why not?"

"Pretty simple, really. Everyone is looking for it. You can't do anything with it. Can't hang it. Can't resell it."

"Hmm." His father sipped the salvaged coffee, looked at him. "Interesting. Guess I'll stick to selling cars." He smiled at his son.

Michael saw the pain in his father's eyes when he didn't return the smile.

"How's your cover letter and resume coming for summer internships, Michael?"

"I'm working on them."

"Want help? I was an English major in college, you know. And I hire people and read resumes all the time."

"I know. And, no, I'm all set."

His father looked at him over his coffee. "Can we talk about something?"

"This is why you came home for lunch, isn't it?"

"It's about your uncle Ted, Michael. He says he feels like you've been pretty ... *distant*. That was the word he used when he described how you've been to him since the fall, Mikey. Anything you want to tell me?"

"No."

His father looked at him for a long time before finally nodding. "Okay, pal. I'm going back to work. Have a good afternoon."

"You, too, Dad."

His father crossed the room, dumped what was left of his coffee in the stainless-steel sink, and rinsed his mug. He started to leave the kitchen, but paused.

Michael watched his father exhale, blowing out a long breath—one, he thought later, the man had probably been holding for months.

"Something changed last fall, Mikey. I know it did. I just want to know what and why."

"I'll get Aleksei after school," Michael said, and ate his sandwich.

When the front door closed, he took out his cell phone and called Donovan Ford. "May I speak to Ted Donovan?"

The voice offered to get him, but Michael hung up.

Knowing Uncle Ted was at work was enough.

———

Uncle Ted's apartment was locked and dark, but Michael knew where the spare key was, and he switched on the light in the main room.

He liked coming up here. Partially, it was the secret of these trips. But more and more, it was his appreciation for what was in the box that brought him here. Just twenty minutes here and there. That was enough.

What was Uncle Ted doing? He was pretty sure his mother knew nothing about it. It was his father who Michael wondered about. And like most things one dwells upon, these questions and doubts had calcified and now had taken on a life of their own. Michael's theory was cemented in his mind: His father knew what was here and had some sort of plan for it.

But that wasn't what Michael was thinking this afternoon, when his mother was at a PTO meeting and his father and Uncle Ted were at work. The apartment was warm. The temperature, it seemed to Michael, never changed in the apartment. Today he simply enjoyed what was there, noticing everything he could, thinking of how much there was to see, of how much he no doubt overlooked.

And he wondered, as he always did, what his father and uncle had planned.

2:15 p.m., Garrett Station

Leaf Ryan didn't look familiar to Peyton. He was in his late fifties, a former state trooper whom Peyton had never met.

"Thanks for coming in to see me," she said when he sat across from her in the Garrett Station bullpen.

The term *bullpen* might have originated with police homicide squads in the 1950s and been used to describe their working space, but an agent at Garrett Station had used the term here. And it stuck.

"Mr. McCluskey required me to do it."

"You didn't want to?"

"I never liked working with Border Patrol agents when I was a trooper up here. And I know that I don't have to talk to you. I'm here voluntarily."

She leaned back in her seat, folded her arms across her chest, and said, "Well, as I said, thanks for coming in. Want something to drink? Coffee, soda?"

He shook his head.

Sixteen desks were arranged nose to nose. Agents sat in pairs facing each other. It had been a big day when Washington had finally allocated a laptop for each agent. Everyone in the bullpen knew agents on the southern border were taken care of first, which, Peyton thought, was as it should be. Still, she'd been shocked to transfer north and learn she'd be sharing an eight-year-old desktop with Miguel Jimenez, who now sat at the adjoining desk. She wondered if he was actually doing paperwork or playing fantasy sports. She looked past Leaf Ryan's left shoulder. Jimenez looked at her and smirked, enjoying watching the silver-haired man give her a hard time.

"So what do you need from me?" Leaf said.

"You worked here as a trooper?"

"Started out in Augusta. They needed help up north, so I offered to be finish up here."

"Surprised our paths never crossed. When did you retire?"

"Two years ago. Kyle offered me a job, so I retired."

"He hired you away from the state police?"

"Pretty much."

"Must've been a good offer."

"I was ready to go." He looked around the room. Peyton knew he wasn't comfortable discussing his financial status with a room full of Border Patrol agents. "But, yeah," he whispered, "it was a good offer."

"What do you do over there?"

"Typical security—patrol, run through surveillance tape, make sure no one has his hands where he shouldn't have them."

"Employees stealing?"

"Sometimes. Caught a guy taking parts last year."

"Tell me about the surveillance tapes," she said and opened a note file on her iPad, typed in the date.

He shrugged and looked bored. She guessed he had seven or eight years before Social Security and Medicare kicked in, but he seemed much younger. He had thick white hair but looked fit. No wedding band. He wore a long-sleeved Baxter State Park T-shirt, jeans, and Timberland boots. She could picture him in a leather jacket riding a motorcycle.

"When Kyle hired me, after the smuggling problem, I installed cameras."

"Around the building?"

"Yeah. I thought the smuggling was taking place in the woods near the plant."

"It was," she said.

"Yup, and they were parking in the plant parking lot sometimes. The camera picks up who comes and goes. In fact, I saw you on the film recently."

She nodded. "Just trying to help you guys out," she said. "Kyle must have told you about the boy I found."

He nodded. "I don't need help."

"This is why you really came here, isn't it?" she said. "To tell me that?"

"I'd appreciate the professional courtesy of you telling me when you're on our land."

"I don't have to do that. You must know that."

"Professional courtesy," he repeated.

"Do you have cameras near the border?"

"That's almost five miles from the plant. These things cost a lot of money."

"So you're more concerned with what's going on near the plant?"

"Wouldn't you be?"

"McCluskey's Processing can afford extra cameras."

"I figure you guys can take care of the border. I'll watch my building."

"And a lack of cameras might give you more work."

"What's that supposed to mean?"

"If someone's smuggling on McCluskey's land, it gives you something to do. And that's job security."

"Kyle does pay very well," he said. "I wouldn't want to lose this job."

"I don't blame you." Leaf Ryan was becoming more annoying and less trustworthy by the second. "So what else has your video surveillance picked up?"

"Nothing this year. I did a presentation for the employees, showed them the equipment. It really curbed theft. Mostly parts that can be used on tractors and equipment. And tools too. But, like I said, that's down this year."

She nodded. It made sense. The people working the plant floor would be mostly men who could and did fix things themselves.

"Thanks for coming in this morning, Leaf. I appreciate your time."

"That's it?"

"That's it," she said, and he stood and walked out.

She watched him go.

Jimenez looked across the desk at her. "That's really it?" he asked.

She shook her head. "But it's enough for this morning."

"Guy seems like an asshole," he said.

"I thought you were a better judge of character than that, Miguel. He doesn't *seem like* an asshole. He is the genuine article."

5:30 p.m., 12 Higgins Drive

Peyton was hosting dinner for her sister Elise, nephew Max, and niece Autumn. The March day had ended with a slate sky. Now it was dark. Elise was teaching middle school, having spent the last two years working and taking classes year-round at the University of Maine at Reeds to finish her degree following her divorce.

"Where's Tommy?" she asked. "I haven't seen him since Max and I got here."

Peyton was at the counter kneading ground turkey and lean hamburger, while occasionally tossing in chives and mushrooms. This was her version of turkey burgers, and Tommy usually ate two.

"And you only saw him then," she said, "because I made him get the door."

"What's up? He mad at me?"

"No. He's mad at *me*."

"Well, he's supposed to be mad at you. You're his mother." Elise smiled, swiveled on her stool to face her sister, and sipped her chardonnay. "I want him to like me, though. I've been his favorite person since he was born."

"Second favorite," Peyton said, smiling, "but close."

The sisters ate together once a week. The nights now shifted to fit the sisters' schedules, but the weekly meals together remained constant. Elise had changed after school before coming over. She wore jeans and a cable-knit sweater. Peyton knew Elise would never dress so casually at work; her sister's work wardrobe, like DHHS worker Susan Perry's, made Peyton envious.

"What did you do to make him mad?"

Peyton told her about the situation with Stone and about her breakfast conversation with Tommy.

"Have you told Stone about Tommy's reaction?"

Peyton shook her head. She was making burger patties now and paused to wipe her hands on a paper towel and sip from her bottle of Corona. Holding the bottle before her, she gently twirled it, watching the lime dance inside.

"How serious are you about Stone, Peyton?"

"I think I love him."

The sisters made eye contact.

"You *think*?"

"I love him, Elise."

"Then the three of you need to come to some resolution, sis."

"Is that a news flash?" Peyton said.

Elise ignored her. "And you know what would be really helpful right now? We should call Mom and ask her for advice. She'll come right over and tell you *exactly* what you *need* to do."

"Oh boy, that sounds just great."

Both sisters laughed.

"Thanks," Peyton said, "but I think I'll stick with you for advice. A few years ago you went through your own tough time, and you came out of it well."

"Well enough."

"*Very* well," Peyton said, referring to Elise's decision to leave an abusive husband and come out of the closet. "I'm meeting Stone for breakfast," Peyton said. "I need to figure out what I'm going to say before then. I'll talk to Tommy tonight and see how that goes."

She crossed the kitchen to the sliding-glass door, went to the deck, and, working beneath the floodlight, started the grill. Only half the deck had been cleared; the remainder was covered with snow. Tommy had offered to clear it, but much of the snow was frozen, and to chip it would mean gouging the wood. Now they'd have to wait for the spring thaw to shovel the other half.

"Hey, a new student was added to my class this week," Elise said, when Peyton re-entered the kitchen, "and I think you know him."

Max had climbed onto a stool at the counter and sat next to his mother, dipping carrot sticks into ranch dressing on the hors d'oeuvres tray Peyton had set out. Autumn, Elise's adopted daughter, had pigtails tied with pink bows and played with a stuffed bear on the kitchen floor.

Peyton took a juice box from the fridge, put the straw in it, and handed it to Max.

"Thanks, AP," Max said, using his acronym for *Aunt Peyton*.

Peyton raised her beer bottle, and Max grinned as they tapped drinks.

"Cheers!" he yelled.

"Agent," Elise said, "do we need to teach my kindergartner to toast?"

"It's a life skill," Peyton said.

"Anyway, I think you know my new student. He's living with Bohana Donovan."

"Aleksei Vann?"

"That's him. He is extremely bright. He read *Crime and Punishment* in Russian."

"He's thirteen."

"Yes."

"And he read *Crime and Punishment*?"

Elise nodded.

"I didn't understand that book in college," Peyton said. "I've read it again since and just barely understand it now."

"The kid is a delight. Wants to learn everything. We talk about it a lot as teachers, but don't see it often—a kid who cherishes the opportunity to learn."

"Where he's coming from," Peyton said, "he probably didn't get that chance."

"Well, he has it now. And he's drinking it all in. He struggles with English but asks for extra work. Asks questions all the time. When he told me about his trip, about a female Border Patrol agent finding him, I thought, *Jeez, I wonder who that could be.*"

"Actually," Peyton said, "*he* found *me*. But, yes, I was the agent. And I don't doubt that he's serious about his education. That's at least part of why his father sent him here. The pro-Russian separatists nearly killed his mother. He's come to live with his aunt."

"And his parents?" Elise asked. "Are they coming here too?"

"His mother requires serious care now, which his father provides," Peyton said. "That's how Aleksei would be granted political asylum. His parents need to be anchored to the Ukraine for him to be granted political asylum."

"They can't follow him here?"

"No. That's one difference between what happened in Texas and this case. Aleksei's parents can prove he is in danger if he stays in Ukraine, based on what happened to his mother. And the parents are not coming. His mother is badly hurt, and his father cares for her."

Elise thought about that. "So Aleksei is really on his own."

"He has the Donovans."

"I heard Bohana is his aunt."

Peyton nodded. "I think she and his parents believe he can have a better life here."

"If that's the reason for sending him, the reasoning is the same as it is for the illegal aliens crossing in Texas," Elise said.

Peyton looked at her; she didn't like where this conversation was heading. "Maybe. But there are differences. This trip was intricately planned and not likely to be repeated. This isn't a simple border jumping. Aleksei also says his father is staying behind to fight Putin."

"Yikes."

"Yeah," Peyton said, "I know. The boy might never see his father again."

———

Tommy might have been eleven, but to Peyton he'd always be that five-pound eight-ounce baby she'd brought home from the hospital in El Paso, Texas, more than a decade earlier. She knew he hated it when she told him that, just like he hated it when she kissed his cheek in public, but that would never change. And if the worst thing she did on a daily basis was love him too much, she wasn't doing too badly.

She entered Tommy's room Wednesday after Elise and her children had left. There were three bedrooms and two bathrooms upstairs. Peyton's first renovation had been the addition of her bathroom off the master bedroom. This allowed Tommy to have his own bathroom, and she routinely reminded him that she'd grown up in a one-bathroom home.

Moonlight pooled on the floor at the foot of his bed. He was reading a Percy Jackson book by nightlight.

She turned on the overhead light.

"How was dinner?" she said.

"Fine."

"Just fine? Am I losing my touch? Usually you eat two burgers."

"I wasn't hungry."

She sat on the side of his bed and looked out his window. He never drew the shades.

"Full moon," she said. "I love nights like this."

"I know," he said.

She nodded. "I want to talk to you, Tommy, about this morning. I know I upset you before school. That wasn't right. I shouldn't have done that. I'm sorry."

He set the book down. "So Stone *isn't* coming to live with us?"

"I want to talk about that, sweetie."

"He's not my dad."

"I know that, and he does too. He doesn't want to replace your father. That's not what this is about."

"What then?"

She looked out the window again. It was a good question: Was this all about her? She couldn't deny it. Sure, Stone would probably be more of a father figure than the biological dad Tommy had. Probably already was, in fact. But that wasn't what this was about. Not if she was being totally honest with herself. She wanted to be happy. Was that selfish? Tommy had always come first. She'd given up her work on the southern border, which had lead to her BORSTAR promotion, to move to the safer northern border. The Border Patrol Search, Trauma, and Rescue unit was an elite group that, when called upon, rescued stranded aliens and agents alike, and she missed that work. The move had also been to allow her ex Jeff Mc-Comb access to Tommy, with hopes that he'd be more involved. Now Jeff was dating a woman with two sons, and Tommy had cried when he saw an Instagram picture of his father with those boys at a Red Sox game.

A cloud rolled past the window, blotting out the moon.

"Sometimes grown-ups want to be together, Tommy. They want to spend more time together. If Stone lived here—"

"What if Dad wants to live here sometime?" he interrupted.

Sometime. She watched his face. Heard the desperation in his voice. Saw tears pool in his eyes. Her son knew Jeff wasn't coming back, and he was trying to come to grips with that, trying to figure out why. Kids blame themselves for adults' problems. She knew it. Had done it herself.

She reached to touch his cheek, but he leaned away from her hand.

"Tommy, this is what you need to know: I love you more than anything. More than Stone. More than your dad. More than anything."

"More than Gram?"

"More than Gram."

"More than Aunt Elise?"

"More than her. More than everyone and anything. Stone is never going to come between us, Tommy."

He rolled onto his side, and she looked at the back of his head. She knew he was crying silently.

She also knew he'd suffered a loss she could never comprehend. When her family had lost the farm, she'd been embarrassed. But her loss, nearly a quarter century ago now, had been primarily material, the emotional tidal wave crashing only when she felt her father's humiliation at trading his beloved farm labor for the green uniform of her high school's janitorial staff. Tommy's pain at living three miles from a father he never saw surpassed anything she'd dealt with at age eleven.

"Stone won't change anything between you and your dad, Tommy," she said.

"That's the problem."

"What do you mean?"

He continued to lie facing the wall, not looking at her.

"Tommy, what do you mean by that?"

He rolled over. His wet cheeks shone in the light. "If Stone lives here, Dad won't need to come by. He'll think he's been replaced."

"Sweetie, that's not true. Your father knows he's your dad. That can never be changed. And Stone knows that too."

But Tommy was shaking his head.

"Tommy, this is a chance for you to have two grown-ups here for you every day. Not just me, but someone else too. I want you to think about that. But I also need you to remember that Stone isn't your father, never will be. I know you have a father. Stone knows it too, Tommy."

He didn't speak. She kissed his cheek and left the room.

FOUR

Thursday, March 6, 7:55 a.m., Gary's Diner

"HOW ARE YOU?" PEYTON asked, seeing the dark half-moons beneath Stone Gibson's eyes, when she joined the breakfast crowd in Gary's.

Gary's still had the green metal roof from her childhood. She could hear the rain tap-dancing overhead.

"I'm okay," Stone said.

"What time did you get here?"

"I couldn't sleep." He stirred sugar into his coffee and looked out the window at Main Street. "Yesterday the snow melted a little, but now the temperatures are dropping again. It's supposed to turn to freezing rain. Roads will be icy."

"And the heavy snow will make hiking a bitch," Peyton said. "But you didn't answer my question. What time did you get here?"

"You're not easily distracted. Let's just say I helped Shirley make the first pot of coffee."

"Literally?"

He nodded. "You're drinking from pot number three," he said. "You missed the one I made."

"You've been here since, what, five a.m.?"

"I read the Sports section twice."

Shirley, the two hundred-plus-pound silver-haired waitress who once slapped Stone on the butt before learning he was a state trooper, appeared with coffee. She'd been at Gary's longer than the specials Peyton had eaten there as a middle-schooler with her late father. This day, over her prominent stomach, Shirley wore a T-shirt that read *70 IS THE NEW 50!*

She poured Peyton a cup of black coffee, said, "Morning, Peyton," and set a tiny carafe of cream down and dropped sugar packets next to Peyton's mug.

"I love being in here when it rains," Peyton said. "That sound on the tin roof. My father used to love it too."

"He told me that once," Shirley said.

"Really?" Peyton said. "He wasn't much of a talker."

"None of the farmers are. But, in here, after a while, they all open up. I know more about the potato business than newspaper reporters do." She pointed to Stone's *Bangor Daily*.

"Farming isn't easy," Peyton said. She'd learned that firsthand. Most farmers in the region relied on an annual loan to operate their farm, which often included their living expenses. If the price of potatoes unexpectedly slipped, or blight razed the crop, the farmer lost it all in a matter of months. If the work or long hours didn't kill you, the stress would. In her father's case, all three contributed to his short life.

Shirley looked around the diner. She and Peyton were the only females in the room.

"No, not an easy career," Shirley muttered, then shuffled off to refill another cup.

"She knows a thing or two herself about hard careers," Stone said. "She still working alone in the morning?"

"You mean I don't count?" Stone said. "I told you I made the coffee."

"Cute. But seriously, where is all the young help she hired?"

"She told me she lets them sleep in if they have night classes at the community college."

It made Peyton smile. There was no doubt Shirley would do that. The woman had brought Peyton's mother, Lois, casseroles for weeks following the death of Charlie Cote.

"There's just Stan in the back," Stone said, "and he wouldn't let me near the griddle."

"Thank God," she said. "I've seen your eggs."

Shirley reappeared and took their orders. When she left, Stone looked across the table at Peyton. "So," he said, "any thoughts on our conversation the other day?"

"Many," she said.

"I'm all ears."

"First"—Peyton looked at him, tried to read his face; damn him, she couldn't—"you know where I stand on this, right?"

"I think so." Then he frowned, his skin creasing near his eyebrows. "That isn't a good start. Your talk with Tommy didn't go well, did it?"

"You didn't let me finish."

"Sorry, but I question people for a living. I know where the conversation is headed."

"Tommy is eleven, Stone. He thinks his father will never feel obligated to be a part of his life as long as you're in it."

"I'd never want to hurt him or do anything that takes him away from his father. Hell, you know my past with my own mother. I wouldn't want anyone separated from a parent. I've been there."

"And you know Jeff is never coming back into my life. He wanted to, for a while. I said no then, and I'd say no now. He realizes that and has finally moved on. It's healthy."

"And Tommy doesn't understand?"

"He doesn't know everything between his dad and me. He doesn't need to know that. Not at age eleven. All he knows is that he loves his dad and wishes he could see him more often."

Stone stared at her, thinking.

"This is complicated," Peyton said, when Shirley crossed the room to freshen their coffees. "Of course, I'd never say a bad word about Jeff to Tommy. That would crush him—not because he doesn't know it, but—"

"Precisely because he *does* know it," Stone said. "And he knows why."

She looked at him. Around them, conversations swirled about crop prices, Red Sox spring training, and Celtics games. But Stone was staring out the window again watching cars move slowly on Main Street like carp roaming a shallow pond.

"You've been there?" she said, slowly stirring her coffee.

He only nodded.

"I want you to be a part of our lives, Stone. A larger part. A constant part."

"I don't want to come between you and Tommy. If he has no father in his life, he sure as hell needs his mother."

"Yes," she said.

They were quiet for a while. Shirley reappeared with eggs for both of them. Peyton ate slowly, watching Stone intently.

"The thing I keep coming back to," she said, "is that you have so much to offer Tommy. You know what he's going through, what it feels like to have a parent..." She didn't want to say it.

But he did. "Make you feel unwanted."

"You know what he's going through, Stone. I want you to live with us. I'm going to work on it."

"If you force it, I'll never have a chance."

"I know that too," she said.

They ate the rest of the meal in silence, Peyton trying—and still failing—to read Stone's expression.

She was finishing her orange juice when her cell phone vibrated. She recognized the number. "Our surveillance cameras are ready to be picked up and mounted near the shack," she said.

4:30 p.m., Razdory, Russia

The man in the bed was dying.

That was clear to anyone who saw him. Clear even to the man himself. Victor Tankov—who, at eighty-one, now barely weighed his age—hadn't bothered to ask his doctor. Didn't need to. He could feel the tumor in his throat growing, and he'd read the statistics. A year, at most.

It was why he'd begun his search in the first place.

The space on the wall across from his bed was now empty.

He'd left Moscow a month ago, moved to the country house, the one near the river. Had even put the Moscow home up for sale. He knew he wouldn't return to Moscow. He knew, too, that in this economy so few people could afford the home that he might die with it still in his possession.

And what then?

It wouldn't be his problem. But Marfa couldn't handle the business. What would become of it all? He worried about her.

He looked at the vacant space on the wall. That was where the gift would go. Could Marfa handle that too?

Through the window he saw Nicolay drag two sleds through the snow, watched as the giant put the old man's grandchildren on the sleds, and saw them ride toward the frozen pond.

He couldn't make out the children's words through the glass of the double-hung window. His hearing started to fail long ago. But he could see their smiling faces as the sleds bounded down the steep hill.

The children—the eldest, Rodia, in particular—loved the country home. The 1860s Victorian mansion had eight bedrooms, seven baths, and a small pond. While renovations had updated the home, care had been taken to retain the period charm. Victor Tankov was a man who appreciated antiquity and craftsmanship. And Marfa had taken note and promised the gift of a lifetime.

His daughter entered the room. "Still in bed?" Marfa asked.

"It's hard to get up," he said, turning back from the window.

She looked at the art magazine on his bedstand. "I knew Art History professors at NYU who read that."

He smiled. "A self-education is an eclectic one."

"Not just eclectic," she said. "You always had a focus. Remember the family vacations? The Louvre in Paris. The Acropolis in Athens. The Met in Washington."

"It wasn't Disneyland," he said.

"No." She smiled.

"You forgot to mention the Hermitage," he said.

"Your beloved Hermitage."

Outside, Nicolay helped the children up the hill. Marfa moved to her father's side and sat on the edge of the bed. When the bed moved, Victor flinched.

"I'm so sorry, Father."

"For what?"

"For the way you feel." She tried to fix his pillow.

The old man waved it off.

"Why don't you ever let me comfort you?"

"When you've lived like I have," he said, "suffering at the end is part of the price."

"What does that mean?"

"It means there is only one more comfort I want. You know what it is."

"Yes," she said, her eyes running to the wall, "but I thought you'd also want me here. I came to be with you."

"I know you did," he said.

"And you don't care?"

"There's nothing you can do for me."

She knew that, too, although she didn't say it. She looked out the window. His timetable had greatly impacted her own. She turned back to him. Looked at him closely. Would he die sooner than she thought? She couldn't have that. She needed to win, to have him see what she'd done. The irony wouldn't be lost on a man who loved practical jokes as much as he did. She wanted to be there when the size and scope of her plan occurred to him.

"Dimitri used to love sliding on that hill," she said.

Victor looked at his daughter. The pain and anger she saw anytime someone mentioned her late brother's name was there. Then it passed.

"He really did," she said. "I can still hear his laugh."

"He had a great laugh. Marfa, take your children and go to the US. Start over."

She shook her head. "Remember years ago? When you were hurt?"

"I was never hurt," he said.

"When your tooth hurt. Remember?"

"When I had three teeth pulled?" he said.

"You were in bed. I picked flowers for you. I lay next to you and read you a story from my story book. I was six or seven."

"I don't remember," he said.

"Of course not."

"Oh, yes. That was when Dimitri made a painting for me," he said. "It still hangs in the office."

"And you remember that, of course. But not me reading to you. Why would I think differently?"

"What?" he said.

"Nothing." She turned to the window. "Why would I think this gift would be any different?"

"What are you saying?" he said. "I can't hear you."

She shook her head.

"Marfa, I wish I remembered more of those days. At my age, it's better to live in the past, because the past is better than the future."

"That makes no sense, Father."

"Yes, it does. It means I know the life I've led, Marfa. I know what is to come."

"You've been very generous with some people. *Some* people would say that. And you know it."

"Generous with some, not so generous with others. But that's in the past now. The businesses are yours."

"But not the money?"

"I'll give you what you need until I'm gone. Then it's all yours."

That wasn't good enough. Not because he'd live forever, but because he wouldn't.

"I'll need full access while I'm negotiating," she said. "Surely you understand that."

"Why can't you give me the figure and let me handle that?"

"Father, I'm talking twenty-four or forty-eight hours from when I start negotiating at most. But I need to control the money. It's a complicated transaction. You must realize that."

"Yes," he said. "It'll be complicated. Good experience for you."

"Maybe a good experience for *you* too," she said.

"What's that mean?"

"Why don't you think I can handle the money?" she said.

"Nicolay will help you."

"I don't need his help. I'm ready."

"I wish Pyotr was still here," he said.

"Why? The divorce is final. He's gone. I don't need him either."

"Yes," he said, "you do. He's very smart."

"I have an MBA."

"And I'm proud of you, but it means nothing. I have a sixth-grade education and I know business better than those professors you had in America. Pyotr had a businessman's mind."

"You can't be serious. He didn't have the stomach for this life. That's why I left him." She shook her head. "You'll never understand."

"Maybe not."

"I'll show you what I'm capable of," she said.

"I hope so," he said.

She turned to him.

"Are you laughing?" he asked.

She didn't answer. But she was smiling. "One day, I'll show you that I'm better than Pyotr." Then, under her breath, "Better than the son you wish had lived."

"Marfa, you don't have to show me anything—"

But she held up her hand, and he didn't bother to finish.

"I like to think of the good times we've had," he said. "Remember that year you studied in New York City, when your mother and I visited?"

"I miss her every day. She understood me and what I go through."

"I'll join her soon."

"No, Father." *Not too soon*, she thought.

He looked at her, reached, and took her hand. "You're so young."

"No, I'm not."

"We both know it's near," he said.

"More time," she said.

"I don't get to say how much I get. None of us do."

But he'd misunderstood. *She* needed more time. Needed him to survive long enough to see just what she was capable of. And *that* had nothing to do with him receiving the gift. Marfa looked out the window.

He asked, "Are you crying?"

She turned back to him, her eyes absolutely dry. "No."

"Good."

"Nicolay is a gentle giant," Marfa said, changing the subject.

"Giant, yes. Gentle, only to those who deserve it," her father said.

"He's been with you a long time."

"When his father went to prison, he was fifteen. I took him in, gave him work."

"The Moscow home is sold, Father," she said.

He looked at her, impressed. "Really?"

She nodded and smiled. "Don't say you want to sell this home too. The fence and security system took six months to put in place and cost far too much."

"But we are safer here because of them," he said and pointed a bony finger to the window. "And the children are safer here."

"No one would hurt the children."

"Probably not intentionally," he said. "You actually found a buyer?"

"I *persuaded* a buyer."

She sounded convincing, but Victor didn't see the something in her eyes that he knew was in his own. He'd never seen it in her eyes. It hadn't been in his former son-in-law's either. But Pyotr was gone now, so that didn't matter. Nicolay, though, had the look. It was why Victor had initially hired him. Nicolay had begun by doing odd jobs, then driving, and finally doing things few others would do. He knew that neither Marfa nor Pyotr were capable of doing those things.

"Send Rodia to a boarding school," he said, startling his daughter.

"What?"

"Rodia," he repeated, "my grandson. Send him to a boarding school out of the country."

"Like you did to me?"

"Yes. Why do you say it like that?"

She didn't answer.

"He's not cut out for this life either," the old man said.

"*Either?* What are you saying?"

He watched his grandson fall off the sled and roll. "You should move. I can set up an allowance."

"You don't think I'm capable of handling the money."

"I can set up an allowance."

"I'm not a little girl, Father."

"It has nothing to do with that. You weren't successful in school."

"I earned excellent grades."

"No," he said, "not that. You called home crying. You let people push you around. You lost the money I gave you back then."

"That was a long time ago. And why would I leave now? The country is headed in the right direction, with the right people."

"Tough people—tough *men*—are running the country."

"I'm not begging for the money, Father. I'm not a beggar. I'm a businesswoman."

"What does that mean?"

She shook her head. He'd soon find out. "You have no idea what I'm capable of. You've never given me the chance to prove myself."

He didn't speak. He was pale and looked tired.

"I have good news about your birthday gift," she said.

"Where does it stand? Is it close?"

"The boy is in place," she said.

"The Ukrainian boy?"

"Yes. He's in America. It won't be long now," she said.

Outside, snow began to fall.

9:10 a.m., McCluskey's Potato Processing Plant

There was no avoiding him this time.

Peyton had hoped to once again park at the back of the lot at McCluskey's, walk to the area near the shack, attach the cameras to various trees, and leave without seeing Leaf Ryan. But that wasn't happening. She rounded the building in her Ford F-150 service vehicle and found him standing in the middle of the lot, hands on hips, staring straight ahead, as if waiting for her.

It was too warm, so the early-morning rain had never completely turned to snow. It was drizzling. For some reason Leaf Ryan wore sunglasses. He took them off and raised one hand for her to stop. His hand was raw and cracked, as if he spent a lot of time outside without gloves.

She stopped and rolled down her window.

"How are you this morning, agent?"

He wore jeans, a leather jacket, and running sneakers. At least there was no way he was hiking several miles into the woods with her, not dressed like that.

"Very well," she said, "and you?"

"Excellent. What brings you here this morning?"

"I'd like to take a walk through the woods, if that's alright."

"It's raining."

"Not hard," she said.

They both knew there was no need for her to seek permission. Three Bushnell wireless hunting cameras, with tree braces, were in the zipped backpack on the passenger's seat. The hunting cameras would send photos to her phone or iPad via text.

"What's the power drill for?" he asked.

A yellow DeWalt drill lay next to the backpack; she needed it to mount the tree braces.

"It was in the truck when I got in," she lied. "Need to use it?"

He smiled. "No, we have plenty of drills."

"Something wrong, Leaf?"

"So you're walking back there again?"

"That was my plan. Have you seen anyone out there recently?"

He shifted and looked down at his Adidas. "Nope."

She'd asked millions of questions to thousands of people over the years. When someone physically turned away from a question, she knew why.

"Okay," she said. "I'll tell you if I see anything."

"I bet," he said.

She pretended not to hear his sarcastic reply.

———

The snow base on the trail was close to thirty inches deep, and the morning's rain turned the snow wet, heavy, and soft. If Peyton hadn't worn aluminum snowshoes, she'd have exhausted herself slogging through knee- and (if she strayed from the trail) waist-deep snow.

A half mile in, she paused to drink water. The inside of her green Border Patrol ball cap was damp. She'd learned to dress in layers and now wore a long-sleeved Under Armour shirt beneath her eight-pound

Kevlar vest, her uniform shirt atop the vest, and her flannel winter field jacket over that. She folded her field jacket and put it in the backpack.

At the shack, she took off her snowshoes and looked around. Leaf Ryan was nowhere in sight. She sat on a fallen tree for several minutes in silence, listening. Only sounds of the forest: birds, branches cracking under the weight of the moisture-laden snow, snow itself slipping and cascading down in clumps to land on the crusty top layer below like stones into hay. No human sounds: coughing, talking, or even shuffling. No one had followed her.

She put on her helmet, climbing harness, and tree spikes, and chose a large maple.

After shimmying thirty feet up, she mounted the first camouflaged camera. The sound of the DeWalt drill shattered the forest's silence. She didn't like using the loud drill, but she felt safe doing so this far from McCluskey's plant.

When all four cameras were attached—pointing at the cabin and, more importantly to her, at the trail coming and going past it—she returned to the ground. She sat on the fallen tree again, drank more water, and ate a Clif Bar.

A coyote led Aleksei Vann to the US, and that was who she wanted to see on the video images. The owner of the shack, at least to her, was secondary. She doubted they would be one and the same. But she'd review the video for both the coyote and the drug dealer, who was important to Stone and Maine DEA. *Quid pro quo* among law enforcement occurred often, and it seemed appropriate here. Finished with her Clif Bar, she headed back to her truck.

Only when she climbed in behind the wheel and took her phone off vibrate did she realize she'd missed DHHS caseworker Susan Perry's phone call.

5:55 p.m., Donetsk, Ukraine

Dariya Vann was at his tiny kitchen table. Both chairs across from him were empty now.

He wished there were dirty dishes in the sink. At least then he'd know Liliya ate something. But the sink was empty.

The apartment was silent. Liliya slept often now. He tried to be quiet and felt terrible when he woke her even to eat. It was odd how "fate stage-managed" everything. He'd read that phrase a long time ago, back when he'd been living in Boston reading American novels. Who had written the line? He couldn't remember, but the phrase was fitting.

Fate had made Liliya a larger part of his life now than she'd been even when she was healthy. Even though her existence depended on him, he felt, after nineteen years of marriage, somehow alone. She was home, physically struggling through each day, and he was out of the house from dawn till dusk most days, trying to earn a meager living.

He took his laptop from his bag and opened it on the kitchen table to continue working on an article he began that morning, a piece for the *Kyiv Post*. Most of the afternoon had been spent on the streets, in retail outlets, and in bars interviewing residents about the economic impact "the war," as he described it, was having on the region. He didn't need to ask about the emotional impact it was having—he saw that each moment he spent at home.

Everything had changed in Donetsk, for the city and for him. Only two years ago, he was discussing national and international politics on a TV set with city and national leaders. Hadn't been walking the streets, trying to get someone to talk to him. Back then, interviewees came to him, dressed professionally. But his TV career—for now—

was over. One too many accusations directed at the prime minister, the producer had told him upon his firing. Translation: too many tough questions asking Donetsk city leaders and the prime minister about being in bed with Putin. It had probably taken a single phone call from the prime minister's office, and five minutes later he was a freelancer.

Next to his laptop lay a thin reporter's pad. He was flipping through the pages of the notebook, looking for a particular quote.

If it wasn't for Liliya—poor Liliya—he might actually enjoy the new career. From a purely journalistic standpoint, after all, freelancing was more rewarding. He selected stories *he* wanted to pursue, asked questions *he* wanted answers to, the Prime Minister be damned.

He found the quote. It was hard to concentrate with the neighbor's kids running in the apartment overhead. The light fixture rattled each time one of the children jumped. Worse were the fights he heard coming from the apartment next door. It seemed to happen every night, drunken shouts always followed by something sounding like porcelain shattering.

"Hi," Liliya said, her voice a whisper.

He looked up, saw her pushing her walker toward the table, and leapt to help her. She waved him off, but she shuffled around the tiny apartment the way he'd seen the elderly do in nursing homes.

Dariya sat down again. "Did the children wake you? I'll go up and tell them to be—"

"No. I couldn't sleep." She struggled to a chair across from him. "I think of him all the time."

"Me too. Bohana says he's going to school. Says his teachers are impressed."

"It's hard when you don't speak English so well."

"Yes. I know, firsthand."

"I'm glad he's with Bohana. She's been so good to us over the years, sending us what she could, now and then, always writing."

"Yes. She always wrote."

"But you said it's very hard to be there when you don't speak English well," she said. "That's why you left."

"It wasn't the only reason," he said.

"But now we've sent Aleksei there, alone, to face that same problem."

"It wasn't the only reason I left," he repeated.

"Then why? One day you just decided to come home?"

"We've had this talk many times. I was homesick. I was young."

"He's only thirteen," she said. Dark rings hung beneath her eyes. Even when she'd waited tables until closing, she'd never looked this tired.

"How do you feel? How is your leg?"

"The leg will get stronger. It's the pain in my stomach. The pain should be gone by now."

He knew that was true. The doctor had said she'd feel better weeks ago. "I want you to go to a doctor somewhere else."

She looked puzzled. "Where?"

"Switzerland."

It made her laugh. "How could I do that?"

He stood, went to the sink, filled a water glass, and set it before her. He did not answer the question.

"I want Aleksei to have an opportunity," she said. "The one you walked away from."

"I didn't just walk away," he said. "Things weren't always like this. Don't forget that. This war has cost me my career, our home, your health."

"And now our son."

"We'll be together again," he said.

"When? I want him to stay in America, to go to school there."

"There are other places."

"What are you talking about?"

"Switzerland has opportunities," he said.

She sipped her water. "And I want to feel better." She spoke to the floor.

"You will." He reached across the table, took her hand gently. "We'll go to Switzerland, live in the Alps, like you've always talked about."

She smiled. "You're dreaming. We could never afford that."

He smelled meat cooking somewhere in the tenement. "I saw a rat going through garbage behind the building," he said. "These people live like animals. They just throw garbage out the windows."

"I miss our home."

"*You're* my home," he said. "Let me make you something to eat."

"No. I'm tired. I'll go lie down."

He watched her cross the room with her walker and turn left into the tiny bedroom.

Feet pounded the ceiling above him again as he returned to his work. Specks of plaster floated down from the ceiling. The WiFi was spotty, but it connected, and he saw the new email and stopped typing. The message was from TEDO1.

Aleksei is doing well. Saw him today. Looks like you. Hope your wife is feeling better. You can cut your travel time in half if you fly the first leg. Buyer is paying for your ticket. What are your plans for going back? OS account is all set. Buyer knows 30 is a deal. It's worth 150M.

Dariya knew the value of it. And he didn't like discussions over email, not about the transaction. Skype or Google Hangouts were better.

Why only two lines about Aleksei? Everything else in the message was repetitive, even unnecessary, except the airline ticket and the offshore account information. That was finally done. But the accounts were supposed to be separate, with fifteen million going in each. The email referenced only one account. What was that about? He'd stopped trusting people long ago. One account and two sellers? He could do the math.

Dariya stood and crossed the kitchen, tossed another log into the woodstove. Late-afternoon sunlight streamed through the small window above the sink. He hated this rented apartment, but the Buk tore a hole the size of a garage door in the house they'd called home for ten years. That home and even that past life, thanks to the war and to his termination, were gone.

He thought of the fifteen million dollars. It wasn't one hundred and fifty million, but it was more than enough. *Fate stage-managed everything.* It was Raymond Chandler who wrote that line. And Chandler was right: circumstances dictate everything in your life. Dariya knew his circumstances changed three months ago when their house shook and screams woke him.

And he knew they were about to change again.

12:30 p.m., Garrett Middle School

"I had meetings scheduled all day and had to find one I could cancel in order to squeeze you in," Garrett Middle School Principal Peter Thomas, Ph.D., said Thursday after lunch.

He met Peyton and Susan Perry at the front door, and they followed him down the hallway.

"Just let me deliver these papers," he said.

"Of course," Susan said.

They waited in the hallway while he entered the guidance office.

"I think he's trying to make sure we believe this year's tax bill is worth it," Peyton said.

"Everyone tries to seem busier than they are," Susan said. "You know how that goes." She was holding a bottle of VitaminWater.

Thomas reappeared, and they followed him.

"Sorry I couldn't meet sooner," he said over his shoulder. "I'm terribly busy. I'm sure you understand."

"Of course," Susan Perry said and glanced at Peyton.

Peyton let it go. The last work meeting she attended had taken place two weeks ago. Mike Hewitt had called all-hands-on-deck after an intelligence report stated more than two thousand Westerners were now part of the Islamic State in Iraq and Syria (ISIS). A principal Western player was from Boston. The former Massachusetts resident's picture was pinned to the sun visor in most Houlton Sector service vehicles.

Maybe she was being egocentric, but what the hell could be so pressing in the world of a middle school principal?

"The fight started in the locker room before gym class?" Susan Perry asked after they positioned themselves around a table in a conference room near the principal's office.

Thomas turned from Peyton to Susan and nodded. He had blond hair cut short, and Peyton had seen him coaching Little League games.

"Tell us about that," Susan said.

"Does this matter require the Border Patrol?" Thomas asked. "I can see why you need to know about it. You're his social worker. But I'm a little surprised that you brought Agent Cote."

"I called Peyton," Susan said. "She has a solid rapport with Aleksei Vann. I'd like her insights when we talk to him."

"I don't think that's necessary. He punched a kid. I'll handle this." Thomas glanced at his framed doctorate, which hung on the wall to Peyton's right.

Was he glancing at it for reassurance? Peyton looked at the pale, lithe first-year principal and thought he probably needed it.

"What do you have planned?" she asked.

"I'm going to teach Aleksei that this isn't Russia. You don't go around strong-arming people."

"He isn't Russian," Peyton said.

"Yes, I know."

"Do you?" Peyton asked.

Susan finished her VitaminWater and set the plastic bottle in a recycling container near Thomas's desk. "What's Aleksei's side of the story?"

Thomas folded his arms across his chest. "I haven't asked him yet."

Peyton uncrossed her legs and leaned forward, forearms on her thighs. "You know there's a bullying—"

Thomas's head shook back and forth immediately, as if the word itself triggered his denial.

"—problem in this district."

"That's inaccurate."

"The newspaper has published several articles about it."

"The paper's definition of *bullying* is fairly broad."

"Who started the fight?" Susan interjected.

"I haven't determined that yet."

"Part of my role is to help Aleksei adapt to his new surroundings," Susan said. "I'd like to get Aleksei's side of the story."

"Just don't tell me how to run my school," Thomas said.

"It's not actually yours," Peyton said, "and since she's a taxpayer, she technically *can* tell you how to run this school."

Thomas looked at Peyton. "And I can ask you to leave."

"Yes, you can ask," she said. "But I won't."

They waited in silence for several minutes before Aleksei Vann appeared.

————

There was no way he'd lost the fight. That was Peyton's first thought when Aleksei entered the office.

He paused outside the door, looked through the glass, and, after checking to see who was there, tapped on the window. Thomas waved him in.

There was an empty seat between Peyton and Susan, and Aleksei hesitated.

"Have a seat, Aleksei," Thomas said.

The thirteen-year-old did.

"Hi, Aleksei," Susan said. "Remember me?"

He nodded.

Peyton loved Susan's soothing voice; everything about the woman seemed to emanate calm. Hell, if she worked with Susan Perry, she wouldn't need to go to the dojo in the evenings and hit people to release her tension. She'd just have lunch with Susan each day.

"And you remember Agent Cote?"

He nodded.

Thomas leaned forward. "We understand there was a problem in the locker room this morning."

Aleksei shook his head. "Нет Проблем." He caught himself. "No problem," he corrected.

Thomas leaned back in his seat and looked from one woman to the other. "See this?"

"See what?" Peyton asked.

"This attitude," Thomas said.

"I see *you* getting frustrated," Peyton said. "That's all I see."

Susan cleared her throat. "May we move on?"

Thomas sighed. "Scotty Champaign was in here an hour ago with a broken nose. He told me you hit him. I'm pretty sure he's also got a concussion. That means he can't play in the basketball game this weekend."

Aleksei sat staring at the man. He was only thirteen, but Peyton could see it in the boy's eyes: he wouldn't break. He would outlast Peter Thomas, Ph.D.

Thomas saw it too. And he didn't like it. "Tell me what happened," Thomas said.

"He push me and tell me go back to Russia."

"And what did you do?"

"I tell him"—he shook his head—"not from Russia."

"Then you hit him."

"No. I did not."

"I think the important lesson we're all learning here, Dr. Thomas," Susan Perry said, "is that some of your students need to be educated in regards to what's going on in the Ukraine. To accuse a Ukrainian of being Russian, given the political climate, *may* be insulting to *some* people."

Aleksei offered no reaction. He stared straight ahead at Thomas.

"I don't think it's *our* kids who have the problem," Thomas said. "Aleksei, I know you punched Scotty. Do you know that I can suspend you?"

A tiny smile creased Aleksei's lips.

"You think that's funny?"

Peyton watched the interaction, saw Thomas's rising fury. Certain attributes and strengths must be earned. Inner fortitude is one of them. And Thomas had yet to earn a substantial level of it. His inability to deal rationally with a thirteen-year-old was sad, and, given what he did for a living, a little scary.

Aleksei sat perfectly straight in his chair and looked Thomas in the eye and finally spoke. "No, I do not think it funny. My mother say education is gift. I not go to school after the war started. So, no, losing my chance—" He thought, trying to piece the sentence together, couldn't, and shrugged. "Education is not funny. I think *is* funny that no one knows how much I value it."

Peter Thomas opened his mouth to speak, then closed it as if it took him a few moments to process what the boy had said. And to process the subtle insult. "What happened in the locker room?"

"He pushed me down."

"What did you do?" Thomas asked.

"I got up. I will always get up."

"And then?"

The metaphor made Peyton smile—he was a kid who surely *would* get up after being pushed down.

Aleksei shrugged.

Thomas shook his head. "Go back to class."

Aleksei looked at Peyton. She nodded, and he stood and left.

When the door closed behind him, Peyton said, "Did you know he's read *Crime and Punishment* in Russian?"

"I haven't read that book in English," Thomas said.

Peyton nodded. "Most adults haven't, never mind a middle-schooler."

"Clearly he's having adjustment issues, Dr. Thomas," Susan said. "Can you work with your teachers about stressing empathy?"

Thomas blew out a long breath. "I can try, but the kid is from a different place. He needs to learn to fit in."

"Assimilation isn't the answer," Susan said. "Embracing differences is."

Peyton stood. "This school *should* embrace him. He has lots to teach the kids here—not taking their education for granted is the first lesson."

"I'll see what I can do," Thomas said, "but we still don't know what went on in that locker room."

"Oh," Peyton said, "I think we do."

8:35 p.m., Razdory, Russia

Marfa was in the kitchen of her father's country home, making popcorn for her children, Rodia and Anna, when Nicolay entered.

"You skate very well," Nicolay said to Rodia and tousled his hair.

The mansion might have been built in the 1860s, but the kitchen was a sprawling sequence of stainless steel, granite, and track lighting. On the island dominating the center of the room, Marfa separated the popcorn into two bowls. A laptop lay between the bowls. It was black with a red sticker on the front.

Nicolay dwarfed nearly everyone he'd ever met. He took a plate of cold cuts and a bottle of beer from the fridge and sat across the kitchen, watching Marfa work at the island. She heard the chair creak under his weight and could feel his eyes on her back as she poured two glasses of juice for the children. She set the juice before the kids and turned to him. "How is Father?"

"Resting quietly. You upset him."

She glanced at the children; they ate and sipped, neither following the conversation over the crunching of their popcorn. She poured a glass of juice for herself and sat across from Nicolay.

"Why do you say I upset him?"

He shrugged. "He was tired after you left his room. What did you say to him?"

"That's really none of your business."

"I helped raise you, Marfa."

"My mother raised me," she said, "and we both know that."

"She's been gone a long time," he said. "God rest her soul." They were quiet for a time. Then he asked, "Why do you dislike him so much?" His beard was thick—she couldn't recall a time when he didn't have it—and white now.

"He's my father. I love him." She drank some juice.

Nicolay rolled a slice of ham around a piece of cheese and bit into it. "Odd way of showing it."

"Not so," she said. "Father knows I love him."

"You ought to make sure he knows it, given all he's done for you."

"My mother gave me all I have," she said. "Father doesn't think I can get out of my own way."

"He just worries about you."

"No. He worried about Dimitri; he thinks I'm helpless. There's a difference."

Nicolay drank some beer and whispered something under his breath.

"What did you say?"

He shook his head.

"I heard you, Nicolay. I heard what you said."

"What I said is true, Marfa. In some ways you *are* helpless."

"And what ways are those?"

"I don't want to have this conversation. You know I think of you as the daughter I never had."

"He doesn't think I can handle things when he's gone."

"I'm only sixty. He knows I'll be here to help you."

"I don't need your help."

He stopped chewing. "You did that time in New York City."

"I was twenty-three."

"That was old enough," he said. "I was on my own at twenty-three."

"You were on Father's payroll at twenty-three."

"I was *working* for your father."

"I'm every bit as independent as you," she said.

He smiled sadly.

"Don't look at me like that."

"I'm confused. I thought you'd want my help when your father passes on."

"I don't want anyone's help. I will run everything."

"Alone? What are you saying, Marfa? I've been with your father my entire life. When he's gone, I'll work for you. And I'll help you."

She drank her juice and set the glass before her. "What kind of help would that be?"

"Help running it all," he said.

"Is that what you do for my father?"

"Your father doesn't need—" He tried to stop before he finished. But it was too late.

She rose and took her glass to the sink. Then she kissed each child on the head and said, "Uncle Nicolay will clean you up after snack, children."

"Marfa, I'm not your nanny."

She shot the large older man a look, her eyes never leaving his as she repeated, "Uncle Nicolay *will* clean you both up. I have important things to discuss with Papi." Their eyes locked.

And then she turned and left the room.

3 p.m., Garrett Station

"Have you spoken to Aleksei Vann about his father?" Mike Hewitt asked Peyton on Thursday afternoon.

She was seated at her desk in the bullpen, Hewitt standing behind her. He held a copy of the translated version of the twelve-page letter Dariya Vann had sent his sister, Bohana. She could see Hewitt's handwriting in the margins of his copy. Jimenez was at the adjoining desk, doing something on his computer.

"No." She turned in her chair to face him. "Not since Bill Hillsdale was here. What's up?"

Hewitt was looking at Jimenez's computer screen. "What the hell are you doing?"

"Nothing, Mike." Jimenez clicked out of the screen, and the US Border Patrol website, set as his home screen, appeared.

"You're playing fantasy basketball."

"Just checking the results, sir. Just taking a thirty-second break."

Peyton had watched Hewitt cry in a hospital room when Jimenez had been shot a few years earlier. The former Marine had sat in that hospital like a father waiting for his son to wake up, day and night, for nearly a week. He was still a father figure to Jimenez, and Peyton knew what was coming.

"Take breaks on your own time, Miguel. If you need to blow off steam, do some sets on the bench press in the back. I'm in no mood to babysit your ass right now. Peyton, come to my office." He walked away without waiting.

Peyton stood, gathered her iPad, and glanced at Jimenez.

"That guy always kicks my ass."

"Because he sees potential," she said and walked to Hewitt's office.

"Close the door," Hewitt said.

She did, and then sat across from him. He had a stack of printed emails on his desk.

"You know, if you got an iPad, you wouldn't need to print everything."

He looked at her. For a second, she thought he was going to bite her head off too. Then he broke into a large grin. "You and your daily technology advice." He reached into his desk drawer and pulled out the latest iPhone.

"What?! Mike Hewitt has an iPhone?"

"Keep your voice down," he said. "This thing is a disappointment. My flip phone worked better." He took out his reading glasses, pressed them into place with his index finger like a librarian, and said, "How the Christ do I turn it on? I know how to turn it off, but I can never get the thing started again."

"It's not a lawn-mower engine, Mike. You don't 'get it started.' You leave it on. Hold the power button down until it comes on."

"Same as to turn it off?"

"Yeah."

"Who designs these Goddamn things?" he said. "Same exact thing to turn it off *and* on." He shook his head. "How the hell was I supposed to figure that out?"

She watched him turn the phone on. He pressed the button, then stared at the phone as if waiting to see if what Peyton said was correct. The apple appeared in the center of his phone, then the home screen. He shrugged and turned it off again and put it back in the drawer.

"What are you doing?" she said.

"No one called. I'm putting it away."

She leaned back in her chair, covering her mouth with one hand.

"What are you laughing at?" he said.

"May I make a suggestion, Mike?"

"You never seem to hesitate to do so."

"Leave the phone on."

"I turn it off when I'm not using it," he said.

"Why?"

"I always closed my flip phone. It's like hanging it up, right?"

"Mike, that defeats the purpose."

"What? Why?"

"Look," she said, then she caught herself, "that's a longer conversation for another time. What did you want to tell me about Aleksei Vann's father?"

"I read the letter you got from Bohana. Nothing very much in it. The boy's mother sounds as if she's badly hurt."

"Nothing in the letter helps us to know who brought the boy here," she agreed.

"Think that's by design?"

She shrugged.

"You get the boy to tell you who brought him yet?"

"I don't think Aleksei knows the man," she said, "and that is definitely by design."

"And the kid's scared to say anything he does know because the guy threatened to kill his father?"

"Yes. I'm trying to gain his trust."

"That might be a slow process. Might be impossible."

"He'll never jeopardize his father's safety."

Hewitt nodded. "His father, given that letter, is about all he has."

"Agreed." She looked at a photo on the wall of Hewitt standing over a slain deer. "Russia's annexation of Ukraine has left his family in shambles."

"Which means Aleksei's not likely to risk what he has left of it," Hewitt said. "So where does that leave you?"

"Bohana knows something, maybe who brought the boy."

"And she's not saying?"

"Nope. Not yet."

"The State Department called this morning. The father, Dariya Vann, wants to visit his son in the US for a week."

"Excellent. If he comes here, we can ask him all the questions we want to."

"Doubtful. Besides, that's not exactly how Bill Hillsdale sees it."

"He thinks the father will try to stay—immigrate or get here and run? Come on, Mike. The boy's mother is severely injured. Dariya can't be away from her for longer than a week."

"Or, at least, that's what Dariya's saying."

"So Bill Hillsdale is nervous?"

"That's not the word for it." Hewitt smiled. "Hillsdale is beside himself."

"This isn't the Texas border. Doesn't he see that?"

"Bill is a nice guy," Hewitt said. "Actually, he's a funny guy too. But he can't see the forest for the trees. And, besides, everybody I know in Citizenship and Immigration Services is paranoid right now. But, Christ, this station went through a similar mentality following nine-eleven."

She nodded. She knew the reaction of the USCIS was predictable, perhaps even understandable to the members of Garrett Station. September 11, 2001, was a black eye on Garrett Station. Two of the 9/11 terrorists entered the US at this border. And members of this station would never forgive themselves, especially Hewitt, who'd been the Patrol Agent in Charge at the time.

What had that failure led to? Community members would say it had led to a royal pain in the ass. In the months following 9/11, agents made a habit of "routine" checks, stopping people to search vehicles. The state police liked it because it slowed drug trafficking. But it also led to a lot of community resentment. Peyton knew that was why Houlton Sector Headquarters had offered local media outlets a press release announcing her return. BORSTAR AGENT RETURNS HOME had been the headline, embarrassing her but putting a hometown face to the agency that had ramped up efforts by inconveniencing residents.

"Is Dariya Vann in the US?" she asked.

"Not yet."

"Is there a timeline for his arrival and departure?"

"I'm waiting for dates."

"For what it's worth, Aleksei told me his father was staying in the Ukraine until Putin had been defeated."

"Well, maybe he sees the writing on the wall."

"I was going to go to Bohana Donovan's to check in with Aleksei after school. He got into a fight today."

"Really?"

"Someone teased him."

"Given his trip to the US, that's probably not a good idea. Must be a resourceful kid."

She nodded. "I'll tell you what I learn. Now, let me see your iPhone, Mike. I'll show you what it can do."

He hesitated, then sighed and opened the drawer again.

3:45 p.m., 31 Monson Road

Late Thursday afternoon, Michael Donovan pulled off Monson Road to a driveway in front of a small Cape-style home, behind which ran the Aroostook River. He got out of the battered 2005 Ford F-150—which his father called "the parts truck" because the pickup's primary use was running parts to and from the dealership—and looked around carefully.

Four months earlier, he'd been granted early acceptance to the University of Maine's Art History program. But recently he'd read several articles and blogs indicating that one's acceptance could be revoked if you were convicted in a criminal proceeding. And since this afternoon the pickup was being used to transport something very different from truck parts, he was leery.

There were no other vehicles in the driveway, no traffic along Monson Road, so he reached beneath the seat, removed the plastic baggie, and walked to the front door. It opened before he knocked.

The boy standing before him, his best friend since age five, looked tired and pale, his head shiny under the hall light, his eyes sunken.

"Howdy, butthead," Davey Bolstridge said with a smirk.

Michael said, "How are you feeling today?"

"I hurt all over, man."

"Well, I brought you something for that," Michael said and closed the door behind him.

Inside, he followed Davey across the kitchen toward the living room and bath at the far end of the house. But they stopped in the hallway and without speaking descended the stairs to the basement.

Michael couldn't help but think about the previous spring when Davey had been Garrett High's 220-pound clean-up hitter. Michael had rarely played, and the kids on the team gave him a good-natured teasing when he produced a small sketchpad from his bag and sat on the bench, glove beside him, penciling scenes of his teammates in the field diving and running. But Davey was different; baseball was his life, yet now he looked like the team's scrawny freshman manager.

Michael thought, too, of what he'd read on the Internet about kidney cancer. About the statistics. About the words *fatality rate*.

Davey went to the basement window and reached for it, tried to slide it open. Couldn't. "The U-Maine coach called the other day," he said. "He asked how I'm doing. Didn't tell him I can't even open a friggin' window."

"You'll be playing there in the fall," Michael said, and he pulled the window open. "That's still the plan." He held up a fist. "Roommates, right?"

Davey gave him a fist pump but didn't make eye contact.

"You still want to study your art?" Davey said.

"It's not *mine*," Michael said. "That's why I love it—it's created for the benefit of humanity. No one owns it. No one has the right to do so."

"I'll take that as a yes," Davey said. "When you talk like that I think you're about fifty years old."

"You're a butthead," Michael said.

"That's better. Glad the coach can't see me. I've got the strength of a first-grader."

"No, man. You're just forgetting that I'm a hulk." Michael grinned and handed Davey the bag.

Davey took it to the workbench, reached beneath it, pulled out the wrappers, and went to work, rolling a marijuana cigarette.

"Being down here can't be good for you," Michael said. "It's cold and damp, and your immune system is weak."

"Don't have much choice. You know my parents."

Michael did know Davey's parents, had known them all his life. They didn't believe in medical uses for marijuana. Didn't believe in a lot of things. But they did believe in Jesus.

"The pain is so bad sometimes. Remember that time I fell out of the treehouse and you thought I was dead? It's like that, all day, all night. This is the only thing that helps."

"It's legal for situations like yours," Michael said.

"Not according to my parents. They keep saying God has a plan."

"And suffering is part of it?" Michael said.

"Actually"—Davey lit the cigarette—"that's right. They say Jesus Christ suffered for us all. And I'm suffering like him."

Two lightbulbs lit the room, casting elongated shadows across the cracked cement floor. Part of the foundation was stone. Several plastic storage containers were stacked on one wall. Michael could see Christmas lights in one of the clear boxes. The washer and dryer were set on pallets to raise them off the basement floor.

Davey crossed the room to stand near the open window. "You should see this place in the spring, when the river rises. You can fish down here." He took a long hit and blew it out the window. "Sure you don't want to try it?"

"Man, we've had that discussion already. It's not for me."

Davey nodded. "Thanks for doing this. The pain, man ... "

"I know. Thought you were coming to school to visit today."

"Felt shitty this morning."

Michael pushed himself up and sat on the dryer.

Davey took another hit. "I saw what your cousin did in the locker room over at the middle school. It was all over the Internet. He getting suspended?"

Michael shrugged. "He needs to relax. It's all I heard about today."

"There's a picture of Scotty Champaign on Instagram. Looks like your Russian broke his nose."

"He's not Russian. And he's not mine."

"Whatever. Scotty Champaign, Mr. Bigshot Basketball Player— the high school varsity coach had him come to a practice last week. Got what he deserved, I'm sure."

Michael shrugged.

Davey said, "Remember the middle school lockers?"

"When we were in seventh grade?"

"Yeah. That sucked. Well, maybe Scotty tried to shove your cousin into one and got more than he was bargaining for."

"Probably," Michael agreed.

Across the basement, the furnace kicked on, rumbling to life.

"When does your mom get home?" Michael asked.

"She's got the last shift tonight. She went to McCluskey's at three. Dad usually gets home around seven. No idea what he does after work."

He took another hit. Michael watched the joint's red tip glow softly in the sparse light.

"You ever get scared?" Davey said.

"Yeah, I guess. Why?"

"Forget it."

"What is it?"

"I mean really scared, like about dying. Ever think about it?"

"Not really," Michael said.

"I do, you know?"

"Yeah."

"You know why? You understand?"

"Of course."

Davey looked out the window. "I don't want to die, you know? I want to go to U-Maine with you in the fall. See college girls. Do college things."

"You will, man. We're rooming there, remember?"

Davey took another hit and closed his eyes. "Yeah, I remember. I sent my deposit in." He blew out his breath. His eyes were red.

"I should go," Michael said. "Dad will be home soon. He'll want to have another father-son talk. That's what he calls them. It's really him telling me how I should live my life, and me nodding."

"At least your old man wants to talk about things."

Michael looked at him, but Davey turned away.

4:25 p.m., 7 Drummond Lane

Peyton had changed out of her uniform greens into jeans and a gray plaid flannel shirt she'd gotten at Old Navy the last time she'd driven two and a half hours south to Bangor. But she didn't go directly home. Instead, she pulled her Jeep Wrangler into the driveway at Bohana Donovan's home Thursday evening.

"I hope I'm not interrupting dinner," she said when Bohana answered the door.

"Dinner?" Bohana held the door open. "I haven't even thought about it yet. I might be Americanized, but I will never understand why Americans eat so early."

Bohana was not dressed in Old Navy discount attire—that much was clear. She wore a cashmere sweater and capris that fit too well to have been purchased at the tiny Aroostook Centre Mall.

Peyton had to comment on the capris. "I love those."

"It's probably too early to wear them, but spring is in the air. Finally."

Peyton smiled. "It doesn't feel like spring today."

They'd moved from the entryway into the kitchen.

"But I ordered them online. Donna Karan. So I simply have to wear them." She smiled at Peyton. "What brings you by?"

"I wanted to check on Aleksei."

"You heard about today?"

"I was called to the middle school."

"The other students don't understand him." Bohana opened the stainless-steel refrigerator and took out two Diet Pepsi cans. "And Scotty Champaign is a bully, according to my son. Would you like a drink?"

Peyton nodded. "Thank you."

"Glass?"

"The can is fine," Peyton said. "I just want to offer Aleksei a little support. Is he home?"

"That's very kind. He's upstairs. Follow me." Bohana led her through the living room, where they paused near a couch on which a teenaged boy lay sprawled. "This is my son, Michael," Bohana said.

Michael lay looking at a book titled *Rembrandt: His Life and Work in 500 Images.*

"You like art?" Peyton asked.

He smiled as if to say *No shit, lady*. She'd always found teenagers much harder to interrogate than adults because you couldn't fool them. This one wore distressed jeans, white athletic socks, and an orange Moxie T-shirt. He needed a shave, and his hair was unkempt. An Art major, if she'd ever seen one.

"Some art I like," he said.

"Not all?" Peyton asked.

"Not everything should be called art. People try to pass anything off as art. But not all of it holds up."

"You're a smart guy."

Bohana said, "He always has been. He was accepted into the Art History program at the University of Maine and will live in an honors dorm." Bohana patted his leg.

"Mom, *stop*."

"Your mother's proud of you," Peyton said.

"It's embarrassing."

"Keeping an eye on your cousin?" Peyton asked him.

"He's not at the high school," Michael said and sat up.

When he did, Peyton smelled his strong cologne. But, she thought, for a split-second, she also caught a faint, ever-so-subtle hint of marijuana. Yet his eyes weren't dilated; nothing about him seemed impaired.

She followed Bohana upstairs, where they found Aleksei hunched over his desk, his left index finger moving back and forth over the page of a textbook, his right hand scribbling notes into a spiral binder.

He looked up when they entered, eyes narrowing momentarily before nodding at the realization.

"Hello," Peyton said.

"I in trouble?"

Peyton sighed. Bohana sat down on the edge of Aleksei's bed. She motioned Peyton to an upholstered leather chair. Peyton crossed the bedroom and couldn't help but think of Tommy's room. It wasn't much larger than the closet in this "guest room," which offered a skylight and flat-screen TV.

"Do you feel like you're in trouble anytime you see me?"

He turned on his wooden chair to face her. "I did not start fight today."

"I know that," she said.

"Then why ...?"

"Why am I here?"

He nodded.

"To see how you're doing. Just to ask that question, and to see if maybe I can help."

He looked at her for several moments, then he turned to look at Bohana. Bohana smiled and nodded encouragingly.

"They tease me," he said, turning back to Peyton.

"The kids at school?"

He nodded. "Call names, and do not like when I answer all questions."

"Watch your prepositions. 'All *the* questions.'"

Aleksei sat looking at Bohana.

Peyton said, "They call you names during class?"

Again, he nodded.

Peyton had no doubt other kids didn't appreciate his academic drive. "You spoke passionately about your education earlier today. Many kids your age don't appreciate their educations."

"No. They do not. I study most of night."

"Maybe too much," Bohana interjected.

Peyton watched her. Bohana looked at him with parental concern, the way a daunting mother might, not as an aunt who'd only known this boy for several days.

He shook his head. "Not too much. It"—he paused, searching for the words—"*is* not too much for me." He smiled at finding the correct verb tense.

"I know you're trying to honor your mother's wish for you," Bohana said, "but you can't live on three hours' sleep."

Peyton was thinking of how much others—including her own son—could learn from this boy. How much Tommy and other US kids could learn from many of the children she'd dealt with during her career. The kids she'd come in contact with overcame third-world problems that dwarfed the first-world issues her own child faced.

"Who knows you're being bullied at school?" she asked him.

He shrugged. "No matter."

She didn't believe that. Not for a second. "It matters. Someone at the school should be looking after you."

"It does not matter," he said. "Not to me."

He was pale and very thin. But his eyes were bright and intense. And there was an energy in them—at thirteen years old, no less—that she hadn't often seen among the people with whom her work usually brought her in contact. The sad truth of the criminal justice system, she'd admit only when she chose to be absolutely honest with herself, was that most people who committed the crimes she dealt with—the pushers, the mules, the illegal aliens, the desperate border jumpers— were born with two strikes on them already. Those people lacked the razor's-edge she heard in Aleksei's voice and the acute light she saw in his eyes. *If* most of the people she routinely dealt with ever possessed these qualities, life had extinguished such hopeful attributes quickly. She didn't want that happening again, not to this kid.

"What do your teachers say when kids call you names?" she said.

"They do not know."

"Of course." She remembered how sneaky and mean kids could be. How it felt to be different. Her difference had been economic. Not quite the same thing, but different, nonetheless.

"I'll be around to help you," she said.

"What do you mean?" he asked.

She felt Bohana looking at her, probably wondering the same thing. "Just that," she said and stood. "I'll be around."

"At school?" he asked.

"Keep working hard," she told him. "And one more thing—have you heard from your father?"

"No," he said.

In the hallway, Bohana closed Aleksei's door softly. As they descended the stairs, Bohana said, "May I ask what you meant by that, Peyton?"

"Just what I said. I'll be checking in."

"I'm acting as his guardian. He's *my* nephew."

"I know," Peyton said.

She didn't want to engage but didn't want to be rude, either. She needed access to Aleksei to find the coyote who brought him here. So she needed Bohana on her side, especially now that it looked like Aleksei's father—the man who hired the mysterious coyote—was arriving soon.

"But my own son had run-ins with some kids last year, and the school didn't do much."

"You'll see that he isn't bullied?" Bohana asked.

"That's not realistic. I wanted to stop by and let him know I'll do what I can. I mean, the school—this community, for that matter— ought to be embracing this boy. He adds diversity, which we don't have much of up here. Aleksei has a lot to teach us all."

They'd reached the entryway. Bohana stood staring at her. Peyton wondered what she was thinking.

"I appreciate your concern, Peyton," she said. But her eyes told Peyton something else: she wanted Peyton to desist, but couldn't (or wouldn't) say that.

Why not?

"It's no problem," Peyton said. "Have you heard from your brother?"

"Why would I?"

"Hasn't he contacted Customs and Immigration Services?"

"Why would he?"

"I thought he was hoping to come here to check on Aleksei."

"Is he?"

Peyton didn't answer. What was this dance they were doing? Bohana must know her brother planned to visit. Wouldn't Aleksei's father have contacted her to see how his son was faring in the US?

"Have a nice evening, Bohana," Peyton said and stepped outside.

The warm day had turned to a cold, dark evening. The breeze stung her face.

6:10 p.m., Tip of the Hat Bar and Grill
Destiny.

That's what Ted Donovan was thinking about, seated in a window booth after work on Thursday.

His navy-blue button-down shirt had his name stitched across the breast pocket and matched his Dickie's work pants. The steel toe of his right boot was worn bare and shone under the bar lights because at work he had the habit of always dropping his right knee when bending to change a tire or examine an exhaust pipe. He shifted uncomfortably and remembered the screwdriver in his pocket, pulled it out, and tossed it onto the table. It clattered near his glass.

"Want anything else, Teddy?" Becky asked him.

He grabbed the screwdriver and looked at it. "Another beer."

"I must be a mind reader." She wiped her hands on her apron and walked toward the bar.

He didn't smile at the joke. Just watched her go, enjoying the way her jeans fit, remembering how she'd looked in high school. She hadn't changed much. Crow's feet now at the corners of her eyes, but, he had to admit, she'd aged a hell of a lot better than he had. Back then he'd been the point guard; she'd been the cheerleader. Now here they were, still in this tiny border town a few decades later.

He finished the Bud Light before him and took the dinner knife from the napkin-wrapped silverware set and worked it like a cuticle cleaner, prying remnants of oil from beneath his fingernails. He hadn't been able to get the grease off his hands before leaving Donovan Ford, despite five minutes at the sink with the gritty GOJO hand soap that always left his hands dry and cracked.

Becky returned, set the fresh Bud Light bottle before him along with a cheeseburger. "Stop using the silverware to clean your fingernails. That's disgusting."

"You my mother now?"

"I'm your waitress. And hang up your jacket. It's dripping water all over the booth." She pointed to his Gore-Tex Ski-Doo jacket and to the pool of water beside him.

He draped it over the back of the booth. "You're worse than my mother."

"I see you more often than she does, that's for sure—every damned night."

He pointed at the cheeseburger. "I didn't order a burger."

She wiped a ring of perspiration from the table. "You don't eat enough. It's on me."

"If I was hungry," he said, "I'd have ordered something."

"No, you wouldn't," she said and tucked the cloth into her apron. "I'm worried about you, Teddy. You come in here every night, drink four or five beers, eat a few peanuts, and stare at paintings on your computer."

She wasn't exactly correct, but she was close enough to make him nervous. He closed his laptop. "How do you know what I look at?"

"Like I said, I wait on you every night. You've lost weight, especially lately. I'm worried about you."

"I look at lots of things," he said, "not just paintings."

"Who cares what you look at? Eat the burger, Teddy, please." She moved off.

On the TV over the bar he saw his brother's smiling face. *Steven Donovan, owner*, the caption read. Steven—walking around the sales lot at Donovan Ford, smiling at the camera, telling the world about the low goddamned prices.

Through the darkened window, Ted could scarcely make out the Aroostook River, black and fast-moving this March night. He'd always had an artist's sensibility and now saw the metaphor that lay before him: football-sized chunks of ice, reflecting the lights from Main Street, danced past and soon were out of sight.

Like the major-market TV career he still thought about a quarter century after throwing it away when he left Emerson College.

He'd gone to Boston to study with budding journalists from the world over. But then in March of 1990 he drove back to Aroostook County, knowing no matter how successful he was at WAGM, a tiny CBS affiliate station, he'd pass on offers to move on to a larger market. He'd have to turn them down. After the second offer—from a Philadelphia station—he quit network news altogether, and he had been working as an automotive technician for his brother ever since.

But he still believed in destiny.

"How's the burger?"

He turned back to Becky.

"Good," he said, "but I won't be able to finish it. Just a few bites. Ever read Dostoyevsky?"

She shook her head. "Are you about to say something interesting again?"

"He wrote that 'an *extraordinary* man has the right to decide in his own conscience to overstep certain obstacles for the practical fulfillment of his idea.' Isn't that great?"

"I love it when you say stuff like that."

He knew she did. Secretly, he hoped it led to something more between them, even if just for a night.

His eyes left her face and refocused on the dancing ice chunks again. He'd read that line hundreds of times. And he'd faced obstacles his entire life. So why shouldn't he be allowed to "overstep" a few? No one else had the guts to take the chance. Hadn't the world been talking about what he'd done for twenty-five years? And maybe he hadn't fully abandoned his journalism career. Looking at art? Certainly. But researching it, too, for a book. And for much more. After all, he was an expert on the subject. His knowledge of art had distinguished him at Emerson.

She looked at him. "Waiting your table is never dull, Teddy. I'll say that."

"I aim to please."

"I've always meant to ask"—she tapped the *Boston Globe*, which lay before him—"why do you read the Boston papers? Why not the local news in the *Star Herald*?"

She was right. He always had a copy of the *Globe*, even if it wasn't that day's edition, and he read it cover to cover. The real answer to her question had two parts, but he shared only one: "I like big-city news."

"You miss doing the news on TV?"

"It's been years," he said. "You're probably the only one who even remembers I was a newscaster."

"I remember because you were so good," she said. "Too good for the little station in this town. I always thought you'd start here and end up on the *CBS Evening News*." She smiled warmly.

"The next Scott Pelley?"

"That could've been you."

"Not a chance," he said. "Thanks, but I'm happier working on cars," he lied, forcing a smile.

Destiny and sacrifice, he thought.

"I respect that," she said. "Growing a beard?"

"Maybe." He didn't like that she'd noticed that, either. In the coming days, the beard would be necessary.

She nodded and pushed her hair behind her ears. He liked the way she wore her hair. Not quite sure why. Maybe it made her look like she had when she'd been in high school, when they'd both been young.

"I like the beard," she said. "Kind of cute." And she moved off again, went to the bar and talked to Peter Dye, the high school history teacher who tended bar four nights a week. Were they an item?

He liked Becky, liked hearing her say he could've been more. But her compliments, even so many years after his decision to quit his TV job, reminded him why he'd given it up: because six years ago, after waiting nearly two decades, he believed he'd found a way to unload what had become his burden. And with that proposed sale, he might achieve his destiny—to become truly "extraordinary," as Dostoyevsky explained.

But that first offer fell through. Now the burden remained—just a while longer—tucked away, like the major-market TV career he still thought about.

7:35 p.m., 12 Higgins Drive

The open floor plan allowed her to watch him from across the house. Finally, Peyton shifted in the living room chair and set her Lisa Scottoline novel on her lap.

"Tommy," she said, "how's the math homework going?"

He was working at the dining room table and shrugged, not looking up. "You just asked me that a little while ago. It's going the same."

He was right. She'd asked that same question not fifteen minutes earlier. But she could see the struggle on his face. And it killed her to watch him—his pencil stuttering across the page, his eyebrows creasing like clenched fists as his face pinched in concentration.

Dishes had been cleared, the woodstove fed. Through the window she could see snow falling hard, and she could hear the backdraft in the chimney. A strong wind was rolling in from New Brunswick, Canada, fighting against the hot air inside the flue. The forecast called for six inches of blowing snow. In this region, where fifty-below-zero temperatures literally occurred, Strong Woman Winter never left without a fight. So a late-season storm was far from unexpected. But unwelcome, nonetheless.

"Might have a snow day tomorrow," she teased. She set her book on the coffee table, crossed the room, and put another log in the woodstove. She'd received a quote for a pellet-burning stove and

119

was setting aside a little money from each paycheck with that in mind. Next fall, the new stove—and a winter without the hassle and mess of wood—would be her Christmas gift to herself.

"A snow day?" he said. "You think?"

She zipped her fleece up to her chin. "Don't risk it, Tommy. I shouldn't have even mentioned it. Finish your work."

But it was not to be.

The power went out five minutes later.

She walked around the house with her iPhone serving as her flashlight and lit strategically placed candles. Power outages were a way of life in Aroostook County.

She heard Tommy chuckling. "Guess I *can't* finish my homework now. Too bad. I *really* wanted to, Mom."

"Oh, I can hear the sadness in your voice." She turned quickly and tickled his belly.

He squealed with laughter. Then, when she stopped, he said, "I'm too old for that, Mom."

"I'll be tickling you on your wedding day."

"That'll never happen. I'm not getting married. I'll be a Border Patrol agent."

They'd reached the kitchen, and she lit the candle on the center island. She pulled out a stool, sat, and he followed suit.

"Border Patrol agents get married, Tommy."

He shrugged.

"I was married. You know that."

"Yeah, but I just think it's better if you don't."

"Don't get married?"

He nodded. His eyes were focused on the candle. Deliberately? Was he uncomfortable?

"Why shouldn't Border Patrol agents get married, Tommy?"

"I don't know. I just think about you and Dad sometimes. It's easier if you're not married."

"A lot of the men and women I work with are married and never get divorced. Your dad and I getting divorced has nothing to do with my job. Sometimes a marriage just doesn't work out."

He looked up. "Well, it's too hard when it doesn't. So I'm just not going to do it."

She opened her mouth to speak, but then she did something wise: she closed it. She got up, went to the fridge, and rummaged in the dark for orange juice. Poured two glasses and returned to her stool at the island.

"You're talking about how the divorce made you feel, and I know that, sweetie. And I'm terribly, terribly sorry."

"It didn't hurt me," he said, tears in his eleven-year-old eyes—eyes that had seen the world get very big very quickly. For a split-second she thought of Aleksei Vann. Maybe the boys weren't so different. Part of her wanted to tell Tommy what really happened: Jeff simply walked out, left her to raise him alone in Texas. But she wouldn't do that, wouldn't turn him against his father, no matter what said father was like.

She would, however, try to provide a better role model for him.

"Are you ready for your karate competition this weekend?"

He nodded.

"You've been working hard," she said.

"Yeah."

"Is Stone a tough teacher?"

He nodded. "But he says I'm ready."

"That's great," she said. "I'm so proud of you, of how you've stuck with it. Not everyone does. Not everyone has it inside them to do it. It takes a lot of work and discipline to earn belts. You ought to be proud."

"I am kind of proud." He was looking at her now, smiling.

She'd positioned Stone into the conversation—had manipulated Tommy to do so and didn't feel great about that. But it was a conversation they needed to have.

"I want to talk about Stone, Tommy."

"What about him? He's my karate teacher. That's all."

"He might be someone you can do things with, someone you can talk to."

"I don't need that. I have you."

"You do have me."

"And *I'm* the man of the house, Mom."

"That's an awful big burden, pal."

"Don't call me *pal*. I'm not a little kid. It's not a burden." He turned and looked at the candle flame.

"Tommy, nothing between you and I would change if Stone moved in. I would never do anything unless I thought it would benefit you. I think this could make your life better. I want you to know that."

"We don't need anybody but Dad."

"Tommy, we still have Dad," she said, but her statement made no sense, and the conversation was getting away from her.

"Well, he can't come back if Stone's here."

She looked at him and inhaled deeply. "Tommy, I don't think you should wait for Dad to come back."

He turned away from the candle to look at her, eyes suddenly wide. She only nodded—knew it would hurt him, but had to.

He got off his chair and started across the room, into the dark house.

"Tommy," she said.

"No. *Don't talk to me!*"

She heard him climb the stairs in the dark and heard his bedroom door slam. She didn't give chase. He needed time. She finished her orange juice, rinsed both glasses, and went to bed.

The house remained dark.

FIVE

Friday, March 7, 7 a.m., Razdory, Russia
"I'm not an invalid," Victor Tankov said.

Although, at eighty-one and unable to walk, he knew that was precisely what he was. In fact, unbeknownst to his daughter, Marfa—sitting bedside with her own three-year-old daughter, who played with her dolls on the floor—he knew he was dying soon. He'd gotten worse since she arrived. Maybe it was the excitement of having the grandchildren in the house. Maybe it was his desire to rejoin his late wife, Dunya, who'd passed long ago. Maybe it was the stress of Marfa desiring to step into his shoes. Whatever it was, although the doctor had told him he had upwards of a year, he knew it was far less.

Esophageal cancer. Stage IV.

"What are you thinking about?" Marfa asked.

His eyes blinked, as if he were coming back from some faraway place. "Your mother. What would she think of her granddaughter?"

"Don't talk like that, Father. It makes me too sad. She was so strong, so inspirational."

"She was stubborn," he said. "I'm glad you're not like her."

"That's an insult."

"I worry about my grandchildren. Take care of me, grant my final wish, then leave the country, Marfa. You're a mother."

"And a businesswoman, Father. You misjudge me—always have."

"I did not mean to upset you."

"I have an education in business, Father."

"Yes, I know. Take it. Go to America or Italy or Canada. Use it. Be safe, and be well."

Outside, the snow had stopped falling. Sunlight shone brightly in the window and reflected off the crusty white landscape surrounding the estate. Nicolay, up early, stood on the frozen pond. Rodia skated around him, laughing as the giant feigned to grab him.

"You sound like Pyotr, Father. He thought I would be content as his housewife, so I left him."

"I know. I should have spoken to you before it came to that."

"What would you have said?"

"Think of your mother. She was fulfilled."

"As a housewife, Father? Is that what you're saying?"

"Why do you ask that?"

"Mother always felt that you held her back."

She saw his face redden. "Don't speak like that. You know nothing of our relationship. I only want you to be happy. Pyotr was a good husband."

"He was a chauvinist."

"I only want you to be happy and safe."

"I'm alone," she said, "and I'm happy now."

"I wanted more for you."

"But *I* want to follow in your footsteps."

He raised his hand and pounded the bedsheets, a sound no louder than someone fluffing a pillow. But it took all his strength. "No," he said. "I don't want that."

Three-year-old Anna started to cry.

"It's okay, darling," Marfa said. She took her daughter in her arms. Victor leaned back, still looking at her. "Don't you see? Look at yourself." He pointed to the wall mirror across the room.

Marfa's reluctant eyes betrayed her and sought out the mirror. She saw herself instinctively rocking Anna as she had when the girl had been an infant and awoke at night.

"You're a mother, first and foremost," Victor said. "That is not a weakness. It just is. Leave. Promise me you will leave."

"The only one who has left is Pyotr."

"I hope you see him again soon. Maybe he'll take you back. Why are you smiling?"

She didn't answer, only thought of the irony of his statement. *If he only knew.* "Remember when you asked Mother if I was gay?"

"I was worried."

"No, just confused," she said. "You're still confused. You don't understand independence among women. I was independent, even at sixteen. I didn't *need* a boyfriend, Father. And now I don't *need* a husband. I'm a strong woman. You'll see just how strong I am."

"When you get me what I've asked for?"

"Sure," she lied. "That's it." Marfa turned and walked out of the room.

Peyton entered the office and handed Miguel Jimenez a Tim Hortons coffee.

"Thanks. What's this for?"

"No reason," she said.

He pushed back from his desk, the wheels of his chair squealing. "I thought you liked espresso in the morning."

"I do," she said, "but I thought I'd bring you a pick-me-up instead."

Much to Tommy's chagrin, there had been no snow day, so they'd stopped at Tim Hortons for a hot chocolate on the way to school.

Jimenez set the coffee on the desk and folded his arms across his chest. "This is because Mike yelled at me yesterday, isn't it?"

"No, I was just thinking of you. The way I do a pain-in-the-ass brother."

"You don't have a brother."

"But if I did, and if he were a pain in the ass, he'd remind me of you, I'm sure."

He smiled at her and reached for his coffee. "Tim Hortons," he said. "This might be the one thing I miss when I transfer back to Texas."

"And my jokes," she said.

"Not so much."

She was still standing, about to head to the locker room to change from jeans into field greens. "Still talking about leaving us?" she said. "Want to go back south, huh?"

Jiminez was a lifer, that much she knew. He'd gotten a tattoo featuring the Border Patrol emblem as soon as he'd graduated from the Academy. But she always knew he wasn't long for the northern border. And she knew why.

"It's home, Peyton. You get that."

She nodded. "Of course. That's why I'm here."

"I knew I'd need experience along the northern border if I ever want a shot at being a PAIC. Now I have that experience."

"You want to be a Patrol Agent in Charge?" she asked. "After seeing what Mike goes through? Fighting for funding, meetings all day."

"Yeah. Why not?"

Her backpack was slung over one shoulder. She set it on her desk and shook her head. "Not me. I like being in the field."

"You can still do some of that."

"Not enough." She pulled her cell phone from the pocket of her fleece and slid it into her backpack with the items she had for hiking: Clif Bars, VitaminWater, extra wool socks, spare gloves, and a rescue flare.

Jimenez set his coffee on the desk and scrolled through a map on his iPad. "What are you up to this morning?"

"I'll snowshoe the area along the Canadian border where Aleksei Vann entered the US."

"The Ukrainian boy?" he asked.

She nodded, left her cup and phone next to the backpack on her desk, and started for the locker room to change.

"Peyton," Jimenez called, "your phone is vibrating."

She came back, saw the name—as did Miguel—and answered it.

"Haven't heard from you in a while," Stone said.

"I know." There were only two female agents at Garrett Station, so she knew she could find privacy in the female locker room.

"How's Tommy?"

"A work in progress."

"Aren't we all?" he said. "Hey, this is a business call. Have you had a chance to review the video footage from your cameras?"

She sat on the chair in front of her locker and looked around the empty room. Ten lockers lined the east wall across from a shower and two toilet stalls. "The video from my tree cameras?"

"Yeah. You've forgotten about them, haven't you?"

"Of course not," she lied.

"Could you take a look at the video this morning? See if we can determine who's growing pot behind McCluskey's?"

"I was planning to snowshoe behind that shack this morning."

"What if I offer to buy you dinner tonight?"

"You're bribing me?"

"And I'll give you a shoulder rub."

"We both know what that usually leads to," she said.

"I have no idea what you're talking about. It was an innocent, friendly gesture."

"Right," she said. "Give me the morning. The cameras have been out there for a while now. It'll take me some time to go through the video."

"Call if you see anything interesting, please."

"You've brought the Maine DEA in on this, haven't you?"

"Affirmative."

"Keddy's," she said, "at six thirty."

"How about my place?"

"I've had your cooking," she said.

"I was thinking more about the shoulder rub," he said.

"I've had that too."

He laughed. "Ouch. Actually, I was thinking Tommy might come with you."

"That would put a damper on the shoulder rub."

"But it would give me a chance to spend some time with him."

"You know," she said, "you're actually a very good guy."

"That's why I offered the shoulder rub."

"We both know why you offered the shoulder rub."

"And it was purely altruistic," he said, laughing and getting in the final word before hanging up.

———

Jimenez was gone, had left for the field, when she returned to her desk with her iPad in a thick rubber OtterBox case.

The field scan option on each camera had been preset for one-minute intervals, and she hadn't reviewed what had been recorded the previous day. Scanning the images sent to her iPad would be time consuming. So Peyton settled into her chair and began the task.

A large doe was caught in one frame. She paused the slide show, looking for human footprints. The snow was crusty and frozen in this image. So she knew it was more than a day old.

An hour later, she reached an image of falling snow. It had come from last night, when six inches had fallen. Looking closely, she saw something near the shack that resembled a boot print. A trip to the site might confirm it as animal or human, or she might find the snow completely covering the track.

The cabin, however, wasn't her main priority. She was hoping the video would reveal people or, more likely, one man—someone who looked like he knew how to enter and leave the US without detection. Someone who could've led Aleksei Vann from Ukraine to the US.

She'd worked through frame-by-frame images, hating desk work more than ever. Her mind wandered. Jimenez had been caught playing fantasy basketball. At his age, before her marriage and Tommy, she'd have used her off-duty hours to scour these video images. Back then, in her early twenties, when fewer than 10 percent of agents were female, professional success and proving herself to be as good or better than male agents had driven her.

A deer appeared in one image. She watched it cross the screen, frame by frame, like a silent movie reel. It sniffed the ground and moved off.

Had she been a better agent back then? Or just unproven and hungry? She knew now she tried to be a better mom than agent. Felt like she failed at that. A lot. Stone said she was too hard on herself, but Tommy deserved the best she had.

She stopped thinking, squinted, and paused the iPad. Scrolled back and let the frame play again.

"Gotcha," she said aloud, took out her iPhone, and called Stone.

11:15 a.m., near the Canadian border
"What's this?" Peyton said, when Stone climbed into her truck and handed her a paper bag.

"It's the least I could do."

She opened the bag and saw a burger wrapped in wax paper atop a container of french fries. "Is this from the Blue Moose?"

"You told me the Blue Moose has the best fries in Aroostook County," he said.

"You drove halfway to Houlton to get me fries?"

"I was checking on Sara."

She recognized the name of the victim in his child-abuse case.

He nodded and picked up the grainy black-and-white photo on the seat between them. "I had to get more testimony."

"That must be brutal," she said.

He didn't have to answer. He was looking at the photo. The radio was silent. They'd met between Route 1A and the Canadian border, several miles behind the McCluskey's Processing plant. She was to hike the trail, snowshoeing when needed, and the burger and fries wouldn't help her. But she didn't want to insult Stone. And she did love fries from the Blue Moose.

"I can't eat the burger," she said, "but I'll eat the fries."

"We can't let the burger go to waste." He reached into the bag.

She smiled. "That's big of you."

"I have to cancel dinner," he said. "I'm staking this place out tonight. Very sorry."

"I understand."

"I knew you would," he said. "You know what it's like."

"To have to drop everything for work? Oh, yeah. Stay warm."

He nodded. "I have a tent and a sleeping bag good for minus forty."

"Are you alone?"

He nodded. Then, in what she knew was an effort to deliberately change the subject because he didn't want her to worry, he said, "I brought a good book." Along with the one printout, she'd emailed photos from her surveillance cameras. He had his phone out and was looking at a photo she'd emailed him.

"I wish the photo was closer and not so grainy," she said, pointing to his phone.

"It looks like a man," he said.

"But the hood and sunglasses make it difficult to determine. And the scarf doesn't help."

"I think it's definitely a man. And he knows what he's doing—the hiking gear, the winter-wear. He's prepared for the climate and the conditions."

"You make him sound like a pro."

Stone thought about that. "Not sure. We're only talking about six marijuana plants. But he's growing them pretty damn well in sub-zero temperatures. Think there's a connection to your Ukrainian boy?"

"Aleksei didn't mention the structure. But he hasn't said much to me. I'm still working on that."

"Trying to gain his trust?"

"Yeah, if we can find this guy"—she pointed to the photo of the man wearing the blue winter jacket with a yellow emblem on the collar—"you can have your drug bust, and I'll question him about what he saw out there."

"I wanted to spend time with Tommy tonight," Stone said.

"He didn't even know we were going over for dinner," she said, "so he won't be disappointed."

"But I am," he said. He dropped the hamburger bun back in the bag, folded the wax paper around the patty, put it inside his backpack, and opened the truck door. "Rain check?"

"Of course," she said. "Be careful."

"You too." He stepped out and closed the pickup door, then waved and started into the woods.

11:45 a.m., Garrett Middle School
Aleksei Vann was sitting at the end of a table at the back of the library in Garrett Middle School. The novel *We Were Here* lay open before him, but he wasn't reading; he was thinking.

About how it felt to be alone. To be unwanted.

About how things had been different back home.

About how this had been his father's idea. *A better life*, his father told him.

Was it? Would it be?

He was wearing new clothes—an Abercrombie & Fitch sweatshirt and Levi's, for starters, thanks to Aunt Bohana. He was doing very well in the high-school Algebra II class, the only eighth-grader in it. But the students laughed when he spoke, repeated his phrases, and took pleasure in correcting him.

The boy at the other end of the table was a sixth-grader. Other eighth-graders were at the round tables, seated in twos and threes, at the front of the library. Aleksei looked at them, watching them talk, secretly text each other with phones under the table, and laugh quietly. The laughter was what he noticed, what he missed. Laughter meant you were part of the crowd. It meant that you had friends. He'd yet to share a laugh with his cousin Michael at the Donovan home, and he certainly hadn't laughed with anyone at school.

But not everyone from Garrett, Maine, laughed. There were other outsiders, even among the locals. He'd seen that, seen how kids treated some others. That didn't change in America. Same as it had been back home. An "in" crowd and an "out" crowd.

In the Fiction row, a girl—Ally, that was her name—with clumps of greasy, shoulder-length blond hair moved her index finger down the spines of books, looking for something particular. She wore blue jeans. Not the tight-fitting jeans most of the other girls wore. Her jeans were baggy, faded, and were usually torn near her knee. Clearly hand-me-downs. He'd never seen her in a winter coat, just a gray Patriots sweatshirt. Her hands were usually stuffed in the pocket. No gloves or mittens.

Aleksei was watching her when she turned and scanned the library, her eyes stopping on him. Then she approached. Had she seen him looking at her? They'd never spoken.

"You reading that?" She pointed to the copy of *We Were Here*.

He shook his head. Outside of class, he spoke as little as he could. It was easier to fit in if no one heard his accent.

Her eyes were on the book, hands hanging stiffly at her sides. "You sign it out?"

He looked at her index finger—raw and cracked. Saw the dried blood.

Her hand went quickly into her sweatshirt pocket. "What are you looking at?"

"Nothing," he said.

"Tell me where you're from, again."

He told her.

"I hear you're in Algebra II," she said. "I'm in the other section. You and I are the only eighth-graders who walk next door to the high school to take it."

"Really?"

"Uh-huh. You like it here?"

She bent like she might take the seat beside him, but then stopped, looking over her shoulder. Two girls—one in a cable-knit turtleneck sweater, the other in a basketball jacket with *Scotty* stitched into the sleeve—were watching from a nearby table.

"It's not home," he said. She had been the first one in his new school to seek him out. "Want sit down?"

She shook her head. "You beat up Scotty Champaign?"

He shrugged.

"I hear that's a good book." She pointed.

He slid it to her. "Take."

"Take it? Really? You don't want to read it first?"

He shook his head.

She snatched it off the table and took a step toward the librarian's desk, then turned back.

"Scotty's a jerk. So are a lot of kids here. He's been teasing new kids or nerds for a long time. A bunch of us were glad you broke his nose."

He didn't say anything.

"You're pretty quiet, huh?"

He just looked at her.

"Joining the math team?"

"Is there math team?"

"Were you on a math team where you were before?"

He nodded. "And skeet."

"Shooting?"

"Yes."

"We don't have that here. I'm on the math team. You should join."

"Okay."

"Yeah, you'll join?"

He nodded.

"It's in room six. Right after school. See you there."

She took *We Were Here* to the circulation desk. As the librarian checked the book out, he was thinking about the math team, about being part of something.

The girl turned and looked at him over her shoulder. When they made eye contact, he smiled at her.

She looked away.

2:15 p.m., 7 Drummond Lane

Michael Donovan ascended the stairs to the one-time attic, now the third-floor apartment. As a precaution, he carried the sudoku book Uncle Ted left downstairs. He could say he was just returning it, if Uncle Ted appeared and asked why Michael had let himself in.

Of course, he'd have to explain knowing where the spare key was. And there was certainly no precautions for the rest of the visit. Never was. Maybe that was partially why Michael loved doing this—the risk.

The first time he'd come here alone and looked at it inside the box and wrapped in plastic, he doubted its legitimacy. After all, it had been missing over two decades. Hidden in Aroostook County, Maine? Eight hours from where it had been taken? But there was something about it—he'd unwrapped and rewrapped it six times now—that spoke to him. The precision, the mastery. Then, of course, when research told him of the telltale marks, he knew.

There were a million reasons to take it. But he didn't. Simply couldn't do that. It wasn't Uncle Ted's future that bothered him. But what if his parents were involved? Could they be? Could they *not* be? It was, after all, their house. But he'd never seen either of them enter the apartment. They gave Uncle Ted privacy. Yet they'd lived in the house since before Michael was even born.

Besides, if he didn't wait to see what Uncle Ted and (maybe) his parents had planned for it, what were his other options? Return it to its rightful owner?

And just who, exactly, was that? The last person you could call the "owner" was long dead. And what would become of his parents, of his family, if he did that?

So, as he'd done several other times over the years, he simply looked. Admired. Twenty minutes was long enough.

SIX

Saturday, March 8, 8:55 a.m., 7 Drummond Lane
Michael woke to a text on his vibrating phone. It was from Davey
Bolstridge: Pain is bad, dude. can you get me some?

Michael read it. Ya, later this morning he replied and grabbed
a backpack from his closet, put on jeans and baggy wind pants over
them, wool socks, and hiking boots.

Bohana stopped him in the kitchen. "Where are you off to?"

"Hiking, Mom. Be back for lunch."

"Your cousin might want to go."

"No. Going alone."

"Where?"

He was taking a water bottle from the fridge. He wasn't going too
far, but he had to sell the hike. He paused, thinking of what to say.

"You must know where you're going, Michael."

"I do. There's a trail behind McCluskey's. Going to take some
pictures."

"You and your pictures," she said. "Ansel Adams is what I should call you." She pointed to one of his photos hanging on the wall in the hallway behind him. "So talented. You said you'll be home for lunch?"

"Probably," he said and headed for the front door.

9:30 a.m., Dojo, Caribou

The Saturday morning atmosphere inside the dojo, Peyton thought, was a cross between a hockey game (bloodthirsty, crazed parents) and a tennis match (upper-crust, subdued spectators). She didn't know which group she fit into; hoped neither.

She sat silently in the back row of maybe thirty parents, separated from the mats by thick plate glass. She noticed, as she did at all of Tommy's events, that she was there alone. She felt like a single mother more at Tommy's events than at any other time. A boy younger than Tommy and wearing a *gi* sat next to his parents in front of Peyton. The man next to him, in a tan Carhartt jacket, reached over and gave the boy's shoulder a gentle squeeze. The boy looked at him and smiled.

Through the glass, she saw Tommy standing beside three other boys. Stone Gibson, as their instructor, was offering last-minute directives. One by one, the boys nodded. Stone pointed to an area in the back corner, and two of the three boys moved off and began stretching. Now Tommy was alone with Stone. The off-duty trooper leaned forward and spoke, his face serene, his smile warm.

Tommy's back was to her, but she knew her son, knew his body language. He wasn't returning Stone's smile. His head was down, eyes focusing anywhere but on Stone's. Still, his back was steady, which meant there were no tears. Eventually, Tommy's eyes found his hands, which fidgeted with his belt.

Tommy typically hung on Stone's every word, especially in the dojo. This day, though, he seemed set on finding distractions. Was Tommy nervous? Or was he seeking anything to take him away from Stone? She knew her son well enough to know the answer.

Stone shrugged and smiled, then patted Tommy on the back, and Tommy moved off to be with the other boys. Stone looked up, scanned the small audience beyond the glass. When his eyes met Peyton's, he shook his head.

11:45 a.m., Gary's Diner

"I need to use the bathroom," Tommy said. He slung his North Face jacket into the booth and walked off. Peyton and Stone had just slid onto the bench across the table from Tommy.

"Maybe I shouldn't sit beside you," Stone said.

"What do you mean?" Peyton asked. She smelled the same onion rings she'd eaten when her father had taken her here at Tommy's age.

"If we sit next to each other, Tommy has to sit alone, across from us. Might send a bad message."

Peyton exhaled. "Like we're ganging up on him?"

"Maybe," Stone said. "I'm just thinking aloud. I don't know what to do. This morning was rough. He won't look at me. He didn't want advice and wouldn't listen to me during his match."

"That's probably why he lost," she said and looked across the diner at the men sitting at the counter. Several talked about the upcoming potato season, about anticipated prices. One wore a tan Carhartt jacket, the kind her father used to wear; the other wore an orange hunting vest over a sweatshirt and hoodie. She turned back to Stone. "Obviously I've been talking to him about you moving in. And obviously you know where he stands on that right now."

"Still thinks I want to replace his dad?"

She nodded.

"Let's try something," he said.

"What?"

"Why don't you leave?"

She looked at him. "Go home?"

"Yup. Leave me alone with Tommy for lunch. I won't mention moving in, just talk to him and about him for a while."

"And if he flips when he comes back and finds me gone?"

"Peyton, he's not going to walk home."

She smiled. "Oh, he just might. You don't know my son."

"I know him well enough. Let's try."

She stood. "Great, I'll run some errands," she said. "Text me if you need me."

"I won't," he said.

"Confident?"

He smiled. "Certainly."

"And foolish." She gave him a quick peck on the cheek.

Then she strolled briskly toward the door, just before Tommy reappeared and said, "Where's Mom going?"

"She wanted to do some shopping. I told her that was boring and you and I would meet her back at your house," Stone said, trying not to emphasize the word *your* too much.

12:10 p.m., near the Canadian border

Michael Donovan, hauling gas for the generator, set the red container in the snow and approached the shack's front door.

He stopped suddenly.

Tracks near the door startled him.

142

He went inside and found everything just as he'd left it—nothing moved or taken. He went back outside and stood near the boot prints. Someone—a man, judging from the size of the prints—had walked to the shack and circled it. So Michael walked back to the trail and followed the tracks north.

He'd never seen anyone on the trail. Michael had stumbled upon the shack one day while taking photos of a red-tailed hawk. Then Davey had fallen ill. And three months later, he'd asked for help. And you don't say no when your best friend is in pain and has cancer. You figure out how to get him what he wants. Even if it means building something that could jeopardize your college acceptance.

He looked at the tracks again. His father and mother would kill him if he got caught. (How ironic, if they were in on what Uncle Ted was hiding.) The fact that he'd never even smoked the stuff and had only learned how to grow it from watching YouTube videos wouldn't matter to them. Nor would it matter to the University of Maine Admissions Office.

He kept following the boot prints. Whoever had been to the shack had come from the north, parking near the Canadian border and heading south toward McCluskey's. The boot prints veered off-trail into the powder at the crest of a rise, as if the hiker had seen the shack and, curious, had been drawn to it.

Michael considered that. A shack in the middle of the woods was an odd sight; he himself had noticed it a year ago. Having seen it on a hike, he'd immediately gone to check it out. "I had to cut branches to get to it, but it's like the bus in *Into the Wild*," he later told Davey. So he wasn't surprised someone noticed it. The question was, had the hiker entered the shack? No snow puddles had been left behind. No evidence that the hiker entered.

His breaths formed tiny clouds in the crisp morning air. The sun was bright overhead. He took off his Oakleys and rubbed his eyes. Recent forecasts had predicted as much as eight inches of snow. Less than that had fallen, but the powder atop the crusty layer made tracking easy. It would've been a good day for hunting. But deer season had come and gone, and he hadn't bothered to get a license this year. His father had suggested they spend a few mornings together in the woods, but Michael had declined. Part of him felt bad about avoiding his father and uncle. Yet it was hard to be around them without thinking of Uncle Ted's apartment. And he couldn't bring himself to mention it. After all, what would he say? *Please explain why we have an international treasure in the attic apartment?*

The shack lay in the valley between two small bluffs. The footprints led him to a spot sheltered by thick balsam firs where the thin cover of snow was packed evenly. Michael's hands were cold inside his gloves. He clenched his fists, then stretched his fingers wide, like an old man fighting off arthritis. A sudden breeze turned the blowing snow into needles peppering his cheeks. Snow careened down the back of his jacket, and he shivered at the icy spiders crawling down his spine.

Someone had created a shelter here. The nylon underbelly of a tent had packed the snow; he knew that immediately. He took one hand out of his glove and blew warm air into his fist, thinking. Whoever had spent the night here had not entered the shack. Had they peeked inside? Had they slept here because the small bluff offered a clear view of the shack?

If the answer to those questions was yes, it explained why the hiker had left the pot plants, the generator, the portable heater, and the heat lamps exactly as they were: because the hiker he was now tracking was actually tracking him, hoping to catch him entering and leaving the shack with pot.

The snow on his spine no longer felt cold. He was sweating, his mind somersaulting.

Davey had never before complained about the pain, but today he said it was bad. He needed the dope today.

Someone—a cop?—had spent the night near the small wooden hut. To watch it? To see who was growing the pot? What if he was being watched now? Maybe he was over-reacting. The hiker, to his knowledge, hadn't entered the shack. So did the hiker even know what was inside?

His best friend since age five had cancer. And he was in pain.

Michael went back down to the shack, got what he'd come for, and left.

6:30 p.m., Donetsk, Ukraine

Dariya Vann watched Liliya sleep. The bedroom was dark save for a shaft of light pouring into the room through the curtains from the street lamps. She lay peacefully beneath a white quilt in the metal-framed bed. Her dark eyelashes fluttered but never separated, and the corners of her mouth rose and fell with the emotions of whatever dream she was having.

He wanted to do more but knew there was really little he could offer her, aside from providing basic care. He helped her into and out of the shower, cooked her soft bland foods, helped her down the stairs when she wanted to leave the tenement to get fresh air. But those things weren't enough. He wanted to *fix* her, whatever that meant—wanted to make her leg finally heal, wanted desperately to take her abdominal pain away. But he wasn't a doctor. And for at least a little while longer, he couldn't afford to get her the medical attention she needed. So he settled for watching her sleep.

He was smiling when she rolled onto her side.

But then she screamed, her eyes opening wide as she sat up, gasping for air like one who breaks through the water's surface after being under too long.

Startled, he scrambled to his feet, his wooden kitchen chair toppling over backward.

"Liliya," he whispered, "you were dreaming. It was only a dream."

She leaned back against the wooden headboard, eyes opened wide, breathing heavily. Then she swung her legs over the bed's edge and began struggling to her feet. He grabbed her by the arm.

"Aleksei," she said, "where is he?"

"It was only a dream," he said, rising and gently easing her back to the bed. "Just a dream, Liliya. There are no more bombs."

She sat on the edge of the bed, her feet on the floor.

"Lay back," he said. "Rest."

"Aleksei shouldn't be there alone. Something's going to happen to him. I can feel it."

"It was only a—"

"No," she interrupted, her eyes focused now. "Not the dream. I just know. I can feel it. Like the day he broke his leg."

"What are you saying?" he said. He was still standing and, although he wasn't conscious of it, he wiped his palm on his pant leg.

She sat ramrod straight. "You know what I'm saying."

He did. When Aleksei had been young and was visiting cousins at Liliya's sister's, somehow (they'd never learned the details; they'd just been happy when he returned home with only a broken leg) he'd fallen nearly thirty meters from a window and was rushed to the hospital. Inexplicably, almost simultaneously with the accident, Liliya, at the counter chopping carrots, turned to Dariya and said, "Aleksei is hurt. We need to get to my sister's."

Dariya sat down again. He'd never forget that day, never forget her gently laying the knife on the countertop, nor the expression on her face. She *knew* something had happened, and she was certain the feeling she had wasn't coincidental. Somehow, someway, she knew it. And her knowledge, no matter how it was gained, had been accurate. A mother's intuition?

Dariya had no idea what to call Liliya's instinctive knowledge of danger surrounding her son. But he trusted her.

And that trust made him nervous now.

He turned on the overhead light. It shook as small footsteps raced across the ceiling above them. He'd asked the children's mother to take them outside to play, told her about Liliya's condition. But he knew it was too cold to stay outside for extended periods of time.

"Please turn on the light," Liliya said.

"It's late," he told her. "You should lay down, go back to sleep."

"No. Turn it on."

The overhead light wasn't bright, but coupled with the street lamps through the curtains, he could see her clearly. She was wide awake. There was no going back to sleep now.

"When are you going to see Aleksei?" she asked him.

"That's what I wanted to tell you," he said. "Very soon. I'm flying there."

"Flying?" She tilted her head. Had she misheard him?

"I know what you're thinking. There's an opportunity to fly."

"I don't understand. We can't afford—"

"No, *we* can't," he said.

"Bohana? Is she paying for you to fly?"

It was an out. He took it. "Yes." She didn't need to know who was paying his way.

"Why didn't she pay for Aleksei? His trip took so long and was so hard."

"You're forgetting he didn't have documentation. He surrendered in order to get into the country. I'm being allowed two weeks only to check on him."

"They're letting you visit?"

"Temporarily. If you weren't ill, I couldn't go."

"That's why you went to see my doctor."

"I needed a letter from him explaining your health. The United States wants to know I'll come back here. That we aren't using Aleksei to move to the US too."

"Use him? What kind of parents do they think we are?"

Use him, he thought. *If she only knew.* He couldn't meet her eyes then, had to look away. It was a good question: *What kind of parent was he?*

She stood. He rose, too, reaching for her. "Be careful," he said.

"You're returning without Aleksei?"

He nodded. "You know that. We had agreed on that. His opportunities are there, not here."

"You're sure?"

"Liliya, look at our lives, at the economy since Putin's invasion. And Putin will only take more."

"Yes," she said. "When will you leave?"

He told her.

Part of her had wanted to stay in the parking lot and follow them.

But Peyton was talking about her boyfriend and her son, after all. And Stone had requested time alone with Tommy. So Saturday afternoon she was home, sitting on her sofa with her Lisa Scottoline novel, when her cell phone chirped.

"Hi, sis," Elise said. "What are you doing?"

"Trying to concentrate on a book I'm reading."

"Trying?"

"Yeah. A lot on my mind."

"Tell me."

Peyton was wrapped in a fleece-lined blanket. The woodstove across the room was roaring.

"Tommy's with Stone. I think we might be forcing the issue."

"Him moving in? That's the issue?"

"Yeah."

"Tough to force it. It would be a big change for Tommy."

"I don't want to be selfish."

"I don't think you are," Elise said.

"But I really do think it would be good for Tommy. He'd have a male role model."

"Oh, I *know* it would be good for Tommy. But we're talking about a huge change for him. It's been just the two of you for almost five years."

Peyton stood and walked to the window. Mid-afternoon sun shone brightly on the small, snow-covered lawn that ran to the tree line.

"I know a little about what you're going through," Elise said. "Max was only a year old when Jonathan left."

"It's not easy being alone."

"No," Elise said, "but I have Max and Autumn, and I've had drinks with a woman named Molly twice."

"Molly? She's new."

"Uh-huh."

"Serious?"

"Oh, Christ, who knows? I was married to an abusive asshole. He left me with one child to raise alone, and I adopted another. And I came out of the closet. Life's too messy to take seriously, isn't it?"

Peyton thought about that. It *was* messy, and especially so for Elise, who'd left out the fact that her former husband, Jonathan, was dead, having been killed in a standoff with Border Patrol agents. The baby she'd adopted was Jonathan's by another woman.

"I don't want Tommy's life to be messy," Peyton said.

"It's messy for everyone, sis. And I hate to say this, but you can't protect him from the world."

"I know that, Elise."

"He's a smart kid. He knows his father's an ass."

"I think he's in denial."

"He's not that innocent, Peyton. He's more mature than you're giving him credit for."

Through the window, Peyton saw a doe tiptoe sheepishly from the tree line and smell the ground. The midday sun turned the snow-covered back lawn to a field of diamonds. She watched the deer cross the lawn cautiously, unable to remember the last time she'd seen a deer on the lawn before dusk. This winter had been a bad one. Close to one hundred inches of snow had fallen, and several days reached forty below zero. This doe had clearly borne the brunt of the Aroostook County winter; she was underweight and probably wouldn't make it to spring. Her rib cage protruded when she stopped to scratch in the snow, desperate to find something that would provide sustenance.

Peyton heard a car in the driveway. "Tommy's home. Have to run."

"Love you, sis."

"You too," Peyton said and retook her seat on the sofa, book in hand, casually, although the book might have been upside down for all the attention she gave it. Her eyes were on her phone. No messages. Stone hadn't sent a heads-up text warning her that Tommy was entering the house upset.

She heard the front door open and went back to her book, giving Tommy space, leaving his time with Stone as happenstance—all the while dying to know how the lunch conversation had gone.

The closet near the door opened. She heard a zipper, then the clatter of boots hitting the closet wall, then the closet door closing. Tommy always kicked his boots off, but at least the mess was out of sight.

"Mom, I'm home."

"Oh, I didn't hear you come in." She stood and went to the hallway. "Hey, nice job at the competition."

He put his hands on his hips. "Mom, I lost."

"So what?"

"So it sucks."

"Tommy, language."

"It's not fun to lose."

She was about to say something about listening to your coach but didn't. Instead, she said, "There are a few cookies left from the batch I baked."

"Didn't you bake them last week?"

"Hey, I never claimed to be Betty Crocker."

"Who's she?"

"No one. What did you have for lunch?" she asked, nudging the conversation in the direction of Stone.

"Cheeseburger."

"I knew it."

"Then why'd you ask?"

"Just a conversation starter."

"I'm going up to start my homework."

She looked at him. "It's Saturday."

"You don't want me to do my homework?"

His comment ended her line of questions. She'd learned nothing, defeated by her son. "Have you had experience being interrogated?"

"What? No."

"I don't believe it," she said and kissed him before he dashed upstairs.

––––––––

"I think I just got outsmarted by an eleven-year-old," she said, when Stone answered.

"I heard that happens to Border Patrol agents all the time."

She was in the kitchen. The microwave beeped, and she retrieved her mug of hot water, took a tea bag from the counter rack, and sat at the kitchen table. She could hear Tommy walking around his bedroom overhead.

"Well, he didn't walk home," she said.

"No, I drove him."

"And he went with you willingly?"

"You think I had to cuff him to get him in the car with me? What are you saying?"

"Nothing," she said. "Tell me how the lunch went."

"Fine. We talked about his match, about what he wants to work on, and about the Red Sox."

"Mention moving in?"

"To Tommy? No. I was just spending time with him."

She knew that was the right thing to do. "I'm over-analyzing the situation, aren't I?"

"Funny, you're so clear and rational at work."

"This isn't work," she said.

"No, it isn't. I just pulled in. I need to let the dog out."

"Okay. I'll let you go."

"I had a great time with Tommy. And, for the record, he laughed at my jokes."

"I never said he had a good sense of humor."

"We both had a good time, Peyton. Let's not press it."

"Got it."

"So," he said, "when can I give you a shoulder rub?"

She grinned. "There must be a bad connection. I think the call is about to drop."

"Hey—"

She hung up on him, smiling all the while.

7:15 p.m., 7 Drummond Lane

"Can I talk to you?" Bohana said, entering the guest room that was now Aleksei's.

Aleksei was surprised to see his aunt, more surprised when she closed the bedroom door behind her. He'd been lying on his bed, wearing jeans and a Garrett Bobcats T-shirt, flipping through pages of his Algebra II textbook. He sat up, swinging his legs onto the floor.

Bohana moved to the bed, sitting on the edge next to him.

Why had she closed the door? She'd never entered his room and closed the door before.

"I have some good news," she said. "Your father contacted me."

He looked at her, waiting.

"He's coming here soon."

"My father? When?"

She told him.

"He call you?"

"Emailed me," she said. "After only letters for so long, I can't wait to see him."

"My mother?"

"He says she's not strong enough yet."

"But soon?"

"Aleksei, your father won't be here long."

"Why?"

"He needs to return to care for your mother."

"He not staying?"

"'He *is* not staying.' You forgot the verb."

"*Is* my father staying?"

She shook her head. "Only for a few days." She reached to put her arm around him, but he stood and moved away.

He was trying to process it. Only a few days? "When will he and Mother be coming to live?"

"To live *here*? Aleksei, I don't think they are. They sent you here to have a better life. You know that. Your father is staying to fight Putin, right?"

He was staring at the floor, but he shook his head.

"No?" she said. "You told the Border Patrol agent and the social worker that."

"He tell me they come here to live."

"Aleksei, you must have misheard—"

"No," he said. "I heard."

"Please don't raise your voice. Did you lie to the authorities, Aleksei?"

His eyes darted frantically back and forth from her to the bedroom door.

"This must be hard," she said. "Your parents love you, Aleksei. That's why they sent you here. We're going to see that you go to college and have a wonderful life."

Bohana knew the realization must've been startling. He now knew things would never be as they'd been. He was living apart from his parents, and that wasn't changing. This was his life now. In this same position, her own son would be devastated. What had Dariya told him?

"When we be together again?" he asked. "My father say he and Mother come to live in US. When?"

"I don't know that. Your father has said nothing about that to me."

He was looking at the floor.

"Listen, Aleksei, I need to talk to you about something else."

"Nothing else matter," he said and stood, hands thrust in his blue-jean pockets.

"It's about your trip here," she said.

"Keep it secret," he said. "I know. I know."

"Do you understand why?"

He nodded. "I don't like him."

"I know. And you don't have to, but your father asked him to help get you here. You can never tell anyone who brought you here."

"On boat, he told me stay in cabin, even when I was seasick. In the woods, when I tell him I cold, he say walk faster."

"You needed to get to the border quickly."

"I don't like him," Aleksei said and turned away from her to face the window.

"That's okay, but you can never tell. You realize that, right?" she asked again, this time her voice was almost pleading.

He nodded, not turning back until he heard her leave his room and close the door behind her.

SEVEN

Sunday, March 9, 10:10 a.m., Garrett Rod and Rifle Club
If you live in Maine, you're tricked by the weather often, and you learn to doubt the forecasters. But on this day the WAGM weatherman had been correct: overcast, flurries, and a high of thirty-five. All in all, residents would gladly take a March day of thirty-five degrees.

Ted Donovan lowered the barrel of his .30-.30 and squeezed the trigger as he exhaled. The round hit the target at the other end of the range, just missing the center.

"You still breathe out when you squeeze the trigger, just like Dad taught us," Steven said to him.

"Of course. Don't you?"

Steven looked through the scope of his .30-06 and fired once, missing the center target. "I don't think about it," he said. "Maybe that's why I'm here trying to get this rifle sighted. I missed a ten-point buck last fall."

"Michael's a good shot. Was he with you?"

"He's a worse shot than you with your old cowboy gun. No, he wasn't with me." Steven looked through the scope again. "Doesn't feel like hunting this year."

"Planning a trip? I'll go with you."

"Teddy, you just had a nice long vacation to sightsee in Paris and Germany."

"What's wrong with that?" Ted was facing him. "Why all the questions? What's the problem? You approved it."

"Just don't ask for any more time off. Bill Neighbor is whining about the amount of time off you get, said some other guys are getting upset."

Bill Neighbor was the service manager, Ted's direct supervisor.

Steven fired a second shot that missed the target.

"You seem stressed," Ted told him.

"A lot on my mind."

"How's Aleksei fitting in?"

"That's what's weighing on me. Everything's turned upside down. The kid just arrives out of the blue, and it falls to us to take him in. We had no idea he was coming. I don't even know how he got here. Nothing against him, he's a very nice boy. But I have my own son."

"And now you're raising Bohana's nephew?"

"Who I don't even know. That's right. You get it. Not sure that thought ever crossed Bohana's mind when she agreed to take him in. She just told me he was her nephew, so she had to take him in."

"How's Michael doing with all this?"

Steven looked at him. "Jesus Christ, you know, I'm not sure anyone really asked Mikey. It's just been crazy—getting Aleksei clothes, going to the school, Aleksei getting in a fight at the school. We haven't really stopped to ask, not seriously, not to really talk about it with Mike."

"Hard on everyone. But it's got to be best for Aleksei to be here, though, right?"

"Of course."

The spot next to them was vacant. Two spots away, a man fired a pistol at a target he'd obviously brought there himself—a life-sized headshot of a female.

"Your ex-wife?" Steven asked.

The man looked at them and removed his camouflage shooting earmuffs. He had greasy blond hair and bad teeth and was maybe twenty-five.

Steven repeated the question.

"You guessed it," the man said. "She ended up with my pickup." He put on his earmuffs and fired four more rounds.

"Nice fucking guy," Ted said to Steven.

Steven nodded. "Misogynist."

"Big word. Guys like him are why everyone hates the NRA."

"Who hates the NRA?" Steven said, grinning.

Ted said, "What's Bill Neighbor's problem with me?" He had to yell over the sound of gunshots.

"He came to ask if the vacation rules are the same for you. I assume some other mechanics sent him in."

"Because I took some time off?"

"Yeah. Four weeks is a lot of time. Plus your two weeks last July. I told him it was unpaid."

"It wasn't."

"You're my brother," Steven said. "No one has to know that."

"Was it *supposed* to have been unpaid?"

"You ever read your employee benefits packet?"

Ted shook his head, lowered his .30-.30, and squeezed off a round. This time, he hit the center of the target.

"Moron," Steven said. "Read that shit. You only get two weeks, not six."

"I've never taken more than that before, so it never mattered. Christ, I'm there before you every morning."

Steven nodded and adjusted the scope, sighting the target. Then he fired, finally hitting the center.

Both men turned when an auburn-haired woman stepped into the vacant spot between them and the man who'd lost his pickup.

———

Peyton looked at the black circular target that stood across the range from her. On the target next to hers, facing the man to her right, a headshot of a woman had been stapled. The man next to her, wearing camouflage earmuffs, raised a .45 and squeezed off a round that not only missed the photo of the woman but missed the target altogether.

The hard-packed snow was level. In the mild winter air, she wore jeans, hiking boots, and a fleece beneath her North Face jacket. She removed her coat, folded it, and draped it over the back of a nearby bench, carefully keeping it off the dirty snow.

In the shooting lanes to her left stood a man she recognized: Steven Donovan, Bohana's husband and thus Aleksei's uncle and the man from whom she'd bought her Jeep Wrangler. She didn't recognize the man with him.

She exhaled and slowly squeezed her index finger, hitting the target easily with the first two rounds fired from her Smith & Wesson

.40. She knew Steven and the man with him were watching. The man on the other side of her fired at a woman's photo—and missed again. Peyton squeezed off five quick rounds, the target leaping with the impact of each bullet. Finished, she raised her protective glasses. There were four bullets arranged in an area the size of her palm.

"You really group your shots well," Steven Donovan said.

"Thanks."

"You look familiar," he said.

"You sold me my Jeep." She removed her leather gloves and told them her name. The air was cold on her hands. "And I'm here a lot." She looked at the other man, who said nothing.

"This is my brother, Ted," Steven said and introduced him.

"You here a lot too?" she asked him.

Ted didn't answer.

"Weren't you on TV?" she asked. "I grew up here, remember seeing you."

Ted smiled momentarily. "That was a long time ago."

"News," she said, "right? I saw a profile you did once on area art collections. Not the usual newsfare around here."

"You've got quite a memory," Ted said.

"These days, he'd rather be alone in the woods," Steven said. "You're a great shot."

It wasn't an exaggeration. Like all agents, she was tested four times a year, firing hundreds of shots with a service pistol, a carbine, and a 12-gauge. An agent who failed to qualify suffered a massive indignity: he or she would acquiesce to individual training sessions before a re-test. Among law-enforcement officials, Border Patrol agents were considered elite marksman. And Peyton had never failed a qualifying session; in fact, she'd never even come close to failing.

"I hear you have a houseguest," Peyton said and smiled at Steven.

"Yes, it's been busy."

"Did you know he was coming?" she asked.

Ted said, "Steven, can you help me sight this rifle?"

"Yeah, sure," Steven said. Then to Peyton, "Had no idea he was coming. We're not close to his father. He writes my wife maybe every other year."

She nodded, turned back to her target, and squeezed off another burst of shots. Then she removed her black earmuffs and watched the man to her right fire at the picture of the woman. This time he hit the picture. A corner of the photo tore free and floated in the air for a few moments before gently landing in the snow.

"Divorce me, huh?" the man said. "How's that feel, you bitch?"

"Excuse me," Peyton said.

He turned to face her.

She set the safety on her .40 and moved closer.

He removed his camouflage earmuffs. He looked her up and down. "Are you learning to shoot, sweetie? I'd be happy to show you how."

"It took you twenty rounds to hit a corner of the target. If you had to shoot your dinner, you'd starve."

"Who do you think you are?"

"Someone who finds you totally offensive. I want that photo removed."

"I brought it here myself. It's my ex-wife. She took my pickup. Just blowing off a little steam. I'm actually a nice guy. Why don't you let me show you how nice I am?"

"I want the fucking picture removed," she said.

"I like a woman who can say *fuck* like that." He smiled at her, showing yellow teeth.

"Go take the photo down now. It's misogynistic."

"It's what?"

"Just go get it."

"How about you and I get some lunch?"

"Take the picture down."

"Yeah, okay, sure. I'm Jimmy O'Connor. Wait right here. Then we'll grab something to eat." He hustled to the end of the range while Peyton, Steven, and Ted waited.

When O'Connor returned, Peyton replaced her sunglasses and went back to work. Several times, O'Connor approached and tried to launch a conversation, but she remained focused on why she was there—firing more than a hundred shots, never missing the target, and tightly grouping shots in various locations on the target board.

She paused to replace a spent clip.

"Christ, you can really shoot," O'Connor said. "Hey, I'm single."

"I can see why," Peyton said.

"What's that mean?" He held his camouflage earmuffs and pushed his Cabela's cap back.

She ignored him.

"What time are we going to lunch?" He looked at his watch.

"I'm not going to lunch with you."

"I don't see a ring on your finger."

"I'm not wearing it."

"Married?"

"Sure," she lied.

"Happily?"

"Very."

"Ever cheat?"

"Get away from me," she said.

"Peyton," Steven Donovan said, "is everything alright?"

She turned to see him approaching.

"Everything's fine. Thanks. This gentleman was just going back to his target. And I'm about to leave."

O'Connor turned back to his target and began firing. He shot faster and more erratically than before. Peyton knew he was angry. She also knew he was unstable.

She was leaning over her duffle bag, putting her .40 away, when Steven said, "Are you okay here with this idiot if we leave?"

She straightened and turned to face him. "Yeah, sure."

"Jimmy O'Connor is a nut." Steven motioned to O'Connor, who was still firing—and still missing.

"I'm fine," she said.

Steven grinned. "Yeah, you seem to be able to hold your own." He turned to the man with him, and they left.

Ten minutes later, Peyton was in the parking lot, walking toward her Wrangler, when O'Connor stepped between her and the driver's door.

"I don't know who you are, but you're a hell of a shot. And I don't believe you're married."

His arms were folded across his chest. She noticed grease beneath his fingernails and wondered what he did for work.

"Move out of my way."

"I just want to buy you lunch."

"No thank you."

"Playing hard to get?"

"Not playing anything. Step away from my Jeep. This is the last time I'll ask."

"You a lezbo or something?"

It wasn't much, but it was enough for her. In three seconds, he was on the ground, writhing, holding his crotch.

"No, but my little sister is," Peyton said, stepping over him. "Enjoy your lunch," she said, started the engine, and drove away.

EIGHT

Monday, March 10, 9 a.m., Gary's Diner

ONE WEEK TO THE day from when she found Aleksei Vann, Peyton and Mike Hewitt saw their breakfast party immediately. Bill Hillsdale from the US Citizenship and Immigration Services sat at a table in back of the diner with a man she'd never seen before and Bohana Donovan. She knew the man was Dariya Vann. He wore a gray sports jacket that looked a decade out of style and a button-down shirt, open at the throat.

"At least it stopped snowing," Hewitt said. "I can finally run outside."

There were three vacant seats at the table. When Peyton and Hewitt arrived, Dariya immediately stood and extended a hand.

"Thank you," he said to Peyton, then looked quickly at Hillsdale.

"Yeah, that's her," Hillsdale said.

"Thanks for what?" Peyton said.

"I told him you found his son," Hillsdale said.

"Actually, Mr. Vann, your son found me," she said and watched his reaction closely. His son had surrendered to her. Wouldn't the man know that? Hadn't that been the plan?

Hewitt also shook the man's hand. Then he and Peyton sat side-by-side at the circular table, across from Dariya, between Bohana and Hillsdale.

"We're waiting on one more person," Bohana said.

"Oh," Peyton said, "is your husband joining us?"

"No. I've hired an attorney for my brother and nephew."

Hillsdale tensed. He frowned but only for a moment. Then he looked across the table at Peyton and offered a broad *I told you so* smile.

"I don't know that a lawyer is necessary for the questions we have," Hewitt said, "but that's certainly your prerogative. Also, if you'd like a translator, there's a local professor we've used in the past."

"That won't be necessary," Bohana said. "My brother speaks English."

Spoons clanged the sides of coffee cups, the bell over the front door jangled, and voices at the counter discussed the season's predicted potato prices.

Peyton looked across the table at Dariya. "I see the family resemblance. Your son looks a lot like you, Mr. Vann."

He smiled. "I miss him very much."

"I bet," Peyton said. "It must've been hard to send him here."

Dariya Vann didn't take the bait. He stared at his coffee, then slowly lifted his cup and sipped, never making eye contact with Peyton. She thought she saw him grin.

"It's only been a few days," Hillsdale said.

"How long has it been since you've seen Aleksei, Mr. Vann?" Peyton asked.

Dariya picked up his water glass and drank.

"How about your sister?" Peyton said. "How long has it been since you've seen her?"

He looked at Bohana.

"Oh, years and years," Bohana said. "Christmas cards, a letter here and there—that's all." Bohana leaned toward her brother and kissed his cheek. "Too long."

Dariya was short, no taller than five-seven. His pale eyes had dark half-moons beneath them, like the eyes of men who worked the eleven-to-seven shift at McCluskey's. But his hands were different; they weren't the hands of a laborer. His hands were smooth, and his belly belonged to a white-collar worker.

"My sister say you good to Aleksei," he said. "Thank you."

"He's a nice boy," she said. "You've raised him well."

Dariya smiled. "He have his mother's heart."

Hillsdale wore a suit and had a briefcase on the floor near his feet. He leaned forward, popped the case open, and removed a stack of papers. To her surprise, Hewitt didn't look interested. He was staring at his iPhone.

The inside of Gary's smelled like it always did—like bacon and syrup.

Shirley, the big-boned owner in a gray sweatshirt, approached. "What are you having?"

"The usual," Hewitt said.

"We don't serve alcohol this time of day, captain," Shirley said.

"Cute," Hewitt said.

"And for you?" Shirley said to Dariya.

He looked at Hillsdale. Peyton could tell he was struggling to keep up with the conversation. His English appeared more limited than his son's.

Hillsdale rescued him. "Bring us each a couple eggs," Hillsdale said to Shirley, then looked at Dariya as if to say *That okay with you?* Dariya nodded.

Peyton leaned toward Hewitt. "Think we should call in the U-Maine professor to translate?"

"Let's see how this goes."

It had been Shakespeare who'd written *Conscience doth make cowards of us all.* She remembered her bearded professor reading that line aloud at the University of Maine and recalled thinking about universal truths. Years later, after more than a decade on the job, she'd come to realize language barriers make *dependents* of us all. She knew Dariya had been a journalist in his home country, but here he couldn't even order an egg without assistance.

The irony, of course, was that if Dariya applied to stay in the US, it would be Hillsdale—the man helping him now—who'd reject the proposal.

"Mr. Vann," Peyton said, when Shirley moved away, "we've got some questions to ask you."

Beside her, Hewitt was hitting his iPhone with his index finger. "Worst decision I ever made," he said under his breath, "getting this stupid ... Can't even check the damned weather."

Peyton leaned close to him. "That's how it always begins, Mike. Next stage is full-blown addiction. You'll be playing fantasy basketball at your desk like Jimenez."

"Not likely," Hewitt said, shook his head, and slid the phone into his pocket.

"Mr. Vann has received permission to spend up to two weeks here visiting Aleksei," Hillsdale said.

"My wife ..." Dariya looked at Hillsdale, searching for help.

"Mr. Vann's wife is ill. She needs constant care."

Peyton was surprised by the amount of help Hillsdale was offering Dariya, given that he told her he was certain Dariya was using his son to forge a permanent place in the country.

Dariya nodded. "Yes. Can't stay away long."

"That's why you let him come?" Peyton said to Hillsdale. "That's the guarantee he wouldn't try to stay?"

"I wanted him to be able to see his son," Hillsdale said. "That's why he's here."

"Of course," Peyton said.

"And I didn't make the decision alone."

Shirley returned with two more thick, white coffee mugs and creamer. "No decaf babies here, right?" She didn't wait for an answer, darting back to the counter to retrieve the coffeepot.

"Mr. Vann, we'd like to know why you sent Aleksei here."

"Don't answer that, Dariya," Bohana interrupted. "We'd like to wait for Bobby Gaudreau, our attorney."

Hewitt looked at Peyton, shrugged, and took out his cell phone again. Peyton watched, dumbfounded as he checked the New England Patriots website.

She cleared her throat.

"What?" he said. "It's not fantasy basketball."

"Only one step away," Peyton said, to which Hewitt muttered something under his breath again.

It wasted twenty minutes, but the lawyer finally appeared.

Peyton saw him pull into the parking lot and climb out of a GMC Sierra wearing a dark suit and toting a briefcase. Bobby Gaudreau was a man who seemed hard to dislike. If you believed the stereotypes about lawyers, Gaudreau was unrecognizable: a United Way volunteer, a PTO member, a guy who read to kindergartners. Yet she knew him—professionally—to be a first-class asshole; he'd successfully defended three deadbeat dads in town.

He entered the diner like the star quarterback entering a high school dance. He slapped several men on the back. "Bring me a coffee, Shirley, sweetie."

When he reached the table, everyone rose. They shook hands all around.

"These two agents have some questions to ask Dariya," Bohana said.

Just then Shirley arrived with Gaudreau's coffee.

"Thanks, good-looking," Gaudreau said.

Shirley—already twenty years his senior and looking even older thanks to thirty years spent working inconsistent shifts—made no reply, only walked off, certainly realizing she was being mocked.

"And I wanted you here for it," Bohana finished.

"That sounds entirely reasonable," he said.

"We'd like to know how your son got from Donetsk to the US border behind McCluskey's." Hewitt had nothing to write with, which always perplexed Peyton, who had her iPad and stylus out.

The bastard had only a two-year degree, but he never seemed to fail to recall every detail of a conversation.

"I want better life for son."

Dariya sat stone still, his legs crossed casually, and Peyton, watching him drink coffee and smile, realized that as a journalist, he'd be entirely comfortable in this setting of asking for and receiving information. He might be more accustomed to being on the other end of the conversation, but he'd know how to answer the questions. They might need to question him in a room in the stationhouse to shake him up.

"Can you tell us how Aleksei got from Donetsk to Garrett, Maine?" she said.

"Not important."

"Mr. Vann," Hewitt said, "surely you see why it would be very important to us. Aleksei might be one of"—Hewitt's eyes darted to Hillsdale—"many others who want to make the same trip."

Hillsdale shook his head, his *I told you so* expression set firmly on his face.

"We know life is hard in Donetsk, sir," Hewitt said.

"No one else coming here. Only Aleksei."

"Who brought him?" Hewitt said.

Dariya looked at Bohana. Bohana leaned toward Gaudreau and whispered something. Gaudreau nodded.

"My client has assured you that his son is not part of a human-trafficking ring, agents, which appears to be your primary concern. So may we move on?"

"Not really," Hillsdale said. Then to Bohana, "Were you aware of Aleksei's trip?"

"Not until after he'd left. My brother sent me a letter saying he was on the way."

"Seems odd that you would have no prior knowledge," Hewitt said.

"I'm not in regular contact with my brother. A Christmas card, a letter here and there."

Hewitt said, "Phone calls?"

She shook her head. "It's why I'm so excited to have him visit."

Shirley reappeared. "More coffee for anyone?"

"How long will we be here?" Bohana said.

"Not much longer," Gaudreau said.

"Don't rush this," Hillsdale said, "or Aleksei will find himself back in Donetsk."

"No," Dariya said. "No. He needs be here. Here he have opportunity. In Donetsk, there nothing. Airport is gone now. Running water gone in some places. People dying in streets. He needs to be here."

Bohana's hand instinctively went to her brother's forearm, a reassuring gesture.

"Um, I'll just bring the pot," Shirley said and drifted back to the counter.

"The possibility that your son will be returned is on the table, for sure," Hillsdale said. "To be clear, the United States certainly wants to help your son; however, there need to be certain assurances. And a certain level of cooperation."

Dariya only smiled, not buying it.

That told Peyton a lot. This was a man who knew what he could and couldn't do and therefore certainly could've arranged for his son to escape the Ukraine's escalating violence and land softly at an aunt's well-to-do home in northern Maine.

"You have power to send him back?" Dariya asked Hillsdale, pronouncing *him* like *heem*, with a long *e*. "You send him back?"

Gaudreau cleared his throat, bringing all eyes to him, which Peyton could tell he enjoyed. "I think, Mr. Hillsdale, we all know the answer to that. Mr. Vann, for very good reason, wishes to keep some facts surrounding his son's brave journey to himself. That's legal and more than understandable."

Peyton could see Shirley approaching with the coffeepot. She held up her hand for Shirley to pause; she did.

"And, of course, our need to ascertain certain facts is also understandable," Peyton said. "Like who the coyote is. If we know that and can learn more about the trip—to the point where we know this is a one-time deal—we'll be satisfied."

"It one-time thing."

"You need not worry, Peyton," Bohana followed her brother.

"Not good enough," Hewitt said. "Sorry, but we can't simply take your word for it. We need to know who brought him here. And we'll want to talk to him."

"I think we have reached an impasse," Gaudreau said.

Hillsdale drank some coffee and leaned back in his seat, his turn for casual. "If the boy wants to have the ability to stay here long-term, we're going to need answers to these questions."

"You'll send him back?" Bohana said.

"There would be a process," Hillsdale said. "It might start with foster care."

"You're threatening my client."

"Nope. Just answering her question."

"The social worker thinks it's better for him to be with me."

"As you will recall, that's a temporary arrangement."

"What if my sister adopt him?" Dariya asked.

"I think this is a good time for this meeting to end," Gaudreau said and stood. Dariya and Bohana followed his lead. All three walked out.

Peyton looked across the table at Hillsdale. "I guess the United States is picking up the tab for the coffee," he said.

"At least your sense of humor has returned."

"And the coffee isn't bad." Hillsdale smirked.

"It's weak," Peyton said. "So what have we learned?"

Hewitt added sugar to his coffee. "That Dariya is desperate for his son to be here."

"Considering adoption?" Peyton said.

Hillsdale was eating a cinnamon roll half the size of a dinner plate. Peyton knew Shirley made them herself, and she guessed it was fresh and delicious. *Focus on the fruit cup*, she told herself.

"And that, for whatever reason, they don't want us to know who brought the boy here?" She shook her head. "It makes no sense, unless the coyote is still here."

"Maybe it's Dariya himself," Hillsdale said.

"That might make sense," Hewitt said. "It's nice to see you like your old self."

"Well, I was taking enormous heat from the higher-ups. Not easy to feel like you're about to be fired when you have two kids in college."

"That's why I never wanted to work in Washington," Hewitt said. "I say something stupid every day. I'd end up working as a fly-fishing guide sooner than I can afford to."

"We need to bring Dariya Vann in and question him again," Peyton said.

Hillsdale nodded. "We should also start the machine working to extract Aleksei from Bohana's home and into foster care. She might know more than she's saying. And this will squeeze her and Dariya to be more forthcoming."

Peyton looked out the window again. The sky was gray, but it wasn't snowing. "I don't like using the boy to get the father to talk. That's cruel. They must know they can't simply adopt the boy to allow him to stay here."

Hillsdale looked at her. "I don't know what they know or don't know. But I'm done playing games. You have a better idea?"

Hewitt looked at her as well. She said nothing.

"That's what I thought," Hillsdale said. "I'm going to call Susan Perry at DHHS."

3:20 p.m., 31 Monson Road

"I'm not sure how long I can keep bringing you dope," Michael said Monday after school.

Davey was stooped over the workbench, carefully rolling a joint under the silver spotlight his father had clipped to the side of the bench. He stopped and straightened to face Michael. "Did I do something? Say something wrong?"

"No, Davey. It's nothing like that. I went out there this weekend."

"To the shack?"

"Yeah. I think someone found it."

"And the stuff inside?"

"Probably," Michael said.

Davey's basement was cold. Michael wore his GHS baseball windbreaker over a dark hoodie.

"We start throwing in the gym next week."

"Pitchers and catchers?" Davey asked.

"Yeah, you coming?"

Davey shrugged and went back to rolling the joint.

"You should come."

"And do what? Clap?"

"Every time I throw, yeah." Michael grinned. "That would be awesome—my own fan club."

Davey said, "Screw you," but smiled as he said it. His hand shook as he tried to light the joint.

"Want me to do that?"

"I got it." After three more tries, he lit the joint and puffed, holding the hit for a long time.

Michael could see the corners of his eyes soften, realizing for the first time that day that his friend's face was pinched in pain. The marijuana alleviated at least some of the discomfort.

"Man, you eating enough?" Michael said.

"Can't stomach much. Why, do I look skinny?"

"A little."

"You're lying. I've lost a shitload of weight," Davey said. "Did you clear the shack out?"

Michael shook his head. "I kind of freaked. Didn't know if someone was watching me. So I took off."

"Watching you?" Davey giggled then.

"Don't be an asshole. That shit's making you laugh."

"No, man. No. Just saying, it sounds funny. Who's watching you out there? I mean, you found the shack by coincidence, right? Even had to cut branches to get to it."

"Yeah. But someone hiked all around it. Even spent the night out there at a spot above it."

Davey took another hit. "You mean so they could look down at the shack?"

"That's what I think. I just walked away."

"What about the generator?"

"I can take the snowmobile and tow it back. I just freaked and left."

"Shit, man, I can see why."

"But you need pot, right?"

"Not if you get in trouble. Forget it."

"Will your doctor get it for you?"

Davey shook his head. "Can't. You're forgetting about my parents."

"He can't prescribe it on his own?"

"I'm not eighteen yet. They have to approve it. And they say no son of theirs is"—he made air quotes with his fingers—"'doing drugs.' The doctor can give me other stuff, but I don't like the pills. They make me feel like I'm in a fog, and they don't even really work."

Michael was looking at the floor, torn between the threat of being arrested and his best friend's needs.

Davey said, "You think it was a cop out there?"

"Who the hell else would spend the night out there?"

"Lots of people tent out in the winter."

"Out there? Shit, there wasn't even a fire—no ring of melted snow, no nothing. I think someone was out there waiting for someone to enter the shack."

"Could've been a hunter. Isn't it bear season?"

"I don't know, man. But most hunters don't sleep in the woods."

"So what are you going to do, Mikey?"

"I'm not sure. I need to get home." He started toward the stairs.

"Mike."

He stopped and turned to face Davey.

"Thanks, man. If you can't do it anymore, no biggie. I get why."

"I can't lose my spot in the Honors program at U-Maine, you know?"

"I know."

"Come to practice next week, Davey."

He looked at the ceiling. "I'd have to wear one of those stupid masks. And everyone will ask how I feel and all that shit."

"People want to see you. It's been a long time."

"Six weeks. Homeschooling sucks."

"Come to practice."

"I'll think about it. What are you going to do with the generator?"

"My father hasn't mentioned it," Michael said. "He doesn't realize it's gone. We haven't lost power for an extended time yet."

Michael turned to climb the stairs.

"Oh, wait. I got something for you." Davey reached into the front pocket of his sweatshirt and quickly pulled his hand out and flashed the middle finger.

Both boys laughed.

10:30 p.m., Razdory, Russia

The days were getting shorter, and he knew that made no sense. March had once been Victor Tankov's favorite month because the days grew longer and hinted at spring. But this March was different; his days seemed shorter. How was it possible?

It wasn't. And he knew what that meant, too, what it told him about the cancer in his throat. That the doctors were wrong. He'd been given a year. He knew he had weeks.

He rolled onto his side and pulled the covers to his chin. One day soon, he thought, it'll all be over, and they'll pull the sheet all the way up.

He stared at the vacant space on the wall.

"What are you thinking about, Father?" Marfa said, entering the room.

"Redemption," he said.

"Redemption?"

"Yes."

"For what?"

"My sins."

She was walking across the room to move the chair closer to his bed but stopped and stood looking at him. She wore a cream-colored sweater, and the huge diamond on her right hand got caught on the opposite sleeve.

"Don't talk like that," she said, trying to ease the ring from the wool.

"Did Pyotr buy that ring for you?" the elderly man asked, his voice barely a whisper.

"No, Father, I bought it myself."

"It looks like an engagement ring."

She freed the diamond, went to the red leather chair along the far wall, dragged it bedside, and sat. "Well, I'm not engaged."

"Are you still married?"

"Father, I have some good news."

"You *are* married? Pyotr is coming back?"

"No. The thing you've been waiting so long for is coming here, though."

"The boy has it?"

"Not the boy." She leaned forward and patted his hand. "I've taken care of everything. Now I need access to the accounts."

"To pay?"

"Yes."

"How much?"

She shook her head. "I'm negotiating. I need full access."

"Full access to my accounts?" His pale eyes were watery. He looked exhausted.

She knew he wouldn't fight it for long.

"How much are you willing to pay?" he asked.

"Probably twenty percent of its value."

"Do you know the value?" he said.

She assumed he did. He knew more about the subject than many of her professors had. "I've done my research," she said.

"Twenty percent would be more than I wanted to pay."

"But you're not handling the negotiations, Father. I am."

"True." He sighed and closed his eyes for a long moment. When he opened them, he said, "You look like an American today."

"Levi's?"

"And the jewelry and makeup. All of it."

"Good, because that's where I'm going. I'll look the part."

"When are you leaving?"

She told him.

"And Nicolay?"

"He's staying here to care for the children."

"He should go with you," he said.

"No. He'll be here. I'll handle this, Father."

He thought about that. "Why don't you take the children with you?" he said. "Stay there. Live in New York. You loved it there. Walk away from this life."

"I'm going back downstairs now."

"Why can't you understand?"

"Understand what?" she asked.

"It's like when I got you into the Sorbonne and you chose McGill in Canada."

"I loved McGill. I *wanted* to go to McGill. That was my choice, Father."

He tried to sit up but didn't have the strength. He'd lost fifty pounds since the diagnosis. He'd been living on Ensure for weeks. "I've always supported you," he said.

"Oh, really?"

"When you came home after New York, I went to your grand opening."

"And then you didn't invest. And when I looked for other investors, no one would touch me."

"What are you saying? Are you saying your business failed because of me?"

"No one wanted to partner with me," she said again.

"You're saying that's because of who I am?"

"No one would give me a loan"—she looked away—"for *whatever* reason."

"I didn't pressure the banks. I'd done enough of that for other things."

"And you obviously didn't believe in my company, didn't invest in it. So the business failed. It never had a chance."

"I see what's going on now," he said.

Panic, like a shaft of ice, shot through her spine. Had she overplayed her hand? Given too much away? Did he know what she had planned for the funds? If she could only get him to give her access.

"What?" she said calmly.

"You want to negotiate to show me what you can do," he said. She heard the ever-present confidence in his voice.

"That's correct," she lied.

"You're a sweet girl."

"I'm a businesswoman, Father."

The door opened then. Nicolay entered the room with a pitcher of water.

"I'll give you access to the accounts until you make the deal," Victor said.

Nicolay stopped pouring water. He looked from Victor to Marfa, set the water carafe on the table near the bed, and then left.

6:25 p.m., Chandler Pond

Monday evening, Stone's entire eight-hundred-square-foot log cabin smelled like whatever was in the oven. Peyton liked the smell but didn't know what Stone had planned for dinner. She had a glass of chardonnay and her Lisa Scottoline novel and was sitting in a Lay-Z-boy chair across the coffee table from Stone and Tommy, both of whom were focused on Stone's fifty-five-inch TV.

"That TV is too big for this house," she commented.

"You say that every time you come here," Stone said and waved the XBox controller. "Kathy St. Pierre found this house for me. She's meticulous. She found everything I asked her for."

"She found my house too," Peyton said. "She dominates the real-estate market up here. She was on HGTV's *Lakefront Bargain Hunt.*"

Tommy, sitting next to Stone on the couch, leaped up and pointed his controller frantically at the TV.

Stone's cabin was clearly a single man's purchase: it had a main central room, dominated by the TV he bought to watch the Patriots,

Bruins, Celtics, and Red Sox; a counter and breakfast bar area; one bedroom off the main room; one bath; and a loft that he used as a den. The property abutted a small lake, and he'd built a dock the previous summer.

Peyton set her glass on the coffee table and leaned forward. "Which one of you is the eleven-year-old?"

Her young literalist raised his hand; Stone, seeing Tommy's hand go up, raised his own.

The sight made her smile. "Glad we're clear on that."

Tommy was focusing, a bottle of red Gatorade before him on the coffee table, the tip of his tongue protruding from his mouth.

"Those remotes look like birds," she said.

"They're not remotes," Tommy corrected. "They're controllers, Mom."

"Sorry."

Stone waved his controller wildly and yelled, "Yes!" as the football player on the TV screen crossed the goal line.

"You look like you're strangling a bat," she said, "the way you wave that thing around."

"I'm scoring touchdowns," he said, "and the controller doesn't look like a bat."

"Stop distracting me, Mom!" Tommy said, but he was smiling all the while.

It had been some time since she'd seen him smile.

"Need me to check on the oven?" she asked.

"The meatloaf will take another twenty minutes." Stone looked at Tommy. "Time for one more game."

"Let's play." Tommy took a drink of Gatorade, the skin between his upper lip and nose turning red.

She set her glass on the table. "You made meatloaf?"

"What did you expect? I give great shoulder rubs, and I cook a mean meatloaf."

When they made eye contact, she smirked. "I've had your shoulder rubs. They're overrated. I'll get back to you on the meatloaf."

"Ouch," he said, smiling.

She lifted her glass, crossed the room, and opened the fridge. He'd tossed a salad. The mashed potatoes were finished and in a casserole dish on the counter. She pulled off the lid. Son of a gun, he'd even added chives, like Tommy loved. Gravy was warming on the stovetop.

She didn't say it aloud, but she thought it: *I could get used to this.*

She sipped her wine and glanced out the window. The ice hadn't thawed, but a raccoon emerged from behind a spruce and sipped at the water's edge where a spring ran to the lake.

Her cell phone chirped, and she went to her purse to retrieve it. She recognized the number and sighed.

Stone heard her sigh and said, "I think we might be eating alone, champ."

Tommy said, "Can we get pizza?"

"You haven't even tried my meatloaf."

"Cote here," Peyton said.

"Peyton, it's Jimenez."

"Yeah, Miguel?"

"There's a problem, and it's sort of your case."

"Tell me," she said, feeling Stone's eyes on her back.

7:10 p.m., Garrett Station

The walls of Hewitt's office were lined with framed photos. Years ago, when Peyton had first arrived at Garrett Station—coming home after

185

her mandatory years working the southern border—the frames held photos of Hewitt's wife. Now the wife was gone and so were the pictures. Instead, the frames held photos of Hewitt fly-fishing, his new passion.

Bill Hillsdale pulled the tab on a can of Diet Pepsi. In a suit, Hillsdale looked like an accountant, but now rocking dad jeans and a faded Washington Nationals T-shirt, he looked more relaxed, like a guy ready to take his kid to an amusement park.

Except he didn't look amused.

He glanced at his watch. "I was supposed to be landing at Dulles right now. My youngest daughter has a hockey practice tomorrow morning."

Peyton nodded. "I had plans too. Supposed to be eating meatloaf."

"Look," Hewitt said, "none of us like eighteen-hour days, but it is what it is." He pointed at Peyton as if remembering something. "You have child care?"

She nodded. "Tommy's spending the night with Stone. Thanks for asking. So what happened?" She took out her iPad and stylus.

Hewitt said, "Bobby Gaudreau called the desk—Jimenez caught the call—and Bobby said he needed to speak to me immediately. Jimenez said he'd leave the message but wasn't giving my home number. So, like the self-centered jerk he is, Bobby said that wasn't good enough. He wanted to talk tonight."

Peyton, writing on the iPad, looked up. "Miguel got off the phone and called you?"

Hewitt nodded.

"Why the rush?" she asked.

"I know the answer to that," Hillsdale said. "It's because Susan Perry at DHHS took Aleksei."

Peyton leaned back and blew out a long breath. "I really hate using kids this way."

"Me, too, but I didn't see any other way," Hillsdale said.

She knew it was true. In the criminal justice system, situations often dictate what is deemed "ethical" behavior.

"So the story, according to Dariya Vann," Hewitt said, "is that he doesn't know who brought Aleksei here."

"He doesn't know the man who brought his child from one continent to another?" Peyton leaned back in her chair and folded her arms across her chest. "Has no idea who that might be?"

"You've talked to him tonight already?" Hillsdale said.

Hewitt nodded. "He came in here with Bobby Gaudreau, wrote his statement, and I took it. Didn't answer questions. I let him go, knowing you"—he motioned to Hillsdale with his chin—"would want a crack at him."

"He says he paid a stranger to bring Aleksei here?" Peyton said.

"Yeah. That's not unheard of."

"Giving someone money at the edge of the Rio Grande and having them take your kid to the other side, where a family member will meet them an hour later, is one thing. This trip would've taken nearly twenty days by ship. There's no way I'd leave *my* son with someone I didn't trust for the better part of a month."

Hillsdale nodded. "I'll need to see the statement. And I'll want to interview him."

"I'd like to be in on that too," Peyton said. "Do you buy it, Mike?"

Hewitt shook his head. "Too convenient. Solves too many problems."

"Where's Aleksei?" she asked.

"With Maude O'Reilly."

Peyton smiled. "Well, we know he's being spoiled. I didn't know she took in foster children."

"I don't know her," Hewitt said. "Only heard about her. Susan Perry likes her a lot, though."

"She was my fourth-grade teacher. She made each student a Valentine's Day card each year, used to bring in warm brownies. Last time I saw her, she was volunteering at the nursing home."

"I guess it was quite a scene when they took the boy from the Donovan home."

"I bet it was," she said. "He's been waiting to see his father. Now his father comes to him, and DHHS separates them again."

"Susan says Bohana was hysterical, threatened to sue everyone from DHHS, to the Border Patrol, to the president."

"Take a number," Hillsdale said.

"I think I'll stir the pot a little," Peyton said and stood. "I'd like to go see Aleksei and maybe Bohana and Dariya in the morning. That okay with you, boss?"

"Just don't push too much," Hewitt said.

"Why do you say that?"

Hewitt moved a pile of papers from one side of his desk to the other. "I heard a story when I went to the gun range this afternoon."

"What did you hear?"

"That you had an—um, how to put this?—*altercation* of sorts there."

She cursed under her breath. "I was being harassed and defended myself."

"I heard you about kicked a guy's nuts to the back of his throat."

"Jesus," Hillsdale said, his hand instinctively going to his groin.

"It wasn't that bad," Peyton said. "He wouldn't leave me alone." She shrugged. "So I defended myself." She stood and started toward the door.

"I want to ride along in the morning," Hillsdale said. "I still think Dariya Vann and his wife are planning to move here. I don't trust the medical documents."

11:55 p.m., Razdory, Russia

The house was dark, and Marfa sat in the leather chair in the great room, staring at the dancing flames. In the mouth of the fireplace they leaped four feet high, their shadows spanning half the room's length. She held a glass of brandy and sipped it, contemplating the future.

"Is everything alright?"

Startled, she turned to see Nicolay. "Yes," she said. "Everything is fine."

"I hope the children were sufficiently washed after lunch today," he said sarcastically.

She looked at him, saw the anger in his eyes. Also saw the shame —he was considered more than common household help; he was part of the family. But she hadn't treated him that way.

"I'm sorry," she said. "Why are you still up?"

He sat down on the hearth across from her. "I heard something." He reached into the pocket of his bathrobe and withdrew a 9mm and laid it on the hearth next to him.

"You're still protecting my father."

"Always."

"We're safe here," she said. "I arranged for the security system myself."

"I don't trust security systems."

"You should trust mine. I screened several companies myself."

"You're always trying to prove yourself," he said.

"I always have to."

"I don't know about that," he said, "but I'll provide your father with security until the end."

"You mean that, don't you?"

"Why would you question it? I'll never let anything happen to him."

"I don't know," she said. "That kind of loyalty is unique." She held the dark glass up and looked at the fire through the brandy. The liquid turned orange when the flames danced behind it.

"I walked you to school for years."

"I remember. That was a long time ago." She smiled. "You didn't have gray hair then."

"If I had no gray hair then it was a *very* long time ago. Rodia asked if I was Father Christmas the other day."

She chuckled. "He means no harm."

"I know. You were the same way."

She shook her head.

"No?"

"No," she said, then stood and tossed another log on the fire.

"What makes you say that, Marfa?"

"I was raised differently. I was alone."

"You had Dimitri."

"No, Father had Dimitri."

"And you spent a lot of time with your mother."

"She died when I was eight. Then I was alone."

"Your father has given you a lot."

She set the brandy on the hearth and looked at him. He was a huge man. She could see why Rodia asked if he was Father Christmas. "He has. Everything. I know. But that's different."

"I don't follow," he said.

"Possessions and love and respect are different things."

"He's been a good father, Marfa."

"Yes." She smiled and patted his hand. "And now I'm giving something back."

"What's that?"

She shook her head and smiled. "A surprise."

He touched his white beard, thinking. "It has something to do with the space on the wall, doesn't it?"

"Has he told you?"

"No. But I heard you talking about the accounts today."

She didn't say anything. The fewer people who knew she'd have access to her father's accounts, the better.

"Can I ask what you're buying him?"

"It's a surprise."

"You won't say?"

She shook her head.

"But it's why you're going to the US."

"Father told you that?"

"He said I'd be responsible for the children for a few days."

"It will be a short trip."

Her father had made sure the 1860s home had not been changed, save for the updated kitchen and added security. And now in the silence of the night, the house creaked, and somewhere a furnace rumbled to life.

"What will you do when he's gone?" Nicolay asked. "Really? I mean seriously."

"When he's gone?" she said.

He nodded.

Then she laughed. "I'm not thinking about that. That's too far off. I like to think short-term."

"But you know he's dying shortly."

She nodded. "And I can think of some things to do when he's gone, as sad as that day will be." She leaned forward and kissed Nicolay's bearded cheek. "I can think of a few things," she repeated and walked out of the room, leaving the brandy glass where it was, knowing Nicolay would take care of it.

10:45 p.m., 7 Drummond Lane

Steven still wasn't getting it, Bohana thought. He never got it.

It was late Monday night. Dariya was in the room that had been Aleksei's, and Michael was in bed. He'd arrived home exhausted and stressed, his mother thought. The last time she'd seen him like that was as a freshman when he failed his Algebra I final. Whatever was bothering him, he didn't want to talk about it.

Steven stood and got a bottle of Geary's Pale Ale from the stainless-steel Sub-Zero fridge. Pots and pans hung above the granite island.

"What do you want me to do? He's your brother, Bohana, not mine."

"What do I want you to do? How about helping me here? Call an immigration lawyer, use a contact."

"Immigration lawyer? He's not staying, is he?"

"Eventually, of course, he'd like to move somewhere, once Liliya is well enough to travel."

"Look"—he sat down across from her again—"I know you love your brother, but what can I do? Neither of us knew he was sending Aleksei here. We couldn't plan for that. We have our own lives, right?"

"I want to help my brother. I always have. And I will continue helping."

"What does that mean, *continue helping*?"

She shrugged. And when their eyes met, she looked away.

"Bohana, did you know Aleksei was coming here?"

"Dariya needed help, Steven. Lord knows we've helped your brother enough—for twenty-five years. He quits school, moves home, and you let him live with us. He loses jobs, and you—we—take him in."

"Not *jobs*. And he didn't lose his job. He quit. I think he was burned out. And I didn't *take him in*. He works for me."

"We renovated the entire attic space for him! Converted it to an apartment for him."

"He contributed some."

"He put in central air," she said. "A ridiculous expense for an efficiency apartment. That doesn't even make sense."

Steven shrugged. "It's what he wanted."

"Well, if I want to help my brother, I have that right. Yes, I knew Aleksei was coming. I didn't tell you in order to protect you."

"So you know this is serious? We're talking immigration laws, human trafficking."

"You're getting carried away. I didn't help get him here."

"This is serious," Steven repeated. "You need to know that. The agents are trying to figure out who brought him here. Do you know the answer to that?"

"What I know, Steven," she said and stood, "is this is family."

And she turned and left him at the kitchen table, twirling his beer bottle before him.

11:15 p.m., Chandler Pond

Late Monday night, following her meeting, Peyton parked her Jeep Wrangler next to Stone's Ford pickup and got out in his snow-packed driveway. The night sky was clear, the stars like ice chips against the black backdrop.

Stone met her at the door, his finger to his lips.

She nodded. "He's asleep?"

He held the door for her. "Yeah." He spoke in a whisper. "We ate without you, watched a little ESPN, then I had him read. I have a collection of Hemingway's stories. I actually think he liked the one he read. It was about fishing."

"You got him to read?"

"He had some trouble."

"He's dyslexic. It doesn't come easily."

They were inside now, and he took her coat. "He's asleep in my bed. I figured you'd go home, and I'd take the foldout in the loft and drop him at school in the morning for you."

"Is he okay with that?"

"Yeah. He suggested it. I was surprised."

"Well, I can stay for a little while," she said.

He nodded and hung her coat on the pine rack near the door. A large salmon hung next to the rack. She knew Stone had caught it in Madawaska the summer before.

She went to the sofa on which Tommy had sat next to Stone playing XBox earlier. Stone sat beside her.

"I like talking to you at the end of the day," he said.

She smiled. "I'd rather be by myself."

"Ouch. What a romantic," he said.

She leaned forward and kissed his mouth. "Just kidding. I can be romantic."

"I know. Believe me." He smiled, stood, and got two water bottles from the fridge. "What happened tonight?" he asked.

She told him about Dariya Vann changing his story. "At breakfast," she said, "Dariya Vann knew who brought his son to the US. By dinner, he didn't seem to know it anymore."

"Think he was confused this morning?"

"I don't think the same father who comes to check on his son—after the boy has been in the US only a week—would put him on a boat with someone he doesn't know. No way."

"Maybe there was a middle man handling the transaction," Stone said.

"That's possible. I'll ask him. I think what I'll find is that Dariya Vann wants to play ignorant on all charges."

"If that's the case, why not say the boy came here on his own?"

"That would have been the smart play. But that would have been hard to believe. Aleksei is only thirteen, and he wouldn't be as sympathetic that way."

"And it would've been much harder to get political asylum without the father to tell everyone how much danger there is back home," Stone said.

"Yes."

"So Dariya has to say he sent his son here. But he doesn't want to say with whom? Why not? Why not just give up the coyote?"

"It doesn't make a lot of sense," Peyton said. "What does Dariya gain by protecting the coyote?"

"Something," Stone said.

She looked at him. "I'm missing it. But, yes, there has to be something to be gained by not giving him up. Aleksei told me the coyote threatened his family. Maybe Dariya heard that same threat."

"But if you take the coyote off the street," Stone said, "the threat goes away. So why not tell you?"

"Maybe he thinks we won't be able to find the guy," she said.

Stone leaned back and stretched his legs before him. He was still wearing jeans and a gray New England Patriots sweatshirt. "Look for the money trail," he said.

"Whoever brought Aleksei here was paid by Dariya, so there has to be a money trail."

"Has to be," he agreed. "And, by the way, I had the shack fingerprinted. We got a few, but they didn't match anyone in the system."

"DEA has no match for anything you lifted?"

He shook his head. "Surprising, I know. The setup in there looks like someone knew what they were doing."

"They know what they're doing well enough not to get caught, apparently," Peyton said.

NINE

Tuesday, March 11, 6:35 a.m., 12 Higgins Drive

As soon as she was sure Stone had finished his first cup of coffee, she texted: Everything ok?

He replied, AOK. Leaving for Tim Hortons, then dropping T at school. Tommy says Relax Mom.

She had to smile.

An hour later, she was back at Garrett Station, standing outside with Bill Hillsdale as they gassed up and scraped ice from the windshield of a Chevy Yukon service vehicle. It hadn't snowed overnight, but the temperature had dipped to eight, so the windshield was frosted.

"It's beautiful up here," Hillsdale said. "I called a realtor to ask about buying a cabin."

"I've got a good real-estate agent for you," Peyton said, "Kathy St. Pierre."

"That's the name I was given."

"She represents three-quarters of the houses for sale. Looking for a summer place?"

"It's preliminary. I'd have to sell my wife and daughters on it first."

"How old are your girls?" Peyton asked Bill Hillsdale.

"Lila's twenty. She's at URI, majoring in Physical Therapy. Kylie's nineteen. She's at George Washington, majoring in Political Science, which is a nice way to say she hasn't got a clue what she wants to do. And Margot's a junior in high school. She's a hockey and lacrosse player. A few colleges have contacted her."

Peyton smiled as she scraped the windshield. "I can tell how proud you are. I can hear it in your voice."

Hillsdale was pumping the gas. "You haven't seen my tuition bills. That's poverty you hear in my voice."

"Well, maybe today will count as overtime."

"What's overtime? Never heard of it."

"Me either," she said. "Hey, I've arranged for a U-Maine professor of Russian to come with us. He's worked as a translator for us before."

"Sounds good."

The gas pump clicked, and he replaced the cap. "You're right," Hillsdale said. "I'm very proud of my girls. So is my ex, Lydia. I worked long hours for a long time and missed too many school events and games. It's why Lydia left. She was always there, alone. She's been there for everything."

Peyton lifted a wiper and let it snap against the windshield. Ice scattered. "It's not easy to make all the events," she said. "I know. I've missed a bunch myself. I don't like it."

"You're divorced, too, right?"

She nodded.

"Joint custody?"

"Technically. I moved back here, in part, to let Tommy grow up near his father. But my ex rarely shows interest in him."

"That sucks."

"Yeah. It does. Tommy's resilient, though."

Hillsdale pulled the passenger's-side door open. "His father will wake up one day and realize what he missed out on."

"It'll be too late," she said and climbed behind the wheel. "This stuff ever bother you?" Peyton slid the truck into drive, and they crossed the lot and turned onto Route 1A.

"What's that? Turning people away?"

She nodded.

"A little. My great-grandfather was an immigrant. I get it. I understand why they do it. And I know that if my great-grandfather had been turned away, I wouldn't be here. This is like our conversation the day this all started."

"Sort of," she said, "except this one's civilized."

"I was an asshole. Sorry."

"I was no better," she said. "I'm sorry, too. And I feel the same way. My family—which doesn't even go back as far as yours—wouldn't be here if not for my grandfather coming from Quebec during the 1920s to work in the textile mills."

They drove in silence for a while.

"Have you looked into Dariya Vann's finances?" she asked. "Seen if he paid anyone to take Aleksei here?"

"A money trail?"

She nodded.

"Nothing stands out," he said. "We have someone looking at that, but nothing's showing up so far."

She thought about that and continued driving.

"Want to stop for coffee?" she asked.

"I'm fine, but stop if you want one."

"No," she said. "At the end of the day," she went on, "it comes down to me having a job to do. I don't create the laws. And given the Taliban and ISIS and Boko Haram, I'm vigilant and diligent in my work."

"That's the first priority now, isn't it?"

"Terrorism? Oh, no question. Last line of defense and all that. We hear it over and over. Contraband is the focus. And the threat of terrorism raises the stakes."

"This was the border where nine-eleven terrorists entered, wasn't it?"

Peyton had been in El Paso when it happened, but the institutional failings hadn't been lost on her. "That's right," she said.

She pulled the Yukon into the Donovan driveway. There was a green Honda Civic parked at the curb. The bearded professor in it was waiting for them.

"No phone call asking if we can stop by?" Hillsdale said.

"No. Not this time," she said.

———

"This really isn't a good time," Bohana said, holding the door open all of four inches.

Hillsdale stood behind Peyton, their breaths riding the morning air like tiny clouds. Mark Rogers stood to Hillsdale's right. He looked like a raven-haired rabbi, except that he nearly had to bend to enter a room. The Russian professor had played basketball at the University of Pennsylvania before earning a Ph.D.

Peyton said, "We're going to need to talk to Dariya, Bohana, either here or at the station."

"He gave your boss what he wanted to know."

"I know he met with Patrol Agent in Charge Mike Hewitt, but we have a few additional questions."

"My attorney can't be here."

"We can wait for him," Peyton said.

"He's in court all morning."

"Would you rather we meet later in the day?"

Bohana stood looking at her, the wheels turning. "What are you going to ask?"

"Just trying to clarify some details," Peyton said. "We can meet at the station later."

"Dariya is only here a couple weeks."

"We need some questions answered."

"This really is quite an indignity."

"I don't think so," Peyton said. "It would be an indignity if I sent a couple state troopers to pick your brother up and bring him in. Actually, I'm trying to spare you and him any and all indignities. I came to you."

"How long will this take? My brother is jet-lagged."

"Not long," Peyton said.

Bohana sat the unwanted guests at the kitchen table and went to get Dariya.

"Quite a kitchen," Hillsdale whispered. "These people are *not* government employees."

"Not hardly," Peyton said.

"Not a university assistant professor either," Rogers said. He wore a tweed jacket and carried a small notepad and pen.

"Thanks for taking the lead outside," Hillsdale said. "I knew you know her. I'll ask Dariya some questions."

"Fine." Peyton pulled out her iPhone.

"Recording this?"

"Planning to."

"Might spook him."

She shrugged and left the phone on the table.

Her iPhone told her it was 8:10 a.m. She had no idea what time that was in Donetsk, Ukraine, but either it was very late there or Dariya wasn't a morning person. Or both. He entered the kitchen, clearly having been awakened from a dead sleep—still in flannel pants and a wrinkled T-shirt, hair disheveled (a cowlick atop his head), and bloodshot eyes resembling a guy who'd come from a bar, not a bed.

"What you want?" he said. "You bring Aleksei back?"

He pronounced *Aleksei* differently than anyone she'd heard say the name previously. He seemed to say the name more fluidly, more rapidly—*Alek-SAY*. Even Bohana, after so many years living in the US, pronounced it more stiffly and Americanized: *Alec-SIGH*.

"Mr. Vann," Hillsdale said, "you realize that neither Agent Cote nor I make the laws, but, like you, we must follow them."

"You're using my son for getting what you want."

"Mr. Vann," Peyton said, "this is Mark Rogers. He's a Russian professor at the University of Maine at Reeds. I asked him to join us in case you have any translation needs."

"I will not," Dariya said.

"Just want to be sure," Peyton said.

"I lived in Boston for a year."

That surprised Peyton. Dariya Vann's English wasn't even as strong as his son's.

"Okay. I'm going to record this conversation so there is no confusion about what was said later on." She reached toward her cell phone as if he didn't have the right to stop her, and the red light started blinking. "We need you to speak openly and honestly about your son's entry into the United States."

"I bring Aleksei here," he said.

"You brought Aleksei here *yourself*?" Peyton said.

He nodded.

"Dariya," Hillsdale said, "this is the third version of the story."

"It was me. I bring him here."

"Okay," Peyton said, "then tell us about the journey, from start to finish."

"Would you like coffee?" Bohana asked, suddenly amiable. The room smelled of cinnamon. She'd baked something recently. Coffee cake before school? Peyton had arranged for her own son to sleep away from home so she could work last night. Hadn't even seen Tommy off to school today. And this Martha-Stewart homemaker was up early to prepare coffee cake?

Hillsdale accepted the offer; Peyton did not.

"My wife get hurt. Very bad."

Dariya looked at his hands. Peyton watched him. He had the face—weathered, wrinkled, eyes tired and sagging—of a man who worked outdoors, a laborer's face; but his hands were thick with manicured nails, the hands of someone who made his living behind a desk. Dariya was twirling his wedding band.

"Putin, you know, taking over. Donetsk a mess. No airport."

Peyton had read about the Donetsk airport, about how fighting between pro-Russian separatists and the Ukraine forces had left it in ruins.

"Liliya need me there. I care for her."

"What are her injuries?"

"Broken bones and stomach."

"What happened to her stomach?" Peyton said.

Dariya thought about that for a moment. "Shrapnel," he said. "Long operation to remove."

Peyton was surprised he came up with the word; maybe his English was better than she thought.

Hillsdale nodded. "So you'll return in a few days?" He knew as much, Peyton assumed, since he'd signed off on the man's stay here.

"Yes, I go back. Doctor says she needs more surgery. But she must get stronger first."

Hillsdale nodded reassuringly. "Why did you send Aleksei here?"

"People dying every day. Boys his age fighting pro-Russians."

"And you have stayed behind to fight?"

"Not like that. I cover the war."

"As a reporter?"

"Yes, I tell the truth."

"Dangerous?"

He nodded.

"When did you decide Aleksei needed to come here?" Peyton said.

"Long time ago."

"Please tell us about the trip," Peyton said for what felt like the umpteenth time.

"I brought him."

"You did?"

"Yes."

"You told Mike Hewitt that you paid someone to bring Aleksei."

"I did myself."

"Alone?"

"Yes."

"Why did you tell Mike something different?"

"To"—he searched for the word, smiled when he found it—"*simplify* things. I thought Aleksei would be take back to Bohana."

"Mr. Vann," Peyton said, "Aleksei led me to believe that you and your wife might be in grave danger if he told me who brought him here. Then you told a similar version of the story but claimed you didn't know who brought your son here. Now you're taking responsibility for his illegal entry into the US."

Dariya said nothing.

"That's three versions of the story," Hillsdale said.

"And Alien Smuggling is a felony punishable by ten years in federal prison."

"You can't arrest my brother." Bohana was on her feet.

"Your brother seems to be highly proficient in getting people here," Hillsdale said. "I'd like to know this isn't—or won't become—a habit."

Dariya shook his head.

Peyton said, "Can you describe the trip?"

"Very long."

"Mr. Vann," Hillsdale said, "we need details."

Bohana got up from the table then and brought more coffee cake from the counter.

"We need to know the date you left, where you went, how much you paid, when you arrived, and who helped you," Peyton said.

"No one helped."

"Tell us how you did it."

"Does that matter?" Bohana asked.

"Yes," Hillsdale said.

Dariya ran a hand through his hair.

His sister reached over and touched his shoulder. "I know it's hard. You were just being a good father. And these people are questioning what you've done." Bohana stared at Peyton.

Peyton smiled warmly and sipped her coffee.

"So you put Aleksei in the back seat of your car and started the engine," Hillsdale said. "Then what?"

"Drove to Hamburg."

"It's nearly thirty hours away," Peyton said.

Dariya nodded.

"Did you do it in one shot? Stop somewhere for the night?"

"One shot."

"Thirty hours?"

He nodded.

"Alone?"

"Yes."

"Then what?"

"Boat."

"Tell us about the boat."

Dariya shrugged. "Cargo ship. I slept the first two days."

"Mr. Vann," Peyton said. "I've done a little research into this, as you can imagine. The trip from Hamburg to Halifax, on a cargo ship, usually takes longer than half a month."

Aleksei nodded.

"Who took care of your wife while you were away?"

"Neighbor."

"Were you in contact with your wife while you traveled?" Peyton said.

"No."

"How long did the trip take?"

He shrugged. "Three weeks."

"And you didn't speak to your ill wife the whole time?"

"No."

"How did you eat on the ship?" Hillsdale asked.

"With the crew."

"And Aleksei?"

"Same."

"What ship were you on?" Hillsdale said.

Dariya shrugged.

"Want me to ask for specifics?" Mark Rogers asked.

"Sure," Hillsdale said.

"I know what you asked," Dariya Vann said.

"Name of the ship?" Peyton said. "Captain's name? Cargo company?"

Again, Dariya shrugged.

"You're not going to tell us?" Peyton said.

"Hard to remember."

"You're telling me you won't answer those questions?" Peyton said.

Bohana said, "That's not what he told you. We should've waited for Bobby Gaudreau."

Peyton moved on: "Where did you land?"

"Halifax. Then we drove—I rent car; I have the rental receipt—to New Brunswick border. And Aleksei walk to you." Finished, he leaned back in his seat and looked from Peyton to Hillsdale.

"How much did you pay for the boat?" Hillsdale said.

"I don't remember."

"Who did you pay?"

"I don't know the man's name."

"Mr. Vann," Peyton said, "Aleksei was asked these same questions." Peyton saw something—not quite fear but certainly concern—cross his face.

"And he told us you paid someone to bring him here. That you didn't make the journey."

"He did?"

"Yes, he did."

Dariya sat up straight in his chair then and looked Peyton in the eyes. "Excellent. He do what I tell him."

"You told him to lie to us?"

He nodded, lifted a piece of coffee cake, and took a bite. "Good," he said to his sister.

"Thank you," Bohana said. She looked pale.

"What purpose would your son's lying serve?" Hillsdale asked.

"Don't like people to know my—" He paused to think, shook his head, and said something to his sister in Russian.

"Business," Rogers translated.

Dariya turned and stared at Rogers as if he'd just remembered Rogers was in the room.

"And you flew back?" Peyton said.

"My wife is ill. Had to get back."

"Do you know what your son told me about the trip?" Peyton said. "And I tell you because, if none of this is true and you really paid someone else to bring him here, whoever that person is should be held accountable. Aleksei said he was locked below the deck of the ship where he got seasick and ate alone. That's a long three weeks, Mr. Vann. I'd even call it child abuse."

Dariya turned to look at Bohana. She sat stoically. Then he spoke rapidly in Russian.

Rogers said, "He wants her to tell him if that's true."

Dariya heard Rogers and looked at Hillsdale then at Peyton.

"He's a good boy," Dariya said. "He did what I tell him."

"You told him to say that?" Peyton asked. "To make all of that up?"

Before he could answer, there was a knock at the back door, which swung open before anyone stood.

———

The man took one step into the kitchen and paused.

"Bohana, is this a bad time?" he asked.

Bohana shrugged, eyes falling to the floor, hands restless in her lap.

Peyton recognized the man immediately. She'd seen him with Steven Donovan at the gun range. He was tall and lean with thinning sandy-blond hair and wore navy blue work clothes. Beneath the unzipped Carhartt jacket, *Ted* was stitched into one breast pocket, *Donovan Ford* into the other.

He looked around the room, his gaze coming to rest on Dariya. Dariya looked at him, then at Peyton and Hillsdale. His sister saw him staring at the agents.

"Yes, Teddy, this might be a bad time," she said. "But help yourself to the coffee."

Peyton and Hillsdale watched the man—waiting to continue the interview—as he not only filled his travel mug but opened the refrigerator and added cream. Peyton looked at Hillsdale, who offered a tiny head shake. She shifted, adjusting the .40 on her service belt that was digging into her side. The eight-pound Kevlar vest was—after all these years—a routine hassle. But the gun digging into her side was an indignity she refused to tolerate. Coffee made, Ted moved to the pantry and took out a bag of bagels, cut one, and popped it into the toaster.

"Friendly neighbors," Hillsdale said. "I wish my neighbors fed me breakfast."

"Oh, I'm sorry," Bohana said. "I should've introduced him. This is my brother-in-law. He lives in the upstairs apartment."

The man failed to acknowledge the statement. When the toaster popped, he took his bagel, wrapped it in a paper napkin, and started for the door.

"You all going to be home tonight?" he asked Bohana.

She shrugged. "As far as I know." She looked at Peyton. "We're having Aleksei over for dinner, so he can spend time with his father." She turned to Hillsdale. "That okay with you, sir?"

"Fine," Hillsdale said.

"I'll be by," Ted said and left.

When the door closed behind him, Peyton said, "So that we're all clear on this, Mr. Vann, you told your son to lie to agents about being mistreated on the ship?"

"Yes."

"I'd like to see the receipt for the rental car you used to get from Halifax to Youngsville, New Brunswick, Canada."

He stood and left the room for several minutes before returning with the receipt.

Hillsdale took it from him, examined it, and put it in his pocket.

"Why didn't you fly here?" Peyton asked.

"Passports," Dariya said cryptically.

"Meaning you don't have them?"

"Aleksei do not."

"Why not get one?" Peyton said. "Or even falsify one for him?"

"Not that easy," Dariya said. "Besides, no time."

"I'm trying to understand how this was time-sensitive," Peyton said.

"After the Buk hit my brother's house, he knew he had to leave."

Peyton looked from Bohana to Dariya. The diminutive man was staring at the crumbs left in his plate.

"So it didn't take you long to line up the ship, the car, and even map the route," Peyton said to Dariya.

"What?" Bohana said.

Peyton saw Dariya scowl at his sister.

"You see what I'm saying, Mr. Vann. Don't you?"

"No. I do not."

"I think you do. From the time you decided to bring your son to the US, it seems like the logistical aspects of the trip took shape very quickly. That doesn't seem possible."

Dariya looked at his sister.

"May I assist?" Rogers said.

"I don't need help," Dariya insisted. Then to Peyton, "You think all of this was planned?"

"Had to be, Mr. Vann. There are simply way too many moving parts."

"No."

"No, I guess there is one scenario that would work the way you've explained it."

Dariya leaned back in his seat and waited.

"You hired someone who knew how to do this and had done it before. Or you spent several weeks, probably months, getting the logistics ironed out before you left."

"You call me a liar?"

It was her turn to not answer.

"I think it's time for you to leave, Peyton," Bohana said.

"That's fine." She stood.

"I'll walk you to the door," Bohana said and did. When she held the door, she said, "I've never seen this side of you before, Peyton."

"And what side is that?"

Bohana started to speak, then stopped. Finally she said, "You can be a real bitch."

"That's on my business cards," Peyton said. "Right beneath my name."

5 p.m., Interstate 95
Rodia. Anna.

Thoughts of them wouldn't let her go. The flight had been long, and the six- and three-year-olds dominated her mind. Marfa tried to focus on what was to be done. But thoughts and memories of her children returned as if part of an unwanted video loop.

Had her father been right? As a woman, was she instinctively maternal? And, if so, would that hold her back? She'd spent years denying her father's theory. Her father had no problem shedding parental duties when business called. "Go play," he'd say. "Daddy's little girl, you go play." Then, years later, "This is something Dimitri and I must discuss. Why don't you go shopping?"

Shopping. The irony struck her for the first time. She was shopping now, alright. She'd turned off the Nokia phone she'd had in Russia (always a Nokia in Russia) and had purchased an iPhone (when in Rome...). Driving seventy, classical music playing, she laughed. She wished she could see her father's face when he realized the enormity of it all. When he realized that, yes, she could have simply waited for him to die—just a few months, maybe a year. She wanted to see his expression upon realizing not only was she taking it all sooner, but also why she was doing it: only to spite him. And, if that wasn't enough, what she was doing now—driving to northern Maine to get (and, unbeknownst to him, *keep*) the gift he treasured above all else—would be the final insult.

The rented Buick Enclave shot north into the midmorning sunlight, had just crossed into Maine, when her iPhone chirped.

She answered it. The voice was familiar.

"It's good to hear you," the voice said. "I've missed you."

She spoke in Russian, "You have no idea how much I've missed you," she lied.

"And our kids?" he said.

"They're home. That will come later. I have to get something first."

"The money?"

"No, not the money," she said. "Something else."

"Well, here's the address for your GPS. I'll be waiting."

Mozart played on the radio. She was glad Pyotr was there already. That meant the house was set. She passed the service plaza in Wells, Maine, not needing gas yet.

Garrett, Maine, she thought, and looked at the GPS. It would take her five more hours.

Where the hell was she going?

And how could it have stayed hidden there for a quarter century?

5:15 p.m., Route 1A, Garrett

Tommy used to say it "smelled like spring" on days like these. It was forty degrees, and Peyton recognized that the early-evening air seemed somehow different after such a long winter. A precursor of what was soon to come, she hoped.

Her thoughts had drifted to Tommy because she planned to miss dinner with him. Again.

Tommy was eating with Lois, who was making shepherd's pie (delicious, but with far too much salt) and crepes for dessert. Given the menu and Tommy's love for his grandmother's French-Canadian cooking, Peyton *almost* felt no guilt about missing the evening meal with her son.

Almost.

But she did feel guilty. Had seen Tommy little in the past twenty-four hours. Worse, now, driving back to the Donovan home, she couldn't say she was providing for him because she knew Mike Hewitt would never okay overtime for a fishing expedition. And that's what this was: another round of interviews with Dariya Vann—just short, she knew, of harassment—which explained her street clothes and the use of her own vehicle. *Off duty, just dropping by,* she'd say.

She hit her blinker and slowed to turn onto the Donovans' street. The truck in front of her turned first, and in the flash of his rearview mirror, she spotted Ted Donovan.

She slowed, leaving space between her Wrangler and Ted's battered Ford pickup. He pulled into the driveway but stopped short, brakes yelping. Peyton rolled past, catching a glimpse of what led to the sudden stop: Dariya Vann, wearing only a T-shirt and pants in the evening's crisp air, shoes untied, stood in the middle of the driveway, holding a garbage bag.

She pulled to the curb at the end of a row of vehicles, five cars away from the two men. This far north, the sun set early during winter months, and dusk was upon them.

Ted climbed out of the truck, approaching Dariya.

Dariya turned to look at the house. Leaned to see in the kitchen window. Nothing. Then he turned back to Ted, whose expression was all business.

Peyton sensed the moment and leaned to roll down the passenger's window.

"I was wondering when we'd get a few moments alone," Ted said extending his hand. "The bank called. Thanks for separating the accounts."

Dariya didn't shake hands. "There were always supposed to be two accounts."

"You don't trust me?" Ted said.

"It's been a long time," Dariya said.

Ted nodded. "And people change."

"Like you?" He pointed at Ted. "My son was seasick."

Ted tilted his head. "What?"

"Aleksei was seasick. And you do nothing. He tell me that."

"That's not true, Dariya. You're exaggerating."

"No. *She* say same this morning."

215

"Who? The Border Patrol woman? You've always exaggerated, you know that? You were like this twenty-five years ago. Remember? Your brilliant goddamned idea? Remember that? Except you left the fucking country. And I got stuck with the merchandise."

Instinctively, she reached for her iPhone to record the conversation. But fifty feet away, the recording would be spotty at best—and maybe even impermissible in court. She slid the phone back into her pocket and leaned closer to hear, peering out the passenger-side window.

Dariya stepped back, shaking his head, disbelieving. "Got *stuck with* it? You? You loved it." His face was red, his finger pointing, shaking inches from Ted's chest. He struggled to find the words "This was all *your* idea. *You* the expert."

"Yes," Ted said, "I am. Even more so now. And I'm saying I'm the one who has done the hard work here. So much work that I should get two-thirds."

"Two-thirds?"

"Yes, twenty."

Dariya took a step back, obviously confused. He started to speak but closed his mouth.

"What is it?" Ted said. "Think about it."

The sun was setting rapidly now, but she saw Dariya's face color. "You fucking think—" he blurted.

"Keep your voice down."

"I'm taking it back. My son here. Think all of that easy? Is that what you think?"

"You speak the language, Dariya. But *I* have the contacts. *I* found the buyer."

"And I met with her. Negotiated price."

"And in a few days," Ted said, "it will be off our hands for good. But let's be clear, I located her, Dariya. I reached out to you, sent you to her. I gave you the details, told you what it was worth, estimated what we could get."

Peyton watched as they stood looking at each other, neither man speaking for what seemed like minutes.

"Listen," Ted said, "I gave up everything. We both know that. You've had a network TV job. Look at me." Ted waved a hand before him, inviting Dariya to look at his shirt front: the same outfit Peyton had seen him in that morning, but now the shirt was covered in motor oil. "This is *my* journalism career," Ted said. "Oil stains and grime."

"That not my—"

"*Fault?* Is that what you're going to say?"

Dariya nodded.

"I know it's not your fault. I know that. But there was nowhere to move here. I turned down an offer in a major city. And then I quit. Where could I go? I couldn't take it with me. And I've been responsible for keeping it all these years. Especially after your fiasco."

"The boat overturn."

"And two hundred million dollars are on the bottom of the ocean," Ted said. "Jesus Christ, what a waste. Look, I've cared for mine."

"The boat overturn. I almost died."

"Well, I took care of mine. And it's come at a price. I even had to put in central air." He stopped. "I can see you don't give a shit. At least I appreciate it. More, I'm sure, than the buyer."

Dariya smiled then and shook his head. "No. Not more than him. His daughter tell me he special. Waited his life to get it. Now he's dying."

"She's granting his last wish?" Ted thought about that. "Makes sense." He nodded, thinking. "So that's why she's willing to buy. She and her old man would know they can never sell it. I wondered about that. It's because they don't *want* to sell it."

"Is ready to move?"

"To be moved?" Ted said.

Dariya nodded.

"Almost," Ted said. "But I want twenty, Dariya. I've earned two-thirds."

"My son, my trip."

"We had to use your son. He'll understand. Someday. That's not a big deal. And, Christ, if you don't want him to know, he never has to find out."

"Me. I know. You aren't a father."

"So?"

"So I *use* my son for this. Send him here."

"For a better life."

"That only part of it. I know what I done. I used my son."

"You can argue with your conscience all you want. I want two-thirds, Dariya. It's my contact."

"Ted"—Dariya's voice was soft in the night, but even in that one word Peyton heard something reminding her of Aleksei's statement about being knocked down (*I got up. I will always get up.*)—"if you take twenty, I kill you."

Ted heard it too. "Whoa." His hands went up defensively. "Slow down, Dariya. This isn't life or death here."

"Ted, my wife need a lot of"—he searched for the word—"treat."

"Treatment?"

"Yes. I get my money, Ted."

218

Ted looked at him, nodded once. Then he moved to the wooden stairs leading to the third-floor apartment. Dariya walked to the line of trash cans. Peyton was low in her Jeep. When she heard the lids clatter and footsteps receding, she looked up.

Dariya re-entered the house. But as he did so, someone—wearing jeans, a hoodie, and a dark jacket with a yellow emblem on the collar—rounded the side of the garage.

The person stood in the driveway, head down, thinking about what had been said. After several moments, whoever it was walked to the front door.

TEN

Wednesday, March 12, 2:35 a.m., near the Canadian border
MICHAEL DONOVAN KILLED THE engine, clicked off the headlights, and walked to the tailgate of his battered parts pickup. He dropped the tailgate and struggled to slide out the six-foot-by-five-foot felt-lined case. It was six inches thick.

He'd taken extra precautions, wrapping the whole thing in thick plastic, making it even more bulky and awkward to carry. He placed it onto a sheet of quarter-inch plywood he'd taken from the basement and into which he'd drilled two corner holes and added a piece of rope. Towing the sheet of thin plywood, he started the long walk toward the shack.

He knew he wouldn't reach it for close to an hour, and the woods at night were dark and full of odd noises. But he had no other choice. His uncle had said in a few days they'd be getting rid of it. And Michael couldn't have that. He hadn't decided what to do about it yet. He knew the item's value, monetarily and intrinsically. Knew all about it's godlike creator. About the act committed twenty-five years ago, a brazen deed. And he'd thought long and hard about those who committed the act. About how, ironically, that had enabled him to have access to it all these years. He'd spent nights staring at the ceiling, thinking about his uncle, speculating about his mother and father.

Perhaps more than anything *that* was what he needed—to know his mother and father weren't involved in what Uncle Ted and Dariya Vann had done. Was that realistic? His father was the businessman in the family. And it all seemed beyond Uncle Ted. Uncle Ted owned art books. Michael had seen them, even read most of them. And Uncle Ted had taken the recent trip to Paris and Germany. Was that trip related to this?

It didn't matter. Not now. Not as Michael trudged down the trail toward the shack. What mattered was hiding it.

At the shack, he dragged the box inside. He pulled a chair across the room and stood on it as he positioned the box in the space above the ceiling. And, as Michael had read, after nearly four hundred years, not much could damage it, especially in a temperature-controlled setting. Summer would bring humidity. (He knew why Uncle Ted's apartment had been kept at precisely seventy degrees all these years.) Of course, the heat lamps and constantly-running portable heater made him nervous. He would have to move it shortly.

The entire drop took two hours. Back at his pickup, he started the engine and wondered how long it could stay in the shack.

Hopefully long enough for him to figure out what to do with it.

3:10 a.m., 7 Drummond Lane

He knew his way around the house and crept into the guest room where Aleksei had stayed. He knew the door would creak. So he turned the knob gently and slowly pushed the door. Inside, he padded across the room until he stood over the bed.

Then, with a stiff index finger, he poked Dariya once on the chest, a firm jab.

"Get your ass out of bed and follow—"

But Ted Donovan never finished his sentence.

In one swift motion, Dariya sat up in bed, his hand emerging from beneath his pillow, the four-inch blade stopping an inch from Ted's nose.

A desk chair scraped the floor when Ted leaped back.

"What are you doing here?" Dariya said, his throat dry, the words rasping. He stood up, the knife falling to his side.

"Put that away. Who sleeps with a fucking knife under his pillow?"

"Someone whose house was blow up."

"You're fucking crazy. Come with me, you asshole."

Ted didn't wait to hear Dariya's reply. He walked down the hall and up the stairs to his apartment.

———

It took several minutes, but Dariya finally climbed the stairs to Ted's apartment. The door was open, the lights on.

Ted was pacing, rubbing his face with his hands. He looked up and stopped moving.

"You leave your knife downstairs?" He went past Dariya, pulled the door closed, and locked it.

"Why you locking the door?" Dariya asked. "It's three thirty in the morning."

"It's been locked for twenty-five years. You, of all people, should know that." Ted stayed near the door. "Where's the knife?"

"Under pillow. It's the middle of the night. What you want?"

Barefoot, Dariya wore only the pants he'd worn that day and a white undershirt. Ted saw no bulges in his front pockets.

"Turn around. Let me see your waistband."

"What?"

Ted repeated the instructions.

Dariya shook his head but did what he was told.

Satisfied that Dariya left the knife downstairs, Ted moved closer. "Got something to tell me, asshole?"

"It middle of the night. Drunk?"

"What?" Ted said.

"Drunk?"

"Am I drunk?" Ted inched closer. He could smell Dariya's breath. "No. But I am mad. Mad enough to kill you, you motherfucker."

"What? What are you talking?"

"Where were you all day?"

"Meeting with DHHS about Aleksei."

"All day?"

"Ask Bohana. She with me."

Unconsciously, Ted stepped back. Hadn't expected that answer. Was Bohana in on it? Impossible.

Or was it?

Then it happened. The surge of anger, his own hand flashing, arm outstretched. In a second Ted's fingers were a vise clamped around the smaller man's throat.

"It's not here. Where is it?"

Dariya, gasping for breath: "Let … me … go."

"It's not fucking here," Ted said. "I checked on it yesterday, and I got up to piss and for the hell of it, thought I'd check, and it's gone." Dariya's eyes refocused, and Ted knew the diminutive Ukrainian understood. He also saw the genuine confusion in Dariya's eyes. His clenched fist went limp. Dariya stepped away from him, gulping air.

"Don't you touch me. Next time I kill you."

"It's fucking gone, Dariya. You hear me?"

"Where?"

"You tell me, asshole."

Dariya shook his head, realizing now. "You think me …"

"Who else?"

"Why would I stay here?"

"If you took it? Where the hell else would you go?"

"I don't even know where you hid, Ted."

Ted thought about that. In his rage and panic, he hadn't considered that obvious fact. The man had lived in Ukraine; how could he know where the hiding place was?

"Yeah, well, no one does. But you're the only one who knows I had it. And you had all day to look for it. No one else."

"Apparently not," Dariya said, surprising Ted with his formal English.

Ted turned from him and went to the third-floor window, blackened from the room's interior light. He stood squinting against the night sky—and noticed Michael's pickup missing from the driveway below.

"If it was warmer," Stone Gibson said, "we could walk the bike trail."

"It would have to be *much* warmer." Peyton took his hand as they walked past the old hotel near the corner of Academy and Main streets in downtown Reeds. "There's still a foot of snow on the bike trail."

He looked at her hand in his. "I'm on duty," he said.

"Well, I'm not. And you're not in uniform, so we can hold hands. We actually look like two regular people."

"With normal, civilian lives. Imagine what that must be like."

"Boring," she said. Peyton's cell phone chirped. She recognized the number.

"When you're as old as me," Stan Jackman said in lieu of a greeting, "you have contacts in lots of places."

"You found something?

"My friend in the Boston FBI office did. Dariya Vann ever mention Emerson College?" Jackman asked.

She wasn't walking anymore. And she wasn't holding Stone's hand now. "No," she said. "Emerson College in Boston?"

"Yeah. If there's a connection, that's it. Ted Donovan and Dariya Vann were both at Emerson in the fall of 1990."

"Were they in classes together?"

"Peyton, I just started looking into it."

Stone was looking at her, eyebrows raised.

"But you're known as a miracle worker," she said, "so I expected you to be further along."

"Of course," Jackman said. "You think they're moving something. I read your shift report. What makes you think that?"

"I overheard a conversation."

"Illegally tapped or spied?"

"Overheard," she said.

"So spied," Jackman said.

Stone was smiling now, correctly guessing what Stan Jackman had said.

"I *overheard* them talking. Ted talked about finding a buyer, and Dariya spoke about negotiating the deal. He said Dariya left the country and left him holding the merchandise."

"And Stone found some pot plants near where the boy was found?"

"Yeah, but only six plants. I don't know that Stone's find has anything to do with it. They were talking about locating buyers. And my sense was they'd had trouble finding one because of resale challenges."

Jackman was silent for a moment, then said, "If the operation is much larger than we think, and they're selling pot out of state, resale would be hard. And that would make sense. Why truck it in to, say, Boston when you can get something home-grown nearby?"

"Whatever it was," she said, "it's been a long process. Ted Donovan was talking about sacrificing his TV career for this."

"I don't know what that's about," Jackman said. "Neither man has a criminal history or anything I see involving pot."

"He's not sacrificing his TV career for six pot plants."

"Has Maine DEA looked into the shack?" Jackman asked.

"I don't think Maine DEA is going to." She looked at Stone.

Stone shook his head. "They don't want it. I'm handling it."

She relayed the message to Jackman.

"Whatever it is," she said, "they're selling it for thirty. That was the figure. They were arguing about who got twenty."

"Thirty grand?" Jackman said.

"I doubt Ted Donovan would throw his TV broadcasting career away for thirty grand."

Jackman paused. "You think they're talking about millions?"

"Yes," she said. "Whatever it is, Ted found the buyer and sent Dariya to negotiate the deal."

"I'll keep tugging at my end," Jackman said. "If I find anything new, I'll call. And I might swing by your place tonight. I got Tommy a new David Ortiz T-shirt."

"That's sweet, Grandpa," Peyton said and hung up.

Stone was checking his iPhone. When she hung up, he slipped his phone in his pocket. He took her hand, and they started walking.

"Maine DEA doesn't believe pot use is on the rise in this area," he said, "but usage statistics don't mean much when you've got a built-in irrigation system. You can grow it and transport it."

"True," she said. "You're talking about the river?"

"This place has always been made-to-order for growing pot," he said. "Has been since I was a kid."

"But Dariya and Donovan sure as hell aren't bringing pot back to the Ukraine."

They passed the bowling alley.

"Does Dariya Vann have ties to organized crime in the Ukraine or Russia?" Stone asked. "You can't take the dope back, but you could send money back."

"You're thinking they set everything up with dirty foreign money," she said. "Launder it here and send that back."

"Turn it into US currency and either wire it somewhere or take it home."

"A thirty-million-dollar pot industry run by Ted Donovan?" she asked.

Stone was staring straight ahead, thinking. "I know. I know. Not likely."

"Virtually impossible," she said. "He works forty hours a week for his brother. And all we have behind this entire theory is six pot plants. DEA doesn't even think that's worth looking into."

They continued to walk, no longer holding hands; now, they were working, both thinking aloud.

"You've got to admit," Stone said, "it's a good theory. Someone in the Ukraine funds a US-based pot-growing operation in a rural area with little law enforcement and a river. You sell the product for US funds, and the dirty money is changed to US currency. Then you send the profits back to the Ukraine."

"And do it all over again," Peyton said. "It's too elaborate, Stone."

"Probably," he agreed.

"Dariya was talking about ships overturning. Said he nearly died and lost his half of the product."

"What's that about?" Stone asked.

"Not sure. What we do know is that Dariya and Ted were in Boston in 1990 together. And that Dariya planted his son here to get back into the US. I'm pretty sure Ted brought Aleksei here."

"Ted?"

"Yeah, Dariya was pissed at him for his treatment of Aleksei."

"What is Aleksei's connection to all of this?"

"He gets Dariya into the US."

"And what does that mean?"

"Good question," she said. "Maybe he really does want Aleksei here to improve his life, and whatever is going on with Ted is secondary."

"Too many questions," Stone said. "Hillsdale must've loved hearing that Aleksei is a plant."

"I haven't discussed it with him," she said.

"You haven't discussed it with him yet?"

"I can't have Hillsdale throw Dariya out yet. I need him here."

"You feds," Stone said. "Always conspiring."

"That's not conspiring. It's playing it safe."

"I'd call that conspiring," Stone said. "Want to walk to Tim Hortons?"

"That's a long walk," she said.

"Yeah, but it's not against regs for a high-paid federal conspirator like you to buy a lowly state cop a coffee." He grinned.

"You've got a nice smile, you know that?"

"And I'll pay you back with a back rub," he said.

"I told you, I've had your back rubs." She smiled. "They're nothing special."

"I'll try harder," he said.

"Then the coffee is on me."

9:30 a.m., Paradise Court, Garrett

"I'm so glad you called," Pyotr said, his Russian, she thought, barely better than his English. "So glad we're back together."

Her head lay on his chest, her eyes steady on the wall. But a slight smile played on her lips. She hated him but was glad he hadn't lost his touch in bed—that would make the downtime during the next few days better.

"Thank you for coming here early," she said, "and finding us a place to stay. A hotel room wouldn't have worked."

The house was a two-bedroom ranch, its interior dated: 1970s paneling, yellow laminate countertop, and shag carpeting. But Pyotr paid a month's rent in cash, said he was a college professor come to the US to research Canada Lynx, a rare animal confirmed to live in only a handful of US states. The whole exchange had taken all of twenty minutes, according to Pyotr. Probably because the house had been for sale for years, and the rental market wasn't good. So the owner, glad for the month's rent, asked no questions.

She hadn't seen him in months. His leaving had been hard on Rodia, who cried for weeks. Anna, at three, occasionally muttered " папа?" But then it passed. It had been hardest on her father, who'd brought Pyotr in twenty years ago as a skinny teenager.

"I understand why," he said. "You're welcome." He ran the back of his hand over her bare nipple. "I missed this. And I missed you."

His hand felt like ice against her skin, an odd reaction to his touch, Marfa knew, especially since she'd initiated the sex.

"It's why I called," she lied. "I couldn't be without you."

He moved his hand up, his index finger moving slowly on her jawline. "You sounded worried that I wouldn't take you back," he said.

"I was." She fought to hold back the grin. "I couldn't live without you. I know that now."

"I thought of you every day," he said.

"Every day?" she said.

"Every day."

"Even two days after you left?"

That gave him pause. She knew he hadn't expected her to know about that.

"She didn't mean anything to me," he said. "I just needed someone to take my mind off you."

She nearly laughed at the cliche.

"None of that matters now anyway. Now we're together again."

"Forever," she said.

He didn't see the smirk on her face.

His breathing was slow, rhythmic. In five minutes, she thought, he'd be snoring softly. Some things never change: following sex, he always fell asleep immediately; she never did.

"Does your father know you're here?"

He was thinking the situation through. She'd anticipated questions.

"He thinks you and I are bringing it back," she said.

"But we're not?"

"No."

"Where exactly are we taking it?"

Pyotr was smart. Her father had been right about that. But he wasn't as smart as she was. That part her father had been wrong about.

"I bought a house in the Alps," she said. And with that lie the game was on. So was the act. She tilted her head, her warm smile looking genuine. "You know how I've always loved the Alps."

"It's where we honeymooned. We'll go back?"

"And live, yes. The children are on their way now. They've missed you."

"Who is bringing them?"

"A nanny. I hired her." That much was true.

"Do you have your own buyer?"

"I have something better."

"Better?"

"Yes, why would I resell? I know its value. And"—she shrugged—"it's the ultimate bargaining chip."

"For what?"

"For whatever we need. Literally a get-out-of-jail-free card."

"To be used when?"

"When and if we're arrested or if my father sends someone."

"Your father doesn't negotiate."

"For this? Are you kidding me? Art has been his whole life. Every vacation we took when I was a child revolved around a museum—a different museum somewhere in the world."

"His life has been about money and power."

"And art," she corrected.

"How are you paying for it?"

He would ask that. Always concerned about the money.

"Father trusts me" was all she said.

"You're negotiating for your father? Using his money?"

"He knows we only have a two-week window, so he gave me access to the accounts." And with that financial admission, she knew she could no longer trust Pyotr. The final step of her plan had been decided. "He doesn't think I'm strong enough to run his operations," she continued, "but he knows I'm good with money."

"We have total control of his accounts?" he asked, blue eyes distant now. He no longer looked sleepy.

"*I* have control of them, yes," she said. "Go to sleep." She stood and crossed to the bathroom.

When she came out, he was snoring quietly. He lay in the middle of the bed now. Still slept with his mouth open, his snore still an endless hum.

She slid into her robe, pulled it tight, and paused in the doorway, looking at him and thinking.

His eyes blinked open. "What are you doing?" he asked.

"Just watching you." *He's no Dimitri*, she thought. "I've missed you."

The lie made him smile.

She could've handled her brother being in control after her father died. Dimitri was older and respected her. And he'd saved Pyotr—three times, no less—from mistakes that would've cost millions. It was her father's reaction to the errors that had offered her a glimpse into the future: each time he laughed it off, a deep, rich, boys-will-be-boys laugh. "Pyotr is learning," her father had said.

But so was she—learning that despite her MBA and her successful boutique, her father had little respect for her abilities. And less for her ambition and fortitude.

Then one night last summer Dimitri left the restaurant in St. Petersburg and was shot once behind the left ear.

One .22-caliber shot had changed everything.

Strategically, it made perfect sense. Taking her father's right-hand man isolated him, weakened his grip on his dominant market share, and left the old man with only Nicolay (also a gray beard), Pyotr, and herself in his inner circle. And to men like her father, she was seen as weak.

"What are you thinking about?" Pyotr asked.

"How mistaken men can be," she said.

"What did I say?"

"Not you." She moved closer, leaned, and kissed his lips, lingering over him a long time.

Then she pulled away.

"It hasn't been easy being apart," he said and held up his left hand. "I never took it off." He showed her his wedding ring. "Where's yours? You should put it back on. We're together again. Forever."

She'd taken hers off ten minutes after he'd left the house for the US.

She kissed him again. "I left mine at father's. I'm so sorry." She had no idea where the ring was.

"What were you thinking in the doorway?" he asked. "You looked angry."

"I was just watching you sleep," she said and pulled the robe tight again.

But, as she descended the stairs, her true previous thought returned: *How would it feel to kill him?*

3:30 p.m., Razdory, Russia

Victor Tankov looked up from his book when Nicolay entered the room carrying a plate of sliced cucumbers and apples.

"I brought a snack," Nicolay said.

"That's not a snack. That's what Rodia feeds the guinea pigs."

Victor hadn't felt well enough to dress—he was still in his robe—but at least this day he sat near the window in his reading chair.

Nicolay smiled. "Not guinea pig food."

"Don't laugh at me."

"You're my boss. How could I laugh at you?"

"I'm not your boss. We stopped that relationship years ago."

"That's true, but you're still my boss."

Victor didn't speak, turning to the window.

"What is it?" Nicolay said.

At his age, in his condition, Victor knew it was time. "I've never said it before, and that's wrong," he said, "but thank you."

"You thank me all the time," Nicolay said.

"No. That's an expression of appreciation for a job well done. And, yes, I do often express gratitude for your excellent work. I'm not expressing gratitude for excellent work now."

"What are you saying?" Nicolay pulled a straight-backed chair bedside, sat, and retrieved a bottle of Ensure from the breast pocket of his flannel shirt. "If you can't eat the vegetables or fruit, promise me you'll drink this."

"That's what I want to thank you for," Victor said. "You've been a true friend for years. When I can count on no one else, I can count on you."

"Yes, you can. You gave me a family when I had none. I have no education, and you've paid me like a doctor."

"I've paid you a fair wage for what you do and what you've been willing to do. And, of course, there is more money to come. You're in my will."

Victor set the biography of Rembrandt Harmensvoon van Rijn down and absently glanced at the empty space on the wall. He put his hand on Nicolay's thick forearm.

"I know, and thank you."

"No need. But you're welcome."

The two men—men who had survived many years doing things few were willing or able to do—held each other's gaze through a long silence.

"Men like us don't often get emotional." Nicolay looked at Victor, saw the pale skin, heard the rasping breath.

"No, not often."

"I have much to thank you for, Victor. You took me in when I had lost my father and had nothing. Helped me support my mother. I can never repay you."

Victor smoothed the flannel fabric on his thighs. His eyes were focused on the floor, but he said, "When Maria died, you were there. Not the children. No one else. You."

Nicolay only nodded, and both men sat looking out the window at the sun-splashed day.

A dry smile creased Victor's mouth. "I'm tired of rabbit food. You know how long it's been since I tasted real food?"

"Months?"

"Seems longer. Sometimes I like to think of the past. About what I did. Where I went. What I ate and saw. I pick one day and relive it in my mind. Is that crazy?"

Nicolay was staring straight ahead. His head shook back and forth. This was the closest his friend had come to admitting his death was imminent.

"I think about a summer day," Victor continued, "when Maria was still alive and Marfa was young. We were in Paris. The sun was shining. We were at the Louvre looking at *Carcass of Beef*. That was a special day. Marfa was eight. She looked at that painting—not in disgust like other children her age. They looked and turned away. She didn't. And I knew then she was like me. She appreciated his work. Saw it for what it was."

"That's why she's getting it for you."

"She wants to be like me. I don't want that."

"This is a hard life," Nicolay said, "for a woman."

"Impossible for a mother. Maria made it possible for me to do the work. I could leave when I needed to, when things got too bad. And I did."

"I remember. One summer you and I went to Milan."

"Yes. A mother, especially a single mother, cannot do that. She has other, higher, responsibilities. And I believe she has different instincts too. But for that I have no proof."

"Mother's intuition?"

"Yes. And that instinct makes a woman put her children before all else. You can't do this work and think about that too."

"She can't slip off to Milan for a summer when things get hot?"

"No, she can't. She provides the children with emotional support. She can't do that and run this from Milan."

Nicolay nodded.

Outside, snow melted and water dripped from the roofline. "How are the children?" he said.

"They're fine. Downstairs. Playing with the nanny."

"Not fine. Children are never fine without their mothers."

"I turned out alright," Nicolay said.

Victor made no reply.

"Something's bothering you." The cherry arms of Nicolay's chair looked like twigs beneath his palms.

"Instinct," the old man said, "has served me well for many years."

"And now?"

Victor looked straight at him. "Something's wrong," he said.

Nicolay's bushy gray brows furrowed. "You think Marfa's in trouble?"

"No. And that's what bothers me."

"If she's not in trouble," Nicolay said, "what could be wrong?"

"I don't know."

"What are you worrying about?"

"Me," Victor said. "I'm worried for me." He looked at the space on the wall again. "I have a bad feeling."

10:30 a.m., Donovan Ford

"Can I talk to you?" Ted Donovan asked his brother.

Steven—in mid stride approaching a man and woman in their sixties who stood alone near a new Ford Escape—stopped and came back to Ted.

"That's Peter O'Reilly," he said to Ted.

Ted turned to see the white-haired man pointing at the Escape's window sticker and nodding encouragingly at his wife as they talked.

"Can this wait?" Steven asked. He turned up the collar of his ski jacket, cupped his hands, and exhaled into them, warming them with his breath. "The O'Reillys bought their last two vehicles from us. This is a slam dunk." Steven smiled playfully at his brother. "Christ, even you could get a commission on this one."

Ted wasn't smiling. "Who is home during the day?"

"What do you mean? I need to go to these people, Ted."

"I need to know who has access to my apartment."

"Access? What are you talking about?" Steven sighed. "Look, it's cold out here. What are you asking?"

Ted could feel his face getting red. The last time he'd had a sensation like this was his first day on-air—so nervous he'd felt nearly out of control. He wasn't nervous now. He was angry. But he was nearing the edge of self-control, nonetheless.

"Someone was in my fucking apartment, Steven. Who was it?"

The elderly man in the red flannel hunting jacket heard the profanity and looked at them, clearly insulted that someone used that language in front of his wife.

"Keep your voice down, Ted. What's wrong with you?"

"Look at me, Steven."

"What?" Steven focused on his brother now. "You're sweating and pale. You sick?"

"I might be. Someone went into my apartment when I wasn't there."

"How do you know that?"

"Because I'm missing something."

Steven's eyes narrowed. "What are you saying? Was it something important?"

"Very."

The brothers stood looking at each other.

Steven started to speak, but then closed his mouth.

"I'm telling you," Ted said, "it was *very* important."

Steven looked at him, their eyes locking. "Jesus Christ," he said under his breath. "I need to wait on this customer."

Then he walked away.

11:15 a.m., Garrett Station

"There's not much there," Stan Jackman said to Peyton.

She sat next to him, looking at printouts and spreadsheets he'd gathered.

Jackman had an office next to Hewitt's in Garrett Station. The office was a concession of sorts: since his heart attack, Jackman was doing very little field work, an unspoken accommodation he hated.

To that end, Hewitt had given him his own office, making him the only field agent to have one.

Peyton looked around the office. "Very nice."

"The framed photos are new. I figure Mike doesn't have to do this. He knows I can't do what I did, and if this was the southern border, he couldn't hide me in here. They'd have me on disability and I'd be retired and bored out of my head. That'll still probably happen, but I'll stay as long as I can."

"You mind doing research?"

"Something like this is fun. I found a shitload on Dariya Vann." He paused. "Is Stone joining us?"

She shook her head. "He's in the woods."

"At the shack?"

She nodded.

"Anyway, Dariya Vann was a big TV reporter in Ukraine. And Ted Donovan was an up-and-coming TV reporter here."

"What happened to Ted Donovan?"

"He walked away from the TV news job to work for his brother."

"For more money?"

"Far less, according to his tax returns."

"You're good," she said.

"I can't do much. But I still know the right questions to ask. Mitch Cosgrove dug up the financials."

Cosgrove was unique among Border Patrol agents—a former CPA. This background offered a rare skill set, and Hewitt had snatched him up when his resume had crossed the PAIC's desk.

"Any idea why Ted Donovan would walk away from TV news?"

Jackman shook his head.

"Think his brother offered him partner status in the dealership?"

"Nothing in Ted's financials indicates that."

"Where does he spend all his money?"

"His Visa bill says he eats at Tip of the Hat most nights. Ten, twenty bucks. Four or five nights a week."

"I'll look into it," she said.

"And he worked at WAGM," Jackman said, "or whatever the local TV station was called back then. I went over there. The place is full of mostly young reporters trying to make a name for themselves so they can move up and move out. No one remembers Ted Donovan. He worked there for about ten years, then more than fifteen years ago, he left."

Peyton thought about that. Ted Donovan hadn't moved up and out. He'd walked away from his journalism career but had remained in the region.

"Did Ted graduate from Emerson?" she asked.

"No, actually. He dropped out."

"Do we know why?"

Jackman shook his head. "Dariya did the same thing."

"What do you mean?"

"Exactly that. Dariya Vann also dropped out."

"When?"

"Here's where this gets interesting, Peyton. Neither man attended a class after spring break 1990."

"Emerson College keeps attendance records for twenty-five years?" she said.

"Not attendance records," he said. "I found something better."

"What?" she asked.

"I'm getting to that," Jackman said, "but before I forget, did you know Ted Donovan traveled to Donetsk recently?"

"I didn't," she said, "but it makes perfect sense."

1:45 p.m., Garrett Station

"Thanks very much for coming in," Peyton said to Dariya Vann.

Stan Jackman sat beside her. Hewitt was to the other side. They were letting her lead.

A manila folder lay before her. She didn't look at Dariya's attorney, Bobby Gaudreau, or Dariya's sister, Bohana, who sat, bookends to each side of Dariya Vann, because she genuinely *wasn't* glad to see either of them. Gaudreau and Bohana would only stall the information-gathering process, and she knew it.

Dariya didn't reciprocate the greeting.

"How have you been since our last talk?" she said.

Dariya looked at her, then at Gaudreau, who took the cue.

"Why are we here, agent?"

"I have no idea why you and Bohana are here," Peyton said, "but Mr. Vann has graciously agreed to meet with me. And I'm here because I work days this month."

"Cute," Gaudreau said. "Stop wasting my client's time."

"I was going to offer coffee. Mr. Vann, you look exhausted. Late night?"

Dariya shifted in his seat. He didn't like the question. Why? What had she said?

"He's jet-lagged," Bohana explained.

"Mr. Vann," Peyton continued, "it must be nice staying with Bohana and seeing people you've missed."

Dariya looked at Gaudreau, who shrugged.

"We're just talking," Peyton assured Dariya.

"Yes, I've missed my sister." Dariya smiled at Bohana.

"And Ted?"

Vann's eyes swung back to Peyton. "Ted?"

"Well," Peyton said, "you went to college with Ted. And about a week ago, Bohana told me she met Steven through a friend of her brother. That brother is you. And that friend would be Ted, with whom you attended Emerson College."

Dariya sat looking at her, the wheels clearly turning. "I guess we both went there," he said after several moments.

Jackman was writing; Hewitt was leaning back in his chair, listening intently.

"I don't remember saying that," Bohana said.

"No?" Peyton said. "We were at your house around three in the afternoon. I was there to see how Aleksei was adjusting."

Bohana said to the table, "I don't recall that conversation."

"Coincidence," Dariya said, dragging the second *i* to a long *e*, "if we both there."

Gaudreau sat like a seventh grader who didn't see the pop quiz coming.

"It must be nice to catch up with Ted," Peyton said.

Dariya shrugged.

"Were you and Ted close at Emerson?"

"No."

"Did you know each other?"

"I see him."

"Where? In what capacity?"

He looked at her, not understanding.

"In class? In the hallway?"

Dariya shrugged.

"Peyton," Gaudreau said, "what are you driving at?"

Peyton opened the folder. "You were both journalism majors and had several broadcast media classes together during the 1989–90 school year."

"Do you expect my client to remember that? That was a quarter-century ago."

Peyton smiled at Gaudreau and looked back to Dariya. "You actually had *several* classes together during an eighteen-month span. And you and Ted were close friends, isn't that right?"

Dariya shook his head. "Not close."

"That's interesting. Remember Frank Griffin?"

Dariya sat up a little straighter. "Who?"

"Oh, I'm sure you remember him. He sure remembers you and Ted. I talked to him this morning. He's retired and lives in Florida now. But he spoke about how hard you worked to learn English."

"I don't know him," Dariya said, but his voice was soft as if he realized the futility of his denial.

"Frank Griffin oversaw a maintenance crew you and Ted were on as work-study students. Frank was in that same job for thirty-five years. Says he never forgets a face. Speaks highly of you both. Says it was clear that you and Ted were"—she shifted her papers in the folder until she found one, pointed to a line of text, and read—"'really good friends. Both good boys.'"

"Where is this going, agent?" Gaudreau said. "Someone remembers my client from more than twenty-five years ago?"

"We're just looking for honest answers," Hewitt said. "Would you like tea, Bob?"

"First time someone's offered tea. No thanks."

Peyton knew what Hewitt was doing: playing good cop to her bad. She went on. "You told me you brought your son here."

Dariya nodded.

She wished she'd been able to record the conversation overheard in the Donovans' driveway. But that hadn't been possible. Now she was forced to rely on memory and to use what she'd learned that night to get more information or to force Dariya Vann or Ted Donovan to say something that filled in a blank for her. At a time when technology dominated information-gathering processes, it was far from a perfect science. And with a lawyer in the room, it was a gamble. But Dariya Vann wouldn't be in the country long. She had to roll the dice.

"That's not true, Dariya. And we both know it."

"I brought Aleksei here."

"Ted Donovan bought a round-trip ticket to Ukraine and flew there just over a month ago. We have copies of his boarding pass. He never flew back, though, never got on the return flight. And we both know why."

"We don't need to sit here and listen to your speculation." Gaudreau closed his briefcase.

Peyton never took her eyes off Dariya Vann. "Because you offered up your son. You needed a way into the country."

"Let's go, Dariya." Gaudreau was standing.

"Come on." Bohana tugged her brother's arm.

Dariya didn't stand. He remained seated across from Peyton, staring hard at her.

"Your son told me what it was like traveling with Ted. I'd call him a child-abuser. You call him a business partner."

"Come on." Bohana pulled her brother's forearm.

This time he stood and followed them out, never turning back. When the door closed behind them, Hewitt turned to her. "You better know what you're doing because you just played your hand."

"Not the entire hand," she said.

"You have more?"

She nodded. "Yeah. I've got more."

7:30 p.m., Razdory, Russia

Nicolay could barely understand what this skinny twenty-something with unkempt hair and tattoos on his ropey forearms said. Although both men spoke Russian, it was like listening to another language. Like the summer he and Victor spent in Milan, and he'd tried to pick up Italian.

"Are you sure Victor Tankov wants me to do this?"

"Yes," Nicolay said. "He's been having computer problems."

"Is the machine slow?"

Nicolay wasn't sure what Yevgeniy meant. "Yes," he said.

"Shouldn't be," the wispy man said. "Plenty of RAM." His fingers danced lightly across the keyboard.

Nicolay watched him; this youngster with a soul patch didn't do the two-finger peck that Nicolay used. Yevgeniy had been here twenty minutes. *RAM space* and *gigahertz*—Nicolay had no idea what those words meant.

They sat side by side in the den, the hulking sixty-year-old and the skinny, pale expert with three silver hoops in his left earlobe. The den was on the first floor of the sprawling country home, one of the Victorian's eight bedrooms converted to an office. Since Victor's health had declined, Marfa had spent a lot of time in this room, on this computer. But Victor—the champion boxer bracing himself against the ropes rather than go down—had insisted on managing the finances himself. For as long as he could. Whatever it took.

It had taken a lot. Now he was bedridden.

And Nicolay had walked in on Victor's conversation with Marfa, had heard Victor promise her full access to the accounts until the purchase. Then Victor said he felt uneasy.

So Nicolay knew what he had to do.

"No," the lanky man dressed in black said, "there's nothing wrong with this computer. What are you having trouble doing? Give me something specific to work on."

Nicolay pointed to the screen. "I need to open that."

"That file?" Yevgeniy's fingers tapped lightly. Then his head shook back and forth. "Well, that's the problem. It's a locked file. You need the password to open it. That doesn't have anything to do with the software or the machine. It's password protected."

Nicolay pulled his chair closer. He understood those words, *password protected*. Knew precisely what they meant to him here and now.

"I need to see what's inside that and to open that email account."

"You need passwords."

"What if I lost them? Can they be opened?"

The skinny man pushed away from the machine and turned to face him, studying Nicolay's face. "This is Victor Tankov's summer home. And you're asking me to break into his personal email. The other file is some sort of financial document or record."

"That's correct."

"I don't think so. I've heard what happens to people who screw with Victor Tankov."

"What have you heard?"

"He put an ice pick through one guy's hand, didn't shoot him until twenty minutes later. Wanted to watch him suffer first."

"You have no reason to worry." After all, Nicolay thought, it hadn't been *Victor* who'd done that. "I'm in charge of this computer."

Yevgeniy looked at him. "You're in charge of it?"

"Yes. The record and email accounts are mine."

"Then how'd you lose the passwords?"

"I forgot them. I have several passwords."

Yevgeniy had heard that before; in fact, he'd even made the same mistake. He sat thinking about the request, balancing it against what he knew of Victor Tankov.

He blew out a long breath. "I don't know."

Nicolay stood and took out his wallet, handed him some money.

"People don't usually pay us in cash."

"This isn't for the bill."

Yevgeniy leaned back in the chair, staring at the money Nicolay held. "Well, it's not like you're asking me to hack into a website or something."

Not yet, Nicolay thought.

"You wouldn't believe some of the requests I get," Yevgeniy said. "Yeah, I can open that for you."

Nicolay leaned back in his chair, looked out the window, watched young Rodia skating on the frozen pond, and waited.

An hour later, when access to the file and email had been granted and the bank account had been opened, he paced the floor of his bedroom, thinking about Victor, about the life Victor had given him, and processing what he'd learned.

4:45 p.m., Garrett High School
"Well, how was it?" Michael asked Davey Bolstridge.

They were alone on the bleachers in the Garrett High School gymnasium following preseason practice.

Michael had been kneeling, making easy tosses to loosen up when he'd seen Davey enter the gym. Wearing the white mask, Davey had shuffled slowly to the sideline. Coach Rowe had hugged him, and one by one, players approached to do the same. Sam Tilton, a sophomore now, who as a freshman had been taken under Davey's wing, had hugged the senior and returned to the batting cage with tears in his eyes.

"I didn't recognize him," he kept saying. "I didn't recognize him at first."

"He's still the same guy," Michael had told everyone.

Now the gym was empty, the last well-wisher having left.

"It wasn't great." Davey pulled the white mask off and flung it. "I felt like a freak, the way everyone looked at me."

The mask floated away from the side of the bleachers, drifting to the gymnasium floor like a discarded paper caught by a wind gust.

"You should keep that on."

"What difference does it make?"

"You don't want to catch a cold. You told me the doctor said it could be really bad for you if you caught one."

Davey looked away, said again under his breath, "What difference does it make?" He turned back to Michael. "I felt like a circus animal. See how they looked at me?"

"They've missed you."

"They didn't want to touch me, like cancer is contagious," Davey said. Then his back stiffened as if kicked in the spine. His face contorted, his hand flashing to his side, his breathing turning to short, rapid bursts. "Jesus Christ," he moaned.

"What is it? You okay? What happened?" Michael was on his feet.

Davey waved him away, fighting to get his breathing under control. "Sit down, dude. Nothing you can do."

"You want water?"

Davey's breathing returned to normal. He smiled at him. "Nothing you can do, Mike. Nothing anyone can do."

"Only the doctors?" Michael said.

"Not even the doctors."

Michael was still standing. "What are you saying?"

"I didn't want to tell you."

"What are you saying, Davey?"

"I'm dying, Mikey."

"You're sick. That's what the chemo was for."

"Mike, when you ask me how I feel, I say okay. On certain days, I do. And a joint makes it better for a while. But I'm not getting better. I never sent in my deposit for U-Maine."

Michael heard the words, but somehow the processing mechanism failed. "No. No. We're rooming together this fall."

"Mikey, it's time for you to take me home. When Mom dropped me off, I told her you'd bring me home."

Michael didn't move.

Davey stood. "Come on, Mike. Let's go. Don't cry, man. That just makes it worse."

"Sorry. I ..."

"I know. Not much to say."

"When?"

"They don't know. Within six months."

"That would be a month into—" The sentence couldn't be completed, the words catching, forced back as if spoken beneath water.

"Let's go, Mikey."

They descended the bleachers, moving slowly toward the gymnasium floor. They drove across town in silence, the only sound in the battered Ford F-150 was sniffling, each teenager thinking about what had been said.

"I didn't want to tell you," Davey finally said. "But I think you need to know."

Michael drove, saying nothing. His mind ran to an image, one he thought of often—Jesus Christ on a storm-struck ship riding devastating waves, his presence a calming influence for a group of terrified sailors.

After he dropped Davey off, Michael headed to the shack in the woods.

5:10 p.m., Garrett IGA

The man across the parking lot seemed out of sorts.

And that made Marfa smile.

Dariya Vann didn't seem like the confused drunks or delusional street people she'd seen in St. Petersburg in recent years. But he had changed. Dariya Vann—the man she'd met at the outdoor cafe in Paris, who seemed confident and even brash—now looked confused. The United States could do that to a person, she knew. She, too, had been a confused outsider for a couple weeks in New York before acclimating.

But Garrett, Maine, wasn't New York City.

Dariya Vann had lost some of his swagger.

She was parked among the after-work shoppers in the IGA parking lot. Americans walked in and out of the grocery store, some pushing carts, others carrying bags. Her rented Buick Enclave idled. It was four degrees (celsius), so her SUV ran with Mozart playing softly. Dariya stood beside a Ford Escape perhaps fifty feet away. Where had he gotten the Ford?

He held a cell phone to his ear. She couldn't hear him but watched him speaking rapidly, his face reddening. Anger? Embarrassment? Then he hung up and slid the phone into his jacket pocket, leaned back against the driver's door, and stood thinking, his idle hand rubbing his temple. Then Dariya opened the car door, climbed behind the wheel, and started the engine.

Marfa reacted to this by sliding the Buick into drive, preparing to follow.

Dariya got out again and started to clear the windshield. What was he doing? The windshield looked clear enough to drive. Was he killing time? Trying to keep busy? If so, why? Was he waiting for someone? Meeting someone here?

He took out his cell phone again and answered a call. He was animated, waving his free hand as he spoke. The conversation ended abruptly, and he hung up, got back in the Escape. This time he pulled away.

Marfa followed. She liked this turn of events. Dariya was upset. At whom? About what? She knew why he was here. What he'd come for. (They had that in common.) Was there a problem? If so—if his travel arrangements had for whatever reason stalled or been altered—he might be more willing to play along with her idea and make the transfer here and not in Germany. There was less that could go wrong that way. She had a jet at the ready; it would land

and take her and her belongings, including what she would get from Dariya, to her final destination. That was far less risky than letting him take it on the boat. When she'd inquired, he'd told her what happened to the other twelve pieces. And showing up unannounced would give her the upper hand.

She followed him to Donovan Ford. Dariya pulled to the back of the lot, stopping between two rows of pickups. Marfa rolled past, turning down a row of Escapes. Was this where he'd gotten the SUV?

A mechanic came out of the building, looked over his shoulder, checking that no one had followed, and walked to Dariya's car. He slid onto the passenger's seat and looked around him one more time.

Marfa turned in her seat to watch the two men. Whatever was being discussed was important, the conversation heated. Dariya was pointing at the mechanic, an accusation of some sort. The mechanic shook his head in denial. His hands before him spread as if to say, *What do you want me to do?*

The conversation was brief. When the mechanic got out and went back inside, Dariya drove away.

Marfa did too. This time, she didn't follow him. Smiling, she went home. She had some computer work to do.

7:30 p.m., Troop F Headquarters, Houlton
Peyton hadn't expected to be in Troop F headquarters at the end of the day, and she guessed Michael Donovan hadn't either.

"Where is he?" she asked Stone.

Stone, responsible for the northern towns in Aroostook County, had an office in the county courthouse in Reeds but came to Houlton two days a week for paperwork and meetings. When the bust had gone down, he'd brought Michael Donovan to the state police headquarters.

"Holding cell." He was in a small office and motioned over his shoulder with his chin as he removed his laptop from his shoulder bag. She saw him open a file to write his report. "I was sitting on the hill above the shack, and he came walking down the trail, wearing the blue jacket with the yellow emblem."

"Same jacket as the guy in the video?"

"Yup. No question he's our guy."

"He confess?"

Stone nodded. "To everything."

"Really?" she said. "Surprised he didn't say he was just using the hunting shack. You said they're pretty communal."

"Yeah, that would've been the smart play. But he was very cooperative. Even helped me pack the aquariums. Asked me if I was coming back to the shack."

"Odd question," she said.

"Maybe."

"What did you say?"

"I told him probably not. And he wanted me to leave the generator there so his father could get it. Wanted me to leave it and the portable heater running."

"Running?" she said. "Why?"

"Not sure. I turned the generator off but left it there for his father. He was so scared I figured he was in enough trouble. Figured I'd let his old man have his generator back. The kid is scared to death. He's crying. His parents are on the way."

"Thanks for calling me."

He shrugged. "You know the family."

"They're not exactly thrilled with me right now," she said. "So that might not help you. How much dope was in there?"

"Just the six plants. Not much."

"What do you think?"

"He's eighteen," Stone said, "and it's a class-D. Could get one to three years in jail."

"Come on," she said.

"I know. Given his record—he hasn't got one—and the reason for growing it, he's probably looking at community service."

"What's his reason?" she said.

"You're not going to believe it." He waved for her to follow him. "Come with me. I'll let him tell you."

———

"What's going to happen to me?"

It was the first thing out of Michael Donovan's mouth. He was in the holding cell, and he didn't wait for Peyton and Stone to get to him.

"Will the University of Maine rescind my acceptance?"

Peyton was in her uniform greens, and her boots slapped loudly against the concrete floor. Stone wore jeans with a 9mm Glock in a shoulder holster beneath his navy blue sports jacket. He didn't bother to lock the cell door behind them.

"Michael," he said, "I can't answer that. Your parents are on their way."

Even in the bad lighting, Peyton recognized him immediately: He still needed a shave, his hair was still a mess, and he wore an orange Moxie T-shirt as he had when she'd first seen him sprawled on the living-room sofa in his home reading a book titled *Rembrandt: His Life and Work in 500 Images.*

Michael Donovan didn't look interested in art right now. His eyes were red, his face pale. "I know what I did is illegal, but it isn't wrong."

"Michael," Stone said, "I'm going to tell you again, anything you say can—"

"I know. You said all that already. I told you I get it, and I don't care. I didn't do anything wrong. Davey's parents did."

Peyton didn't speak, but she listened carefully.

"Davey Bolstridge is dying. Cancer. He's been my best friend since preschool. He's in pain."

"You're saying the marijuana was for him?" Peyton asked.

Michael nodded, wiped his nose with the back of his hand. "He's dying." The words were choked off in a sob, and the octave changed —his voice seemed to get higher—when he continued. "I knew he was sick. I saw him losing weight. We were going to room this fall at U-Maine. Now he's dying. He's in pain."

"Medicinal," Stone said quietly. "No sale. He watched a video on YouTube to see how to grow it and says he gave it all to his friend to alleviate the pain."

Michael nodded.

"Michael," Peyton asked, "why didn't you do this through your friend's doctor? Have him write a prescription?"

"His parents wouldn't have it. No oxy. No nothing. 'God has a plan.' That's what they kept saying, 'God has a plan.'"

"And you didn't think that involved suffering," Peyton said; it wasn't a question, rather a statement to herself spoken aloud.

"Not like this. Some days he can't move. The pain—I can see it on his face—it's unreal. His parents just stood by and watched. So in the afternoons, after school, I'd bring him some dope. We'd go downstairs and he'd smoke. I knew it was helping him."

"Michael, did you smoke with him?" she asked.

"Never. Not my thing."

Stone said, "So if I ask you to pee in a cup, we wouldn't find anything?"

"I don't smoke it. Never have. I'll pee. Besides, I'm playing varsity baseball this season, and I heard they test once in a while."

"If you're clean," Peyton said, "that'll help you."

"What will happen?"

"We'll have to see," Stone said.

Michael looked at him, his eyes pinched, fighting the tears. "Did you take my phone?" he said. "I can't find it."

"No," Stone said. "Did you drop it in the snow at the shack?"

Michael didn't respond. He clearly had no idea. His night was going from bad to worse.

"This is going to be alright, Michael," Peyton said.

"What I did was okay?"

"No. But things will be alright."

"Will I lose my place in the Art History program at U-Maine?"

"I don't know about that," she said and heard the boy's soft sobs as she and Stone left the holding cell.

———

"I'm at a loss," Bohana said. "I don't know what to think. My son was growing pot?"

"Yes, ma'am," Stone said. "He's admitted that."

The conference room seemed small, Peyton thought. She and Stone sat across from both Donovan parents, their son—who wore handcuffs but no leg irons—and Bobby Gaudreau, who had taken a yellow legal pad from his briefcase and was scribbling notes.

"Can I get anyone coffee?" Stone asked.

Bobby looked up from his notes. "Let's move this along, Stone. Michael has no record and is no risk for flight. You know that. So please take his handcuffs off."

Stone ignored him.

"Why is it that every time I turn around"—Bohana was looking at Peyton—"you seem to be there?"

"I'm sorry that our paths keep crossing," Peyton said.

"Did you have any idea Michael was growing marijuana?" Stone asked.

"Of course not," Bohana said.

"I can answer your questions," Gaudreau said.

Steven was shaking his head. "*Did we have any idea?* Does that even need to be asked? We're better parents than this. My wife's on the PTO, and I've sponsored a Little League team for years."

Michael's head was down. To the table, he said, "I didn't grow it for me. Can't anyone understand that?"

"Michael," Gaudreau said, "please stop talking."

"Who, then?" Steven slammed his fist on the table. "Jesus Christ, Michael, what were you thinking? Are you a drug dealer?"

"Of course not. It wasn't for me! It was for Davey. He's in pain. I was trying to help him."

"*Help him?*" Steven was shaking his head. "Haven't we taught you anything?"

"You?" Michael started to rise. "Oh, *you've* taught me a lot, Dad!"
Stone put his hand on his forearm, easing Michael back to his seat.

"Everyone stop talking, *please*," Gaudreau said.

"Yeah, I've learned a lot from *you*, Dad! Like, how about the attic?"

"What attic?"

"Bullshit," Michael said.

"What's he talking about, Steven?" Bohana said.

"I have no idea." Steven looked at Stone. "Has bail been set?"

"Not yet, sir."

"What about the attic?" Peyton said to Michael.

Michael was looking down again, but Peyton could see the tears falling from his cheeks, pooling on the table.

"We both know what was in the attic apartment, Dad."

"What did you say?" Steven said. "Your uncle's upset about something being taken from him. Do you know about that, Michael?"

"No," Michael said softly, his head shaking slowly. "Nope."

"Everyone stop talking," Gaudreau said.

"Why is she here?" Bohana asked Stone. "Does she have to be here?"

Peyton stood. "No, I don't. But before I leave, I'd like to ask a quick question: Steven, why did your brother give up his TV career?"

Steven was staring at his son. "Huh? What?"

"Why did Ted leave WAGM?"

"No idea, lady. That was a long time ago. Said he wanted a change. Now leave us all alone. What's it got to do with my son?"

Peyton wasn't sure. But she had the adrenaline rush that the visceral sensation of progress made on an investigation always offered.

Marfa collapsed onto Pyotr. Seconds later, she got her breathing under control, rolled off him, and started toward the bathroom.

"Hey, I didn't finish," Pyotr said.

"I did," she said and closed the bathroom door and peed. She emerged from the bathroom completely dressed, crossed the bedroom, and went downstairs.

"Marfa!" she heard him call behind her.

She couldn't stand this 1970s house. *It won't be long now,* she told herself. She sat at the kitchen table, making sure her back was to the wall and faced the open doorway. The upstairs was quiet. He was probably finishing alone.

She focused on the computer and checked the accounts. The money was all there, and she could access it. She was tempted to move it now and forget the plan altogether. But the money was secondary. That was for her selfish desires (no more 1970s decor). The other—the item Dariya Vann had—was for her father. She needed it to truly show him what she was capable of. She imagined him seeing it—only in a photo, hanging in *her* apartment, no less—before he died, realizing how wrong he'd been about her.

She heard Pyotr descend the stairs.

"You can be a real bitch, you know that?"

"Certainly." She looked up and smiled. "Judging from your crotch, you seem to have taken care of what you needed to."

"To avoid blue balls."

"What was her name?" she asked. "The one people saw you with in St. Petersburg the day after you left me?"

"What? Is that what this is about?"

"Partially."

"Why are you bringing her up? That's all in the past."

She powered down, closed her laptop, and came around the table. "I know it is." She leaned to kiss him. As he closed his eyes and prepared for the kiss, a grin crossed her face. She pulled back and slapped his cheek, hard.

"You bitch!" he said again.

When he reached for her, she moved quickly, avoiding his hand.

"*Now* we're even," she said. "*Now* we can start over."

He looked at her, assessing. "You finally forgive me?"

"Now I do," she lied. "Come with me. We have something to do."

He would be useful to her for one more night.

9:30 p.m., Tip of the Hat

Mitch Cosgrove had told her Ted Donovan's credit card statements indicated frequent trips to the Tip of the Hat, and Peyton had missed dinner anyway. So, after stopping by her home to change and to kiss both her son and her mother, she entered Garrett's most popular restaurant-bar.

She slid onto a barstool and, as she always did anytime she entered the Tip of the Hat, flashed back to her summers during college: Elise, Peyton, and a host of others, would gather here after a day of shitty college-kid summer work to play pool, eat pizza, and drink pitchers of draft beer. That group had included Pete Dye, her now-ex-boyfriend, who taught US History at the high school by day and made mortgage payments by tending bar at night. Pete was approaching now, flashing his ridiculously cute surfer smile.

"Haven't seen you here in ages."

"Been busy," she said. "How are you?"

"With someone," he said.

"That wasn't what I asked, Pete, but I'm happy for you."

"Thanks. I started dating her about a month after we ended."

"That's great. Can I have a turkey burger and a Molson?"

"Sure," he moved off, called out the food order, took a bottle of Molson from the cooler, and returned. "Glass?"

She shook her head.

"I heard you're with a state cop."

"It's busy for a Wednesday, huh?" she said.

"Playing coy?"

"Playing discreet," she said.

Nearly every booth was filled; four couples were spread around the bar. Some inhabitants she recognized immediately. Some she'd gone to school with, others she'd seen and registered peripherally— people whose faces were familiar. She was good at remembering faces; most agents she knew were.

"Here you go."

She turned back to Peter, and he slid the turkey burger to her. It had lettuce and tomato slices.

"That was quick," she said.

"They're popular. Jimmy has them ready."

"The sign in the window says, *Burgers made fresh*," she said.

Pete shook his head. "You never change."

"What's that mean?"

"You're ultra-cynical."

"No," she insisted. "I'm an optimist."

"Want ketchup?"

"No, I'm good. You ever see Ted Donovan in here?"

"Teddy? Sure, three, four nights a week," Pete said. "Becky"—he pointed—"usually waits on him. She's patient enough to do it. He sits by himself and plays on his computer for a couple hours. Never tips."

Peyton saw Becky cross the room and return to the bar. Pete moved to her, leaned close, and whispered something. Becky looked at him, then at Peyton. She came down the bar.

"Hi, Becky."

"Don't I know you? You went to Garrett High."

Peyton nodded. "About a hundred years ago."

"Didn't we all? You played basketball."

"I did," Peyton said and reached in her purse. "I was the short one running for her life. I'm here on business and pleasure tonight." She slid a business card to Becky. "Do you know Ted Donovan?"

Becky read the business card. "US Border Patrol?"

Peyton nodded.

Becky smiled. "Teddy? Sure. I wait on him several nights a week. He comes in and drinks three or four beers, eats peanuts. Never orders a meal. Gets so wrapped up in whatever he's doing on his computer. Last week, I made him eat a burger. I paid for it. The guy's sort of pathetic. Just stares at that computer like my ten-year-old on his phone."

"Nice of you to feed him. You must really care about him." Was this a mistake? If Becky cared that much about Ted Donovan, there was nothing preventing her from calling to say a Border Patrol agent had been asking questions about him.

"*Care* might be too strong a word. We don't actually talk. He plays on his laptop and says weird shit once in a while."

"Tell me about that."

Becky looked around.

"Some place we can go?" Peyton said.

"I'm on the clock."

Instinctively, Peyton said, "This won't take long." In truth, she had no idea how long it would take.

———

They were in the back office. The desk had framed photos of a man Peyton recognized as Tip of the Hat owner Bill Schute with a silver-haired woman (Schute's wife) and three little girls (Schute's granddaughters). Becky sat in Schute's swivel chair. A newspaper article from the *Star Herald* was framed and hung on the wall behind his chair. The headline read SCHUTE FAMILY BUYS TIP OF THE HAT.

"Tell me about 'weird,'" Peyton said again.

"He quotes Dostoyevsky and weirdos like that once in a while."

"What's he say?"

"I don't remember the exact quotes."

"In general?"

"Something about extraordinary men overstep boundaries because they can."

"Because they can?"

"Yeah. That's the gist."

Peyton shrugged. Not much she could do with that. But she'd remember the line, search it later. See if anything interesting turned up. "Anything else you can tell me?"

"What are you looking for?" Becky said. "Is Ted in trouble?"

"Not at all."

"You wouldn't be here if he wasn't."

"I'm interested in him as part of something I'm looking into. That's really it."

Becky shrugged. "I tell him he could've been one of those guys you see on the network nightly news shows. He likes that."

"Ever say why he gave it up?"

"Not really. I asked. He says he's happier working at Ford than he was at WAGM. I don't believe him."

"Why?"

"Not sure. Just the way he says it. He just goes back to looking at art on his laptop."

"Art?" Peyton said.

"Yeah. He looks at art the whole time he's here."

"Anything in particular?"

"He looks at a lot of pictures," Becky said, "but there is one I've noticed him looking at a couple times."

Peyton was sitting up straight. "Can you describe it?"

10:35 p.m., Drummond Lane

The car ride home wasn't talkative, but it wasn't silent either: his mother cried, and his father swore under his breath.

And Michael wasn't about to start a conversation. The big cop had turned off the generator, which meant the insulated shack wasn't being heated. The Explorer's external thermometer read forty-three. That wasn't great—far from the constant seventy degrees of Uncle Ted's apartment—but it was above freezing, and the air was dry. He wondered if he'd be alone long enough to get back to the shack in the coming days. He also wondered about Ted, about what his father had said in the conference room. Ted knew it was gone.

His father pulled the Explorer into the driveway next to his mother's Escape. Uncle Ted's old F-150 pickup was there.

All three climbed out of the Explorer.

"It's late," Bohana said. "Let's all try to get some rest. I'll set up a meeting with the guidance counselor in the morning."

"Mom, why would you do that?"

"Michael," his father said, "the University of Maine is a big school. They'll find out about this."

"Your name will be in the police section of the Goddamned *Star Herald* within two days," his mother said.

His father nodded. "It's much better to get out in front of it."

"What's that mean, *Get out in front of it?*"

"It will probably mean"—his father sighed and blew out a long breath—"you writing a letter to the director of the Art History program explaining what you were doing."

"We need to see what the judge says," Bohana said. "Maybe the judge will dismiss the whole thing."

Michael opened the front door and entered through the mud room into the kitchen. Uncle Ted and Dariya Vann were seated at the kitchen table, neither man speaking. Four beer bottles and a deck of cards were on the table between them.

"Dariya," Bohana said, "did you see Aleksei?"

"Twenty minutes."

"That's all?"

"He was going to math team," Dariya said.

"He joined the math team?" Bohana said. "That's excellent."

"Where were you?" Ted asked.

Steven shook his head.

"Don't want to talk about it?" Ted said.

"Correct," Michael's father said. "What have you guys been doing? Catching up?"

"More like discussing problems," Dariya said.

Ted and Steven locked eyes.

"Remember what I mentioned at work?" Ted asked.

Steven nodded. "Michael, your uncle thinks someone was in his apartment. You didn't go up there, did you?"

"I don't have a key," Michael said, not answering the question, but not lying either.

Steven nodded, then turned to Ted. "Still no luck finding whatever you lost?"

"No luck," Ted said, looking at Michael as he spoke.

Michael felt a twinge at the back of his neck. Uncle Ted's eyes never left him. The conversation overheard in the driveway told Michael the two men planned to move it soon. He couldn't let that happen.

"I'm going upstairs," he said.

"Want to stay, play cards with your uncle and me?" Dariya said.

Michael turned to him, saw a desperation in Dariya's eyes that frightened him.

"No, thanks," he said.

Ted's cell phone vibrated on the table. He glanced at it absently at first, then he pulled the phone closer and read. He slid the phone to Dariya, who read, shrugged, and nodded.

Both men stood.

"Where are you going?" Bohana asked.

"Out," Ted said.

————

The house was sixty-two degrees and he felt cold. Michael didn't go to bed. In the dark, he stood near the window, looking out at the night.

And thinking.

Why did Dariya and Uncle Ted want him to stay up with them? Did they know he'd taken it? They did know it. He could see it in his uncle's eyes. What had they wanted to say?

He felt suddenly cold, as if a draft had entered through the window frame.

Oh, God, what had he done?

If Uncle Ted had waited more than twenty-five years to cash in, there was too much at stake to let his nephew stand in the way. Based on the conversation he'd overheard, the number was thirty million dollars.

His father either genuinely knew nothing about it, or was a great actor.

What was he going to do? The night before, he still hadn't known. He couldn't turn his uncle in. It wasn't that he wanted to protect his uncle so much as he needed to protect his mother and father. They'd housed the item—and its thief—for half a century. Could they possibly be considered innocent? Would anyone believe them? He wasn't even sure he did, entirely. But he would protect them. And it was more than innocence and guilt. It was the item itself and its creator. Who had the right to *own* it? If Uncle Ted and Dariya moved it, it would be lost again.

As soon as possible, he'd return to the shack, get it, and leave it somewhere where it would be found by the *right* people. And no one would know where it had been these past twenty-five years.

The question was how to avoid Uncle Ted and Dariya until then.

11 p.m., *Tip of the Hat*

Marfa had a bad feeling.

She didn't like the look on the American's face. He looked scared, like he was in over his head and he knew it. And the little Ukrainian looked angry. About what, she had no idea.

They were at the Tip of the Hat shortly before closing time Wednesday. Pyotr sat next to her, sipping draft beer and glancing menacingly at Dariya. He asked about the little man's accent.

"I'm from Donetsk," Dariya said.

"What's your name?" Pyotr asked.

Dariya shook his head.

"I'm Ivan and this is my wife Sonya," Pyotr said.

"Can we all speak English, please?" Ted said.

Marfa liked that. She could speak both languages but didn't want the two men across from her to know it—not yet.

Pyotr ignored him and continued in Russian. "Your town has been at the center of a lot of the fighting."

"Yes," Dariya said. "A lot of fighting. You're from St. Petersburg?"

Pyotr confirmed that.

A waitress appeared. "Hey, Teddy. Who are your friends?"

"Just relatives," Ted said.

No one at the table spoke.

"Another round?" Becky said.

"Four vodkas," Ted said.

"No." Marfa shook her head. "I hate vodka."

"Great accent," Becky said.

"Rum and Coke," Marfa said, "and another round of beer."

Becky nodded and moved toward the bar.

"You're both from St. Petersburg," Dariya said.

"No need to know where we're from," Marfa said in Russian, "and we're not here to talk politics."

"English, *please,*" Ted said.

"It's not politics." Dariya stared at Marfa, still speaking Russian. "It's my life. The fighting almost killed my wife. She needs medical care."

"Once Ukraine falls," Pyotr said, "Putin will take care of you all."

Dariya grabbed a water glass and tossed its contents in his face.

Pyotr was on his feet. Dariya followed suit, coming up to the younger man's shoulder.

"What the hell was that?" Ted said. "What did he say?"

"Hey!" Pete Dye called from behind the bar. "Hey, Ted, what's going on over there?"

"Nothing. Everything's okay, Pete."

"Doesn't look like it."

Pyotr looked at the bartender and sat down.

"Enough," Marfa said. "We're here to talk about the transaction."

"What about Germany?" Dariya said, retaking his chair. "That was the plan."

"I have the money now. Let's make the exchange here. It's easier for you. Much easier."

Dariya looked at Ted and translated.

"What?" Ted said. Then to Marfa, "Are you moving it yourself?"

"I have a private plane on standby. Where we're going is none of your business. Nor is it any of your concern. I can wire the money once you've completed your delivery."

Dariya looked at Ted.

"I don't like changing plans," Ted said.

Again, Marfa had a bad feeling.

"How long will it take for the money to go through?" Ted said.

Marfa shook her head. "No more than twenty-four hours. Once I know you have it and can deliver it, I'll start the transfer."

"We're going to proceed very slowly, very carefully," Dariya said. He was speaking to Marfa but looking at Pyotr.

"I understand," Marfa said.

"We'll pick a public place to show you it. When we see the money in the account, we will meet to give it to you."

Marfa looked at him. "I don't like that. That leaves you holding both it *and* the money for a period of time."

Ted shook his head. "I've had the fucking thing for twenty-five years. I want to be rid of it."

Marfa looked at him. She thought he was on the level, but she still didn't like it.

Dariya didn't like Pyotr. He was like all the others Putin had in his back pocket. She probably was too. But she was smart—and sexy, if Dariya was being honest.

Dariya turned from Pyotr to Marfa. "You'll hear from us. We have your text number." He nodded for Ted to follow.

Ted stood.

"I thought you might have a celebratory drink with my husband and me," Marfa said.

"We'll celebrate when I have the money and can help my wife," Dariya said, then to Pyotr in Russian, "And when Putin is defeated."

Dariya and Ted walked out.

ELEVEN

PEYTON WAS AT HER desk beside Stan Jackman when Hewitt entered.

"What time did you two get here?" Hewitt asked.

"Christ," Jackman said, "Peyton never left. She called me in around eleven."

"Eleven p.m.?" Hewitt said. "You woke him up?"

"It's okay," Jackman said. "Worth it. Besides, I know how you love to pay overtime."

"Overtime gives me heartburn. And you both know that."

Across the bullpen, Agent Bruce Steele chuckled. Steele was the station's K-9 agent; his German Shepherd, Poncho, lay at his feet. "They started out being very serious. Then things got giggly around two in the morning. Then they were giving each other high fives around five a.m. Made my night shift more interesting anyway."

Hewitt tossed his coat onto a chair and moved to Peyton's desk. "You two worked all night?"

She nodded, leaned back, and sipped her coffee. "Fresh pot," she said. "I brought Starbucks from home and brewed it myself. I'll sacrifice one cup, if you're interested."

"Peyton, what's going on?"

"We need to search Ted Donovan's house and look at his computer."

"Ted Donovan?"

"That's right," she said.

"Let me get a cup of coffee," Hewitt said. "Meet me in my office."

———

"Ever eat at the Tip of the Hat?" Peyton asked Hewitt, when he sat down behind his desk across from Stan Jackman and her.

"As little as possible," Hewitt said.

"Well, there's a waitress there named Becky. Ted Donovan's such a pain in the ass, she's the only one who'll wait his table. So she knows him a little." Peyton told Hewitt about her interview with Becky.

"Paintings?"

"Yeah."

Hewitt looked at Jackman, who nodded.

"Paintings?" Hewitt said again.

"She described one painting that Ted seems to look at a lot." She smiled and turned her laptop so he could see it.

"That's a painting of a sinking ship," Hewitt said.

"Not sinking," Peyton said. "Far from it. It's called *Storm on the Sea of Galilee*. Rembrandt painted it in 1633, and it shows Jesus calming the storm on the Sea of Galilee as depicted in the Book of Mark."

Hewitt was rocking back and forth gently, his hands clasped behind his neck. He stopped rocking and drank some coffee. "I'm not seeing things coming together here, Peyton. What am I missing?"

"You know how it goes. Sometimes it's one big thing. Sometimes it's a lot of little things."

"That break a case open?" Hewitt said.

"Yeah. There are a lot of little things that are adding up. Ted Donovan earned distinction at Emerson College for his research into art. And he and Dariya were both journalism students. Who better to know how to find out where the paintings were, how much they were worth, and how to get them? They're trained researchers, Mike. And Ted just flew to Ukraine a few weeks ago, but he never flew back. He was on a ship with Aleksei."

"Planting Aleksei to allow Dariya into the country?"

"That's what I believe," she said.

"Why would he need to do that?"

"Not sure. It gets Dariya here, though."

"And why does he need to be here?"

"This is where this gets really interesting, Mike," Jackman said. "This is where we started high-fiving."

Peyton said, "Both men left Boston in late March of 1990. We know that."

"And?"

"Mike," Jackman said and pushed a manila folder toward Hewitt, "take a look at this."

Hewitt opened the folder. "*Boston Globe* articles."

"From March 1990 until today," Peyton said. "All about the Isabella Stewart Gardner Museum heist. This is what we were doing all night."

"You think Ted Donovan was connected to this?"

"Two men walked in there in the middle of the night on March 18, 1990, dressed as cops, tied up the two security guards, and walked out with nearly half a billion dollars worth of art."

"And you think one of them was Ted?"

"I think Ted and Dariya might have been the guys," Peyton said.

"Peyton, when people talk about 'the crime of the century,' this one gets mentioned."

"I'm telling you, Mike. We need to get the FBI agents working this up here. A lot of little things add up, things Dariya and Ted have said. And the timing fits. They were both there, then they were gone. And Ted's background makes this plausible. And, as journalists, they'd know where to find information on how to get in and out of the museum and even how to sell the stuff. And Dariya's arrival tells us something."

"What's that?"

"If I'm right, they're moving it."

Hewitt looked down at the clips. "Thirteen works of art? Some of these things are five feet tall."

"We need to look into this, Mike," she said.

"Let me call Boston," he said.

———

Peyton went back out to her desk and texted Tommy, glad—for maybe the first time—she'd gotten him an iPhone.

U UP?

YES

She flipped to her recent calls and re-dialed his number.

"Hi, Mom."

"Good morning, pal. Are you dressed?"

"Yes. And my teeth are brushed and my hair is combed and Gram is making pancakes."

"Pancakes? She spoils you." She tried to joke it off but couldn't. *Not spoiling*, she thought. *Just being responsible.* By contrast, Peyton had worked a double shift, and the last breakfast she'd made her son had been a bowl of Cheerios with a sliced banana. "Sorry I haven't been around too much the last couple days."

"Gram says you're really busy at work."

"Yeah." She looked at the bullpen. Three agents were fanned across the room. One was typing, another was reading pages from a folder, and the third was adding water bottles and granola bars to a field pack. "Too busy sometimes. I'm sorry."

"It's okay. Karate was good last night. I think I can win my next match."

"Oh my god," she said, "I totally forgot you had karate last night. Did Gram take you?"

"No. Stone."

"Stone took you?"

"Yeah. He came over and told Gram you were busy and said he could take me. I need to go now. Gram wants to quiz me. Spelling test today."

"I love you, Tommy."

"I know. I love you too." He hung up.

She slid her phone into her cargo pant pocket and couldn't help smiling. For a single mother in law enforcement, it really *did* take a village.

And she was glad as hell Stone lived in it.

Yevgeniy, the skinny man with the tattooed arms, was back. Nicolay didn't think he liked him. Had a lot of trouble understanding him—gigahertz this, RAM that—but he had to admit the little man knew his way around a computer. The arrangement was cash.

"I want to read emails on this computer," Nicolay said.

"That could take forever," Yevgeniy said. "Want me to search for something?"

Victor was upstairs sleeping. He'd slept a lot these past few days, and that worried Nicolay. The eighty-one-year-old never seemed hungry either.

"There are three different email accounts on this computer," Yevgeniy said.

"I'm only interested in the girl's."

Nicolay was amazed at the speed with which Yevgeniy's hands worked on the keyboard. They seemed to float across it.

"Is there anything in particular you want me to search for?"

"Anything having to do with money or travel," Nicolay said.

The door swung open and crashed against the wall. Three-year-old Anna ran into the room pushing a doll in a tiny stroller. The stroller slammed into the wall near Nicolay and overturned, the doll spilling onto the floor.

"My doll is hurt," Anna said. She lifted it to him.

Nicolay took the tiny doll in his massive hands and kissed it, his white beard sweeping across the plastic face. "There, there. All better." He handed it back to the little girl.

"Thank you, Uncle," she said and went out.

Yevgeniy smiled and watched the girl go. When Nicolay turned back, he said, "I might have something" and pointed at the screen.

Nicolay put his reading glasses on. He looked at the airline receipts. "Can you tell me who bought those?"

"The name on the receipt is a man."

Nicolay saw Pyotr's name on the receipt. They were divorced. Was she traveling to see him? "Are there any emails from him?"

"A bunch."

"Any recent?"

"Two days ago." Yevgeniy opened the email. "It's directions."

"To what?"

Yevgeniy told him.

Nicolay leaned back and thought about that. What did it mean? "Print that email out," he said. "I need you to reopen the file you opened for me the last time you were here."

"The financial stuff?"

Nicolay nodded.

"I showed you how."

"Well, I can't do it. I need you to do it."

It took Yevgeniy all of two minutes. "It looks different," he said.

Nicolay reached into his pocket and retrieved cash. "That's all," he said. "You may go now."

When the door closed behind Yevgeniy, Nicolay replaced his reading glasses and leaned close to the computer screen. Yevgeniy had been correct.

The account looked very different now.

———

"Victor," Nicolay said, "I think there's a problem."

Victor was in the leather chair near the bed. The old man's head rolled toward him. Nicolay saw liver spots beneath Victor's thin hair; his eyes were watery and looked tired.

"What kind of problem?" The blankets were pulled nearly to his chin as he lay in bed.

"Financial."

Victor felt a tightness in his chest that hadn't been there before.

Nicolay crossed his legs, admiring his freshly polished shoes. "What is Marfa getting you?"

"The gift of a lifetime."

"And you're paying for it?"

"Of course I'm paying," Victor said.

"And you gave her access to your accounts?"

A fist clenched Victor's chest. "Why do you ask? She did the hard part—she found it."

Nicolay pointed to the space on the wall across from the foot of Victor's bed. "A painting?"

"A Rembrandt, Nicolay. Not a painting." The old man's pale face colored, his breath quickened, a little boy's excitement flashing in his eyes. "A *fucking Rembrandt*." He coughed and struggled to catch his breath.

"Lean back. You're breathing hard, Victor."

"It's the one I've loved since I was a boy. I think it's his greatest work—symbolic and religious and hopeful. It's everything I love in Rembrandt. It's been underground for years, but Marfa found it."

Nicolay pursed his lips. "Marfa found it? There's a little Dimitri in her after all."

"No. Dimitri was a businessman. She's got an artist's eye. Always had it. Even as a little girl. Remember that afternoon I told you about? At the Louvre? Even then she could spot great works. She should go to America, maybe become an art critic."

"I think you insulted her, Victor. How much will the painting cost?"

"Not nearly what it's worth. It's worth five times what I'm paying."

"A good investment."

"It's not about that."

"What, then?"

Victor pointed to the space on the wall. "About owning a piece of greatness and beauty. That's all. I don't have much time. It's all I've asked of her."

"You've asked more than that," Nicolay said.

"What do you mean?"

"She's more like you than you know, Victor."

"You always say that. You know how I feel about that. This life's no good for her. I don't want it for her."

Nicolay knew it was no use. He was torn. He loved the girl like a daughter, but Victor had taken him in at fifteen. Victor had provided for him on several levels, giving him a home, replacing the father he'd lost, and promising him an inheritance.

"And Marfa has access to the accounts?"

Victor looked at Nicolay.

"Are you okay? Victor, your face looks red. You're breathing hard."

"My chest is a little tight this morning. You've mentioned the accounts three times. What is it?"

"The other day, you said you had a bad feeling."

"Yes."

"There's a problem, Victor. But I don't want you to worry. I'll take care of everything."

Victor struggled to sit up in bed.

"Don't," Nicolay said. "You're out of breath. Lie back."

Victor fought to position the pillows. His breathing was labored; the tightness in his chest turned to an ache. "Tell me, *goddamnit.*"

Nicolay uncrossed his legs and leaned forward. "The accounts are empty, Victor."

"Empty?"

"Are you saying she took my money?"

"Can you slow your breathing? You're worrying me, Victor."

"You called the banks?"

"Yes. It's not a clerical error."

"This is about the business. She's angry. She's never understood."

"No," Nicolay agreed.

"Have you heard from her?"

"I tried to call and text. Her phone is off or the number has changed. I'll continue to try."

Victor looked out the window at the overcast sky. A crow was perched on the powerline.

"You're breathing hard, Victor. Lie back. I'm going downstairs to get water and to check on Anna and Rodia. I'll be back in a few minutes. Everything will be fine. I'll take care of everything."

Victor watched the door close behind Nicolay. Marfa? His daughter? His money? His instincts *had* told him something was wrong. For so long, he'd survived on instinct and prediction. But when it came to his daughter, he hadn't wanted to see it coming. The tightness in his chest worsened. The pain intensified and spread across his chest to his left arm. Marfa didn't understand. Never had. His sandpaper breaths were labored, and he began to gasp.

Outside the window, the crow was still on the powerline. He wouldn't think of Marfa this way. Not here. Not at the end. He thought of that glorious Paris afternoon at the Louvre, of the little girl looking at *Carcass of Beef* with awe and appreciation.

The crow flew away.

———

"The children are fine." Nicolay closed the door behind him. "And I brought you water." He took a step into the room and looked up.

And he knew.

"Oh, God. No. Not now. Not like this."

He checked Victor's arm for a pulse, which confirmed the fact.

Nicolay leaned over his dead friend and kissed the old man's cheek. "Together for forty-five years." He sat heavily in the leather chair. "Friend," he said. "Father." He looked at the old man, whose eyes were frozen in repose.

"I'll take care of everything," Nicolay said. "I'll make it right."

7:50 a.m., Garrett High School

Michael saw Uncle Ted's pickup as he crossed the parking lot walking toward the school. The truck approached, and Ted rolled down his window.

"Got a minute to talk, Mikey?"

Cars and pickups drove past them. Uncle Ted was alone. That made the unexpected visit better. Michael didn't trust Dariya Vann. He seemed to be angry all the time.

"Not really. School starts in a few minutes."

"We need to talk, Mikey. Won't take long."

"About what?"

"We live under the same roof, Mikey. You really can't avoid me. Get in."

Michael looked at him. Ted pointed to the passenger door. Michael thought about it and finally rounded the hood and slid onto the passenger's seat. Morning sunlight reflected off the dashboard, making Michael squint.

"What is it?"

"Were you in my apartment, Mikey?"

"I don't have a key."

"That isn't what I asked. Something very important was taken."

"Like what?"

Ted looked at Michael. "I think we both know."

"Not me," Michael said. "No idea."

"How long are you going to keep this up?"

"I don't know what you're talking about, Uncle Ted."

Ted leaned back, resting his head against the back of the seat. He exhaled loudly, reached into his pocket, and removed an iPhone, tossing it onto the seat between them.

"You left this under my sofa."

Michael looked at his iPhone.

"Where is it, Mikey?"

Michael stared at his phone then looked up at Ted.

Ted smiled. "No harm done. I just want it back."

Michael didn't speak. He was staring at the phone.

"You want money? Is that it?"

Michael shook his head. "You don't own it. No one can own it."

"What are you talking about?"

"It wasn't created to be owned. You don't get it."

"Listen—"

But he didn't. Michael picked up his phone. What had he just said? What had he done? How could he have been so careless?

He opened the door and ran.

8:20 a.m., Paradise Court

Marfa hated the lighting in this damned 1970s bathroom. She was doing her hair in the mirror.

"I don't trust either of them," Marfa said over her shoulder. "Did you see how they looked at each other?"

"Yes." Pyotr was on a chair near the window in a corner of the bedroom, sipping coffee.

"How do you like the coffee?" she asked.

"Strong. You made it differently." He coughed. "It's bitter."

"You think?"

"You—" He didn't finish.

She could hear him retch.

"I made it a little differently, yes," she said. "You sound like you're gagging, sweetie."

She liked the way her hair looked. She went on to her mascara. If the formica countertop and ugly yellow backsplash weren't enough, the single damned light made it nearly impossible to do her makeup.

Pyotr coughed. She heard the foot stool overturn.

"*Marfa, help me—*"

"Oh, I thought you liked strong coffee."

"*Please!*"

"I think you do like it," she said.

She moved the mascara brush slowly, lengthening her lashes. He was gasping now. She stepped back to examine herself in the mirror. She liked what she saw. The hacking in the other room grew louder. When she stepped out of the bathroom, Pyotr was on his hands and knees.

"*The coffee!*" he gasped. "*You—*"

"Oh, you spilled your cup, sweetie," she said. "There goes the security deposit."

He tried to crawl toward her.

"Is the coffee too strong?"

She descended the stairs. As she pulled her coat on, she heard a soft thud overhead. She closed the door behind her gently and went out.

9:15 a.m., Garrett Middle School

"I like your new clothes," Dariya said.

Aleksei smiled. "Bohana bought them."

His father noticed how easily he smiled here. They were walking around the back of the school. The guidance counselor had called Aleksei to the office when his father asked to see him. It was in the mid thirties, but the sun was warm. Aleksei wore a blue winter coat; Dariya wore a leather jacket.

"Your hands are dry and cracked," Dariya said.

"It happened when I was in the woods, Papa. I need to get back to class."

"I just wanted to see you. Do you like your new school?"

"Very much. I'm learning a lot."

"And the people?"

Aleksei shrugged. "How is Mother?"

"I'm getting her the treatment she needs."

"What does she need?"

"Surgeries," Dariya said. "Several."

A boy and girl walked around the corner of the building, holding hands. Dariya saw them, thought of his own son, and wondered about Aleksei's shoulder shrug and change of subject.

"Are you happy here?" Dariya asked.

"Yes."

"Do you want to stay?"

"I want to see Mother. I want to know she's okay."

"She will be. You can stay with Bohana until I get things set up."

"What does that mean?"

"We're moving to Switzerland after your school year."

Aleksei stopped walking. "Leaving Ukraine?"

His father nodded.

"I just came here. Now we move again?"

"I'm here to conduct business. It will allow us to move, Aleksei. You need to trust me. In Switzerland, people don't live the way we have had to. It's beautiful. Mountains. Snow. And there's no fighting there."

"And Mother?"

"She'll be well there."

Aleksei nodded. "What do you need to do here?"

"That's not your worry, son. Have you seen your cousin today?"

Aleksei shook his head.

"Do you have his phone number?"

"I see you spruced the place up," Frank Hammond said, entering the bullpen. Two other agents were with him.

Peyton saw a black Suburban parked outside.

"We don't all have federal budgets," Hewitt said, shaking Hammond's hand. "Good to see you, Frank."

And, to Peyton's surprise, she thought Hewitt meant it.

"Aroostook County is always two months behind Boston in terms of weather," Hammond said. "I'm freezing my ass off up here, again."

"Welcome to The County," Hewitt said.

Hammond was the FBI's executive assistant director of the criminal investigative division. He worked out of a glass office in downtown Boston. He had a little more gray hair than he'd had the last time she'd seen him, but he still looked like a guy who ran 10Ks. He wore a *Boston Strong* T-shirt, jeans, and New Balance running shoes.

Hammond looked at Peyton. "I hear you might have some information I'd be interested in."

"Are you the lead agent on the Gardner Museum heist?"

"I am now. It's been twenty-five years. The lead agent has changed numerous times."

"Follow me," she said.

———

Peyton was at the whiteboard in the makeshift conference room. Hewitt, Hammond, Stan Jackman, and two FBI field agents, who looked far too young, fanned out around the picnic table.

"You guys hold all your meetings around picnic tables?" one of the young agents said.

"It's also our break room," Jackman said. "If you get hungry, I'm sure there are leftovers in the fridge." He pointed.

The FBI agent smiled.

Hammond made introductions. The annoying agent was Steven Ramirez.

"Hope you don't need me to go undercover," Ramirez said. "Not a lot of brown people up here."

"You have any agents in Boston who are housebroken?" Peyton said to Hammond.

"Yes," Hammond said. "Ramirez doesn't get out much." Then to Ramirez, "Shut up."

After Peyton's debrief, Hewitt looked at Hammond. "You have the warrant?"

Hammond nodded.

"That was quick," Hewitt said.

Hammond shrugged. "A lot of people have been looking for this stuff for a long time."

"We going in hot?" Ramirez asked.

"No," Peyton said. "The son and father probably won't be home. And Ted Donovan is most likely at work. His sister-in-law might be home."

"Ramirez can pick Ted Donovan up at his work," Hammond said. "I'd like to interview him and would like your help, agent."

"Of course," Peyton said. She smiled politely but bristled inside. It was her case, after all. Except, she knew FBI and ICE had jurisdiction on a case with national and possibly international implications.

"Where's Dariya Vann?" Hammond said. He was staring at Dariya's name on the whiteboard.

"Wildcard," Hewitt said. "We have no idea what he's doing."

"Armed? Dangerous?"

"We just don't know," Peyton said. "He doesn't have a violent past."

"That we know about," Jackman added.

"That we know about," Peyton concurred.

"Let's roll," Ramirez said. He was the first one out the door.

11:30 a.m., Tim Hortons, Reeds

"Where's your husband?" Dariya said when Marfa approached the table carrying a large shoulder bag and a latte and sat across from the two men.

She nodded to Ted and said in English, "He won't be joining us."

"Thank you for speaking English." Ted smiled. He liked looking at this woman named Sonya. He could smell her perfume over the aromas of donuts, coffee, and lunchtime soup.

"I want to be sure we are all clear on where we stand," she said.

Dariya was alright with the husband bowing out. He was a Putin sympathizer. Dariya looked around. A couple men at other tables sat quietly, reading newspapers. It seemed odd, the atmosphere so different here: People were relaxed. No one looked scared.

"There a reason why he won't be joining us?" Ted asked her.

She sipped her latte. Dariya saw her lipstick mark on the glass as he slurped his black coffee.

"For one, he didn't exactly find your friend, here, amiable."

Dariya said, "So you're handling transaction?"

"That's how it looks," she said.

"And money? You have our money?"

"I have it," she said. "And the painting? I'd like to see it."

"It's magnificent," Ted said. "I've studied art for most of my life. There's nothing like it."

"And it's been authenticated?"

"Of course," Ted said. "We took it ourselves."

"And you can prove its authenticity?"

Ted turned to Dariya. "Have you discussed this with her before?"

Dariya shook his head.

Marfa recrossed her legs and bobbed her ankle. She smiled at him.

"Like I said, *we* took the painting. I've had it for twenty-five years. I study art, always have. It's the real thing."

"We don't need talk about twenty-five years ago," Dariya said. "No one needs to know about that. Just now. Just sale."

"I'm paying a lot of money," she said. "I'd like to know it's authentic."

Ted laughed. "You can't be serious."

"It's a lot of money," she said again.

"Lady, if you find a stolen Rembrandt that thieves have had *officially* authenticated," Ted said, "fucking call me. *We* took it. The last thing I'm about to do is call someone in to examine the fucking thing. On the contrary, I've been *hiding* the thing for half my life. That's why we're selling this to you for a fraction of what it's worth."

"I want to see the painting," she said.

Dariya was leaning back, arms folded across his chest. "And we want to see money."

"Fine." She reached into her shoulder bag and withdrew her a black laptop with a red sticker, opened it, and turned it for them to see. She pointed as if tutoring them. "Here are your accounts. They're empty. Here's my account."

Dariya was silent.

Ted said, "Holy shit."

"Now I want to see the painting," Marfa said.

"We'll call you," Ted said.

12:15 p.m., 7 Drummond Lane

"What is that?" Bohana said. She was standing in the front door.

Hammond explained the details of the federal warrant again.

"Bohana," Peyton said, "I know this is a lot to take in, and that it comes on the heels of a long night, but you need to let us in. Let's make this as painless as possible."

"I'm not leaving my house."

"You don't need to, ma'am," Hammond said.

Peyton saw Bohana look at Hammond's black FBI jacket.

"This is like a TV show," Bohana said. "A black SUV, the FBI jackets, men wearing rubber gloves, putting things in paper bags."

"We need to go to the third floor," Hammond said. "Will you open the door for us?"

"That's my brother-in-law's apartment."

"Yes," Hammond said, and Bohana looked at him, a realization crossing her face.

"This is about Ted?"

"We need to go to the third floor, ma'am."

———

The apartment was small, a three-room efficiency. But it was neat, clean, and had nice furnishings. It also had an air duct near the ceiling that Peyton saw Hammond staring at. He moved closer and examined the wall-mounted temperature setting.

Drawers opened and shut, the closet was quickly searched, soil samples were taken from shoes, and Ramirez, wearing an LA Dodgers cap, went to work on the computer, turning it on and finding it to be password protected. He closed the laptop and bagged it.

"Frank," a young blond agent said, "come take a look at this." Her name was Sally Hann. She wore glasses with green and orange frames and had freckles.

They had pulled the sofa away from the wall.

Hammond examined the carpet beneath the sofa. A large spot was flattened. "Something in a heavy box was here for a long time," he said. "Measure the spot."

Hann nodded, went to work, and told him the dimensions.

Peyton, Hewitt, and Jackman stood back and watched the feds work.

"You can't take my brother-in-law's computer," Bohana said. "That's personal property."

Hammond took his cell phone off his belt. He looked at Hewitt. "It's Ramirez." Then to the phone, "Go, Steven." He listened, eyes running to Bohana. When he clipped the phone on his belt again, he said, "Mrs. Donovan, do you know where your brother-in-law and brother are?"

"No idea. First the school calls to say Michael is off somewhere playing hookie, and now this."

"Michael didn't show up at school today?" Peyton said.

"I told him he'd have to meet with the guidance counselor and probably write a letter to the University of Maine. I think he's avoiding both."

"Can I talk to you?" Hammond said to Peyton and Hewitt.

They followed him out of the efficiency and down the stairwell.

"We've got a problem," Hammond said. "Ramirez can't find Ted Donovan. He never went to work. Didn't call in sick." He pointed up the stairs to the apartment. "His sister-in-law will tell him about this. So now we have a serious flight risk on our hands."

"Shit storm," Hewitt said.

Hammond nodded. "That's what this is turning into."

"You have BOLOs out on both men?" Peyton said.

Hammond nodded. "That flattened spot on the carpet matches the approximate size of the painting you're talking about."

They went back into the apartment.

Bohana was waiting for them. "What is this about? What are you accusing them of?"

"We just have some questions we'd like to ask them."

Bohana turned to Peyton. "He's lying. Peyton, what's going on?"

"We just need to talk to Ted and Dariya," Peyton said. "That's really all. Once they help us make sense of a few details, all this goes away."

Bohana looked at her. "What details?"

"I can smell your soup from here," Peyton said. "The whole house smells great."

"You can't do this," Bohana said. "Do you know that? You can't just come into someone's home and take their personal belongings." She pointed to the bags. "Those are Ted's shoes, his laptop."

"The sooner we can speak to him and clear this all up," Hammond said, "the sooner he can have everything back."

Peyton was studying Bohana's face. Her expression said Bohana knew Hammond was lying, which Peyton knew would lead to problems.

12:30 p.m., 31 Monson Road
Michael looked at his phone, which had just vibrated. The text was from Aleksei. He hadn't expected that.

The school had called his mother to report him absent, and his mother had called (straight to voicemail, he'd made sure) twice and texted three times urging him not to skip the meeting with the guidance counselor at one. Then his father had gotten in on it, leaving two more voice messages. No word, though, from Uncle Ted.

He'd been at Davey Bolstridge's since he ran, and now the boys were sitting on living room chairs watching ESPN.

"It's cool that you took the day off to hang with me," Davey was saying. "You see that LeBron highlight? It was sick."

"Yeah." Michael was looking at the floor. Davey's home was maybe a third the size of the Donovan house. The living room furniture was worn, the carpet stained. Michael saw the way Davey looked around the Donovan home any time he visited. The last time he'd been over, he'd asked how big the flat screen was in the great room. *Looks like a movie screen,* Davey had muttered.

"Jaspar pissed on that spot on the carpet," Davey said. "The other two stains are him as well." He pointed. "Every time it thunders, Jaspar pisses on the carpet. I think my father will shoot him when I'm gone."

"Man, stop talking like that."

"Isn't that why you came today? Spend time with me before I'm gone?" As if the thought triggered it, Davey flinched in pain. "Motherfucker, that was a bad one," he said. "Sometimes it feels like a knife right in my side."

"Dude, I'm so sorry I fucked up and got busted. Now I can't help you."

Davey was breathing hard, but he waved that off. "No, man. No biggie. Shit just happens. I hope the U-Maine thing works out. And thanks for coming. It's cool that you wanted to hang out. So that's all, huh. Just to hang, not because I'm dying?"

"Yeah, man. Just to hang."

"Dude, you looked like you ran a marathon when you got here. Why'd you park in the back?"

"Because it's plowed, and I wanted to leave the driveway clear for your parents."

"Nice of you. Mom will probably invite you to eat with us."

Michael was staring at the text: ARE U AROUND? NEED HELP W/ SOMETHING @ SCHOOL. CAN U WLK NXT DOOR?

What did Aleksei need? Aleksei thought he was in the high school around the corner from the middle school.

"My mother will be home around four," Davey said. "I'm not hungry, but she's making spaghetti, if you want to stay."

"Thanks, dude. I need to take off for a little while, though." Michael stood up. "Things are a little rough at home. Can I sleep here tonight?"

"Of course. Where are you going?"

That was a good question, Michael thought.

1:45 p.m., Logan International Airport, Boston, Mass.

Nicolay toted one duffle bag and stood at the rental counter.

"Is a compact car okay?" The small man behind the counter had dreadlocks. Nicolay always wondered about dreadlocks. Crazy Americans. How did he wash his hair?

"I've got a Ford Focus."

"I don't *feet* in that," Nicolay said.

295

"*Fit?*" the young guy behind the counter said. "You want something bigger?"

"Yes," Nicolay said. "In hurry."

"Okay. I have a Camry, but it'll cost twice as much."

"Fine," Nicolay said. He handed the clerk a credit card. If he charged things, he'd have at least until the end of the month before creditors discovered there was no money in the accounts. Selfishly, he also knew his inheritance, which Victor had discussed with him numerous times, was tied to those accounts. So this was business, but it was also personal on several levels. After all, he'd been the one to start the funeral arrangements. That job should have been Marfa's; she was Victor's sole living relative. But she was gone, and Nicolay figured she'd lost that privilege anyway. Victor always said he wanted to be cremated, so that was what Nicolay had done. The ground in the St. Petersburg cemetery was frozen; the service to place the urn in the ground would have to wait until June.

"Would you like to fill out a form to become an advantage member and save ten percent?"

"*Nyet.* No." Nicolay pointed to his watch. He didn't have time for this. He was tired, the past twenty-four hours were a mad dash, and he was meeting someone in the Common in thirty minutes. The man would have something for Nicolay that he needed but hadn't been able to bring on the plane.

"Would you like to purchase any maps today, sir? Don't sound like you're from around here."

Nicolay didn't answer. He took the car keys and walked out the door. Maps weren't necessary. He knew where he was going.

Outside, he went to the car, opened the trunk, and tossed his bag in. He remembered how easy these trips had been years ago, in his thirties and forties. Once, he'd landed in Burma at 8 a.m., done what Victor had asked of him, walked casually away from the scene as cops descended upon the place, and was back on a plane before lunch. The thought made him smile.

These trips—business trips, he called them—had been easy twenty years earlier. He still took the trips and did the jobs. But now they took so much more out of him. This day, he was bone tired: The funeral arrangements, making sure the nanny was set, and, of course, this trip was different—it was about Marfa.

Why did she hate Victor so much? Why couldn't she understand?

He pulled the Camry out of the lot and looked at the GPS on the dashboard. The voice spoke English, and it was hard to understand, so he concentrated on the screen's blue line.

Marfa. Like Victor, he, too, had memories: playing dolls with her when she'd been Anna's age; it had been him, not Victor—who was fifty when she was born—who'd built her tree house; and he'd been there at her graduations from McGill and NYU. Until the day before, a photo of him with her at Christmas stood on his nightstand. Years ago, she'd called him *Uncle.* Until the day before, she'd been the daughter he never had.

This trip would certainly be different.

He thought of the children, Anna and Rodia. In this life, in this *business,* he thought, children were often orphaned. He knew that happened. Knew, too, that he'd been responsible for it in the past. But he'd never known any of them. He told himself it might not come to that.

But, although he hadn't cried in years—not since Victor's late wife Dunya had passed so many years ago—for the second time in two days, tears streak his cheeks. He knew what he had to do, and there was no avoiding it.

3 p.m., Garrett Station

"We have everyone and everything in place," Frank Hammond said. He held an energy drink, forearms resting on the picnic table.

"Bohana's phone?" Peyton asked.

"We're listening to every incoming and outgoing call. And Ramirez is outside the house."

Peyton was staring at the whiteboard. She was reading from a list of circled words. "You have a trace on Ted's cell phone?"

"He hasn't used it."

"So he knows we're looking for him?"

"Or he just hasn't used his phone today," Hammond said.

"I guess it's possible," Peyton said. "Ted will show up."

"If they're in the area. If they have the painting, they probably aren't in the area. And given the dimensions of the flattened spot on the carpeting, they have the painting."

"Thirteen works of art were stolen in that heist," Hammond said. "Think they have only one?"

"Who knows?" Peyton said, but then she thought back to the conversation she'd overheard in the Donovans' driveway. "I think they lost the rest."

"Lost them? You're talking close to three hundred million dollars worth of stuff."

"I overheard Dariya say a boat overturned," she said.

"Jesus Christ," Hammond said. "I'm going to be sick, if you're saying what I think you are."

"I don't know," Peyton said. "It was a cryptic conversation between Dariya and Ted."

"Think Dariya would leave his son and take off?" Hewitt said.

"Probably," Peyton said. "He used him to get in the country, and the boy is probably safer here than in the Ukraine."

"Bohana said her brother's been staying with her," Hammond said. "We'll see if he shows up there tonight."

The microwave over the stove beeped, and one of the FBI agents got up and took ramen noodles out.

"You feds are starting to like our meeting room, aren't you?" Hewitt said.

"An army marches on its stomach," the agent said. He looked like a weightlifter to Peyton.

"Roosevelt said that, right?" Hewitt said.

The agent nodded. "I think so."

"You want to find Dariya Vann," Peyton said, "stake out his son."

Hewitt turned to Hammond. "The son is at a foster home. Foster caretaker's name is Maude O'Reilly."

Hammond nodded.

Hewitt turned back to Peyton. "We are. Sandy Teague is at Maude O'Reilly's house for now. But you have a relationship with the boy. He might talk to you."

Sandy Teague was the station's other female agent.

"Think he knows where Dariya is?" Peyton asked.

Hewitt shrugged.

"I can relieve Sandy," she said.

"No," Hewitt said. "Tomorrow morning. Go home. When was the last time you slept?"

She didn't answer, only stood and started for the front door. "Call me if something breaks," she said over her shoulder.

3:25 p.m., 12 Higgins Drive

"Hi, pal." She met Tommy at the bus. "Tell me all about karate last night."

"We worked on a lot of things. It was fun. Stone said I'm improving. I can tell I really am."

"How was school?" She took his backpack. They were walking up the driveway. He had his winter coat unzipped, something that drove her crazy. It was only thirty-four degrees, after all.

"I did well on my spelling test."

"You got it back already?"

"No. I just know I did."

"That's great," she said, and held the front door for him. What a difference a year makes, she thought. A year ago, he was in the Special Ed room during his free time, believing he was the "dumbest kid in school."

He kicked his boots off into the closet. They banged against the back wall, but she let it go.

"The new ways of studying the words are really helping, huh?" she said.

He nodded. "I like bouncing the ball as I say the letters. It helps me remember things." And sitting on the ball also helped him to concentrate when he worked at his desk.

She unzipped his backpack and took his lunchbox out. They walked to the kitchen. She left the L.L.Bean lunch cooler on the counter, then poured him a glass of milk.

"It was nice of Stone to get you. Gram told me about it."

"Gram really likes Stone." Tommy smiled.

"What about you?"

"I like him too. He likes cool things."

"Like what?"

"Karate, the Red Sox, XBox."

It made her smile. "Let's have an early dinner," she said, and yawned.

"I told Stone I invited Dad to my karate match last weekend. I kept looking for Dad during the match, but he never showed up."

"That's why you were distracted?" she said.

He shrugged. "He was probably with his new family."

"He doesn't have a new family, Tommy. He's just dating someone with two sons."

"I saw him with them at a Red Sox game. It was on Facebook."

Jeff was such an asshole.

"You still come first with him, Tommy," she said. "I'm certain of that."

He didn't reply. He sat staring at his milk.

"How come you didn't tell me you invited your dad?"

"I wanted him to come—he said he'd be there—and you could see that he wants to be with us again." He wasn't looking at her, and his shoulders started to shake.

She knew he was crying.

"You did that because I mentioned Stone moving in?" she said.

He only shrugged, but it was all he needed to do.

Michael didn't see Aleksei. And he wondered why the text asked him to meet in the back parking lot. It was never lit, and the cloud cover made the back lot even darker than usual.

The inside of the truck was warm. He'd drove around Garrett for a while, thinking. Now he cracked the window. He thought about Davey, about how he flinched and spoke of the "knife" in his side. What must that feel like? And there was no way to help him now.

And now his younger cousin needed help. He looked around the parking lot and slid the truck into park. His headlights illuminated nothing of consequence—a dumpster, milkcrates, cardboard boxes. The last text message Aleksei sent made it sound like whatever was going on was serious: I REALLY NEED YR HELP.

He knew it was Aleksei because he had Aleksei's phone number saved to his Contacts. He'd had to save it when his mother insisted he take Aleksei to the basketball game with him. He did, but he sure as hell didn't sit with Aleksei. He went there to see Jenny. (He couldn't care less about the boneheads who played basketball.) And when he and Jenny went below the bleachers, he lost track of Aleksei, so he texted him when it was time to go home.

Now he texted WHERE R U?

This whole thing felt wrong. Aleksei was supposed to be at Mrs. O'Reilly's house. She'd been Michael's grade-school teacher, so he knew she was nice but strict. If Aleksei was supposed to be there, she'd make sure he was there.

He slid the truck into reverse and started to back up.

Then he saw headlights behind him.

She smelled vomit.

She checked her hands. Had she gotten it on her? She didn't see anything, but Pyotr's shirtfront had been crusted with his dried vomit, and the smell seemed to be following her. She'd left the Buick's windows cracked to try to alleviate the problem when she'd entered the bar.

Pyotr had been a large man, so it had taken Marfa several hours to dispose of his body. She had to wait until after dark and then to drag the stiffening corpse down the stairs, through the hallway, and into the back seat of the Buick. And, of course, there had been the disposal location to consider. It had taken longer than an hour to find a secluded spot that didn't require dragging the body too far from her car, but was still remote enough to allow it to go undiscovered for days or longer. She wasn't sure the spot would work, but she couldn't leave the body in the house for the landlord to find. The discovery of a naked body in the woods was a far better option.

Next, she'd showered and sent three messages to Ted Donovan. He'd finally responded, cryptically saying they were reluctant to move the painting before the actual sale, but that he wanted to "talk things over" with her, wanted to meet at the bar in the Reeds Inn and Convention Center.

She didn't trust him and wasn't in a hurry to talk. So now she was sitting across the room from him, the Thursday-evening crowd providing plenty of cover, watching him for a while. So far, he was alone. College kids were at the bar, reminding her of her time in Montreal at McGill. She wore a winter ski hat and glasses and sat at a tall table in the back. She been in bars where old men watched sports on TV, and some drank vodka in the morning. Those were depressing places. This bar was different. College kids bantered back and forth. Most drank beer, and the place was dark. A boy and girl were kissing across the room, and a band was setting up in the front.

She saw Ted check his phone, a draft beer before him. He typed something.

Her phone vibrated. ARE YOU AT THE BAR?

ON MY WAY, she replied.

She saw him shake his head. She wondered where Dariya was. Probably with the artwork.

After thirty minutes, she figured Dariya wasn't coming. She pulled off her hat and slipped it, along with her glasses, into her purse. At the next table, a college boy was looking at her. She winked, and the college kid blushed. The guy next to the young man slapped his friend's arm.

She moved to the bar and sat down beside Ted.

"Where did you come from?" he asked. "I was watching the door."

"Where is Dariya?"

"Why? Sonya, I thought you and I could get to know each other. For instance, I don't even know your last name."

"That's right," she said. He had no idea he didn't even know her forename. "And I doubt Ted is your real name. And that's fine. This is business. Do you have the painting?"

"Of course."

"Here? In your car?"

"No, like I said, I don't want to move it twice. That's too risky."

"I'm starting to think there's something wrong here"—she looked directly at him—"like you're FBI or something, and this whole thing is a setup."

"What?"

"You heard me. I'm starting to think there's something wrong. I want to see the painting. And you're running out of time."

"That's what I wanted to meet you about," he said. "We'll have the painting for you in the morning."

"The morning?"

"Yes, now why don't you let me buy you a drink?"

She shook her head. "Call me when you're ready to do business. Tell Dariya I'm leaving town tomorrow, and I won't be coming back. So it's now or never."

She stood to go.

Ted's cell phone vibrated on the bar. He looked down. The text was from Dariya. He's w/ me. Where to go with him?

"Sonya, where are you staying?"

"That's none of your business."

"If it's secluded, we need your help," he said.

TWELVE

Friday, March 14, 12 Higgins Drive, 2:10 a.m.
PEYTON NEEDED A GOOD night's sleep, but didn't get one.

When Tommy had gone down at the usual hour (9 p.m.), Peyton followed suit. She'd gone to bed with her Lisa Scottoline novel but woke two hours later with the hardcover book under her. Unable to fall back to sleep, she returned to the book but couldn't concentrate. After two hours of thinking about Ted Donovan, Dariya Vann, and a painting that had been missing for a quarter century, she finally drifted off.

She was dreaming about a ship in a storm with a man asleep on the deck while those around him scurried to and fro. She was one of the scurriers—until a rumbling vibration and annoying gong woke her. She reached for her cell phone, the call terminating the dream before she learned how it ended.

"Yeah?" Her voice was raspy, her throat dry and sore. Had she been snoring?

"Peyton, this is Bohana Donovan. I don't know who else to call. They're all missing."

"Who?" Peyton asked. "Who's missing?" She rolled onto her side, saw the clock, and ran her hand through her hair, trying to clear her head. "Bohana, tell me what this is about." She was sitting up now.

"Neither Dariya nor Ted came home tonight. And Michael still isn't home. I called his best friend, who admitted he spent the day at his house. But he says Michael left before dinner."

Peyton was struggling to take it all in. "Start again," she said.

"I don't know where any of them are. Steven and I have been waiting up all night."

8 a.m., Garrett Station

"We don't usually do missing persons," Mike Hewitt said. "Up here, with so few local and state police, we go as backup on a lot of calls, but we don't usually do missing persons."

"Unusual circumstances," Peyton said, "call for unusual actions."

"These are desperate times?" Frank Hammond smiled.

Peyton wanted to say, *Desperate enough to get FBI agents out of bed before nine*, but Steven Ramirez, the one she wanted to insult, wasn't in the room, and besides, she liked Hammond.

They were sitting around the break room picnic table. There were paper coffee cups, sugar spilled on the table, and new notes on the whiteboard: "Dariya Vann," "Ted Donovan," and "Michael Donovan" were written on the board with the last known sighting of each. Nothing there helped Peyton.

"We knew neither Dariya nor Ted came home last night," Hewitt said. "The stakeout came up empty."

"And Maude O'Reilly's house?" Peyton asked. "Did Aleksei come home?"

"He was home after math team practice as planned."

"Does he know his father is missing?"

"Not that we know of," Hewitt said. "Sandy Teague couldn't have known because she was with Aleksei all night, so we assume he knows nothing of it. Sandy is at the middle school now. We thought you were the logical choice to talk with him, Peyton."

"I'm to relieve her?"

"That's right," Hewitt said.

"BOLOs came up empty?"

Hewitt nodded.

Peyton looked at Hammond. "Even with the feds looking for Ted's pickup?"

Hammond nodded. "And we added Michael to the BOLO list."

"Because you think there's a connection between Michael and the other two men?"

"They're his uncles." Hammond shrugged and bit into a blueberry muffin. "No place has better blueberries than Maine."

Peyton said, "Yesterday, Bohana thought Michael was avoiding the consequences of his drug bust."

"What drug bust?" Hammond said.

Hewitt filled him in.

"Could be separate," Sally Hann, the young female FBI agent who'd measured the flattened carpeting at Ted Donovan's apartment, said. She pushed her green and orange glasses into place.

"The boy is planning to major in Art History, or something to do with art," Peyton said. "I remember his mother mentioning it."

"What are you saying?" Hammond said.

"Peyton," Hewitt said, "something make you think he's involved?"

"They all lived under the same roof. He and his uncle were apparently interested in art. It's something they had in common. Now they're both missing."

Hammond looked at Hewitt. "What do you think?"

"I don't know," Hewitt said. "You guys must've been building profiles on these guys for years. How does it fit?"

"After twenty-five years," Hammond said, "I think it's safe to say our profiles have been for shit. That's pretty obvious."

Hewitt smiled.

"Ted had a lot of art on his computer," Hann said. "He was meticulous. Pictures in folders. His Internet Explorer history showed he was constantly reading articles related to the Isabella Stewart Gardner Museum heist and keeping up with the stolen artifacts' values. And there's at least one deleted email suggesting they are selling one painting."

"Do you know which painting?" Peyton asked.

"No. It's not named."

"If the teenager is in on it," Hewitt said. "It changes things."

"We need to find them," Hann said. "Frank, I think it's time to bring the media in."

"That'll force their hand," Hammond said. "Either drive them further into their hole or make them run. And after all this time, I don't want the artwork damaged, if we can help it. Especially if you think this painting is all that remains."

"It's been twenty-five years," Hann said. "The FBI has never been this close. Let's splash the uncles' faces on TV."

"I agree," Hewitt said. "It might be time to smoke them out."

"Let me think about it and make some calls," Hammond said.

"I'm going to the Donovan home before I go to the school," Peyton said. "You okay with that, Mike?"

"Yes," Hewitt said.

8:35 a.m., 7 Drummond Lane

Peyton was thinking she'd give her left arm to have a kitchen like this one. But she pushed kitchen envy aside and tried to focus on the situation at hand: Bohana, sitting across the island from her, eyes puffy and red, hand trembling as she held a pen, looked at her notes. Steven was beside her, rubbing her back.

"I'm trying to write things down," Bohana said, "as I remember them—when Michael left, what Davey said—"

"Who's Davey?" Peyton interrupted. She'd been writing on her iPad with a stylus.

"He's Michael's best friend. That's where Michael went yesterday instead of school."

"Have you talked to Davey?"

Bohana nodded. "Briefly."

"Peyton, would you like tea?" Steven said.

"That would be great."

Steven stood and went to the counter. The two women remained at the granite island. It was black with white specks; the track lighting overhead reflected off it.

"I talked to Davey briefly on the phone," Bohana said. "He told me Michael left after lunch."

That didn't exactly jive with what Peyton had heard before. Who had said Michael left the friend's home before dinner? It could be a difference of four hours. Someone had gotten the story wrong—or intentionally changed it.

"Did he say where Michael was going?"

"He didn't know. I asked that right off."

"Has Michael done anything like this before—gone off without telling you?"

"Never." Steven sat down next to his wife again and put two cups of tea before the women.

Bohana was shaking her head.

"So his leaving was totally unexpected?"

"Of course," Bohana said.

"Well," Steven said, "maybe not *totally* ... no, forget it. It *was* unexpected."

"You hesitated," Peyton said.

"It's just"—Steven looked at Bohana—"Michael hasn't been the same this year. Am I right?"

"It's just the college-application process, Steven. It's just the pressure. He's the same great kid."

"Bohana, even Ted said Mikey was cold toward him."

"He's never really liked your brother."

"Why is that?" Peyton said.

"No idea," Steven said. "Mikey and I used to hunt each fall. This year, Mike didn't want to. He just didn't want to engage with the family this year."

"That's an exaggeration, Steven," Bohana said.

Letting the parents squabble over who was right would no doubt prove fruitless. Peyton moved on. "Bohana, where do you think his two uncles are?"

"I have no idea, Peyton. Why are you asking? Do you think he's with them?"

"I have no theories. Is that what you think?"

"Don't you dare put words in my mouth."

"No one's putting words in your mouth, Bohana. Your brother and brother-in-law are at the center of an FBI investigation. They disappear on the same day your son disappears. It's a logical question. Some might say the thought that Michael is with them is a sound deduction. Any thoughts, Steven?"

"Mikey doesn't like either uncle," Steven said. "I can't see him being with them. I think these are two different issues."

"Yes," Bohana agreed. "Michael is running from a problem—one he created, no less. He needs to return and accept responsibility for his actions."

"Simple as that?"

Bohana nodded. She hadn't touched her tea. "I'm sure of it."

"How can you be?"

"I can be sure of it because I'm the boy's mother."

"There's another way," Peyton said.

"What way is that?"

"You'd know Michael wasn't with them, if you knew where they were."

"Is that what you're accusing me of?"

"Bohana, I'm not accusing you of anything. Please be clear on that."

"I think it's time for you to go now, Peyton."

"Bohana, the woman is trying to help us."

"I don't think so, Steven."

"Everyone wants your son to come home safely, Bohana. I hope you know that. I'm a mother too. If my son was missing, I'd be terrified. My heart goes out to you."

"I'm not sure I believe you," Bohana said.

"That's unfortunate." Peyton stood, rinsed her mug, and left it in the sink on her way out.

———

She'd just gotten behind the wheel of her service vehicle when the CB chirped. It was Hewitt.

"Call me," was all he said.

CB radio transmissions were never private, so anytime something important needed saying, cell phones were used, despite the spotty reception in some areas of the region.

"Mike," Peyton said, "I'm sorry I haven't made it to Maude O'Reilly's yet. I just finished up with Bohana and Steven Donovan."

"It's okay. I have some information for you. We found Michael Donovan's pickup behind the high school."

"He wasn't in it?"

"No, but his wallet was there. It was empty."

"Are you thinking robbery? Foul play?"

"Or the empty wallet was left as a distraction. There's something else: Aleksei gave his cell phone to his father."

"Why?"

"Dariya asked him for it. Aleksei apparently has no idea where his father is. But Dariya went to see him at school yesterday, about the time we were searching Ted's place. He asked for his son's phone."

"Can you locate the phone?"

"It's not on. The last transmission was a text sent to Michael Donovan."

"When was that?"

"After Aleksei gave his father the phone, late yesterday afternoon."

"It sounds like a family reunion," Peyton said.

"Maybe. The FBI is going to give some of the story to the media."

"Someone needs to go talk to Michael's best friend," Peyton said.

"He was the last person to see him."

"You do it. Everyone else is in the field."

11:30 a.m., Paradise Court

The woman his uncles called Sonya brought him a sandwich. No silverware. Just a plate. Michael didn't know who she was, but she was pretty. He hadn't slept at all the night before, and he was tired.

"Your uncle told me you have the painting," she said casually and sat across from him.

She had an accent a little like Dariya and Aleksei's.

The kitchen table had a formica top and chrome legs. It reminded Michael of something he'd seen in a Johnny Rocket's.

"I don't know what you're talking about," he said.

Uncle Ted had surprised him when he'd produced his cell phone. And Michael had panicked and run. He vowed not to panic again.

"Oh, I think you do," she said. "Your uncle tells me you love art. That you're going to college to study it."

The sandwich was ham with cheese, lettuce, and tomato. Only a little mayo.

"Would you like to know why I want the painting?" she asked.

It was the first time any of them admitted part of the plan to him.

He chewed and swallowed, not answering, and took another bite of the sandwich.

"My father is a Rembrandt aficionado. And he's an old man, dying of cancer." She shrugged and looked down casually. "I just wanted to do something nice for him, to give him something he thought he'd never be able to have before he died." It sounded believable, even to her.

"It wasn't created to be owned."

"What are you saying?" she said.

"You don't have that right," he said.

She pushed back from the table, crossed her legs, and looked at him. "I'm being lectured by a teenager?"

He only shrugged.

"How do you think the museum acquired it?" she said. "Isabella Stewart Gardner bought it. So spare me." She stood and started toward the kitchen sink.

He turned to Ted. "Do my parents know?"

"About what?"

"Are they in on it?"

"No, Mikey," Ted said. "Just me."

"It was in their house for twenty-five years. And so were you."

"You think it looks bad for them?" Ted asked.

Michael nodded. It was the first time he'd engaged in conversation with any of them.

"You're worried about them," Marfa said and put a dish in the sink. "You can help them by helping us. The sooner we get the painting, the sooner it's out of your parents' lives."

He pushed the sandwich away.

"It's up to you, Michael," she said.

"You can't hold me here."

She stopped and turned back. "We don't *want* to hold you here."

In fact, he was a major problem for her. Ted and Dariya were a lot to deal with already. She wasn't sure how the money-for-the-painting exchange would go, but her plan didn't involve a financial transaction. It involved Ted and Dariya going the way of Pyotr. But this was a boy, no older than seventeen.

"We'd be happy to pay you for the painting," she said. "But I must tell you we're not going to play games for long, Michael. There are ways to get you to tell us where it is."

"*It wasn't created to be owned*," Dariya repeated. "Crazy. Everything can be owned. Everything has price. Everything." He was across the room and turned on the TV.

CNN flashed Breaking News across the screen: *Authorities claim break in quarter-century-old art heist. Manhunt is on.* The news anchor promised an update momentarily.

"What?" Ted moved across the room. "What's this?"

His face and Dariya's were splashed on the TV screen.

"Oh my God!" Ted said.

"*Nyet!*" Dariya yelled.

Ted looked at Michael. "Look what you've done!" He started toward the teenager.

Marfa cut him off. "Everyone sit." She turned to the TV. "Let's see what they say."

"We need to move," Dariya said.

"No," she said. "Let's see what they say."

Kate Bolduan was on CNN saying, "There may be a new development in a twenty-five-year-old case. According to sources, the FBI is in northern Maine looking into a possible lead…"

Marfa looked down at her Nokia phone. Another text from Nicolay. This one wasn't asking about the account. This one was direct: YOUR FATHER IS DEAD. CALL ME, he had texted in Russian.

"You will tell us where it is!" Dariya shrieked and leapt at Michael, knocking him out of his seat.

"No!" Marfa yelled.

And everyone turned around to see her 9mm Glock.

"I've known Mikey his whole life," Ted said. He helped Michael up. "I held him the day he was born. He's a smart, rational guy. He'll tell us where it is, right, Mikey?" He moved close to Michael, leaned, and whispered, "I don't want them to hurt you. Just tell us."

Marfa was staring at her phone. "Just don't hurt the boy. I'll be right back." She picked the Nokia off the kitchen table and left the room.

"Where are you going?" Ted said.

"Don't touch the boy," she said, staring at the phone and walking outside.

11:35 a.m., WalMart Parking Lot, Reeds
Nicolay answered on the first ring. He was in the Camry, a guitar case in the trunk next to his bag now.

"Tell me about Father."

"Why did you do it, Marfa? He loved you."

"He loved Dimitri. Mother loved me."

"She's been gone a long time," he said and thought, *Maybe that's why. Maybe that's what it's all about—because she didn't have a mother.*

"I always wanted to please him. But it couldn't be done. So I'll beat him at his own game."

"No you won't, Marfa."

"Watch me."

"No one can beat him now."

"You're lying," she said.

"He had a heart attack. I told him about the accounts, about what his only daughter did. It killed him, Marfa."

"I don't believe you. This is about the money. You want me to think it's mine now anyway so I'll come back. That's what you're trying to do."

He smiled at that. *Let her think that.* She didn't need to come to him; he'd come to her. His GPS said he was four miles from the address he'd found in her email, and the clear cell phone reception was nearly a confirmation.

"The money *is* yours," he said, "but not all of it. And you know what I mean."

"He promised you something?"

"Quite a lot, Marfa. I think we both know that."

"He's not dead."

"Where are you?" He wanted to see how much information she'd give him. He also wanted to know what she was up to—why northern Maine?

"Far away," she said.

"What are you doing? When are you coming for the children?"

"How much money did Father promise you?"

He told her.

"That's out of the question," she said.

"That's a fair amount," he said. "I worked for your father for forty-five years."

"That's too much."

"Are you coming back for your children? They miss you."

She hung up.

12 p.m., 31 Monson Road

When Davey Bolstridge opened the front door, he looked ill. Terribly thin with a sallow face. She feared Michael Donovan's prediction—that his best friend was dying—was correct.

She introduced herself, and he invited her in.

She followed him to a sparse living room that reminded her of a bachelor pad. Davey's laptop was plugged into the TV, and *Blue Bloods* was streaming. The sofa was tired, and the carpet had several large stains.

"Am I in trouble?" He sat on the sofa. He wore nylon athletic shorts and a faded Garrett High Baseball T-shirt that looked like he wore it often, but which hung off him as if two sizes too big. Clearly, he'd lost a lot of weight.

"Not at all," she said, taking the Lay-Z-Boy across the room.

His blue eyes darted around the room, as if searching for help or waiting for something bad to happen.

"I need to ask you some questions about Michael Donovan."

"You're the Border Patrol agent who was in Houlton with him the other night, the one at the state police barracks?"

"I was there with him," she said. "That's correct."

"He described you."

"And what was his description?" She saw a faint smile cross his face but let it go.

"Is everything okay? His mom called here all freaked out last night. Mikey came here yesterday. He looked like he'd run a marathon when he got here."

"Did he run here?"

"No, he drove. He said he'd just come to hang out. But, from what his mother said, it seems like he was in trouble. I don't think he wanted me to worry. He knows I have my own problems."

"You're sick? You're the one he was growing pot for?"

"Yeah," he said and flinched. "They say it's on my spine now. Hurts bad sometimes. Mikey was just trying to help me. He never once smoked."

"I believe you," she said. "He sounds like a good friend."

"You really mean that?"

"Yes, why?"

"Not many cops would say that about someone who grew dope." She shook her head. "I'm not a cop. And I think you might be wrong."

He sat in silence for a moment.

"Why do you think he looked so harried when he arrived here yesterday?" she asked.

"*Harried?*" He chuckled. "Never heard anyone use that word. Anyway, I don't have a clue. And he parked behind the house. When I asked why, he said it was plowed, and he was saving the driveway for my parents. I thought he was just being nice."

"And you don't think that now?"

"I don't know what to think."

"Has he contacted you since he left yesterday?"

"No. And I sent a few texts."

"Tell me how he looked when he arrived."

"It wasn't so much his breathing. He was sweating, his hair was messed up, and his face was red. His mother said she didn't know where he was. Is he in trouble?"

"We don't know, Davey. You've known him a long time?"

"Since as long as I can remember. We were going to room in college. But…"

He didn't finish the sentence. He didn't need to. Was he even eighteen? He had seen his last Christmas. Her mind ran to Tommy. Was she spending enough time with him? Her roles of mother and agent clashed far more often than she'd like. This week had been a perfect example.

"Where do you think Michael might be? Is there any place he might go?"

"To hide? Not really, just the shack in the woods. But you know all about that."

She did, but no one had looked there.

1:15 p.m., Garrett Station

"Change in plans?" Peyton asked as she entered the front door.

"Yeah." Hewitt was holding a manila folder. "No need to go to the shack again."

"You found Michael?"

"Possibly. We'll follow it up before you hike a couple miles in the woods."

Peyton saw Sandy Teague sitting at her desk with Aleksei Vann.

"We had Sandy bring Aleksei here," Hewitt said. "He didn't want to leave school. He's missing a math test."

"Wish some of that would rub off on my son," Peyton said. "Why does he need to be here?"

Hewitt looked around to make sure Aleksei was out of earshot. "Because we don't know what Dariya is up to, and he's used the boy once. I don't want him doing anything stupid."

"You're talking about a potential hostage situation," she said.

"Just taking precautions. That's all."

"Tell me about Michael," she said. "His friend says he looked pretty rough yesterday."

"Ever hear of a StingRay?"

She nodded. "Phone tracker, yeah."

"We found his phone," Hewitt said. "ICE is on the way. We probably won't wait for them, but they're coming."

ICE was Homeland Security's branch of law enforcement, the Border Patrol's investigatory brethren. She knew things were moving along now. She'd missed something.

"What's going on, Mike?"

"Logan Airport surveillance picked up two people entering Boston from St. Petersburg, Russia, in the last few days." Hewitt opened the folder and handed Peyton two photos: one was of a man in his sixties with a thick white beard; the other was of a woman, much younger, wearing dark glasses and designer clothes.

"Who are these people?"

"This is Victor Tankov's longtime right-hand man, Nicolay Fyodorov. Tankov is a notorious Russian mafia figure. He's also personal friends with Vladimir Putin. He's one of the guys who had assets frozen by Obama in an attempt to squeeze Putin into leaving the Ukraine."

"This is where Dariya Vann comes in," she said, "isn't it?"

Hewitt nodded. "The woman is Tankov's daughter, Marfa Tankov. Remember when you said Dariya's arrival was important because it shows they're getting ready to move the painting after twenty-five years? Well, it would make sense that these are the buyers."

"That's why ICE is coming aboard."

"Victor Tankov is notorious. And artwork is a hot item right now among organized crime members. Usually, there's no black market for stolen Rembrandts because there's nothing you can do with them. You can't display them, and it's hard to sell them because you can't have anyone authenticate them. But Tankov is dying. Cancer."

The comment reminded her of Davey Bolstridge, who wasn't a criminal. Just a simple teenager who wanted to go to college and room with a friend.

"So Victor Tankov wants to own the painting before he dies?"

Hewitt shrugged. "Or he wants it for the reason most people like him do: It's a great bargaining chip, should he—or Nicolay or Marfa—get caught. Two years ago, a guy convicted of fraud, murder, and money laundering copped a plea and got only ten years in a federal country club when he traded a Rembrandt."

Peyton shook her head. "That's disgusting."

"The judge said the Rembrandt was worth it. And now all of those guys know about it."

"So Victor Tankov sent Nicolay and Marfa to get the painting?"

"That's what it looks like."

"How is he buying it, if his assets are frozen?"

"I said *some* of his assets are frozen. He has lots of assets and more cash than you or I can imagine, Peyton."

"Do we know where they are?" she asked.

"Ramirez is working on that."

"Where does Michael Donovan fit in?" she said. "His parents deny that he'd have anything to do with his uncle."

"Maybe, but it's becoming harder and harder to imagine that he's not with them." Hewitt took the pictures back and slid them into his folder.

She looked at the one conference room in the back. Ramirez was there. He had a laptop open and something Peyton had never seen before.

"That looks like an old VCR," Peyton said.

"That's the StingRay," Hewitt said.

She'd never seen one before, but knew it acted like a cell tower and tricked a cell phone into giving it data. It could also locate cell phones, even when they weren't in use.

Peyton was in the break room spreading cream cheese on a bagel when she heard the commotion.

"Frank," Ramirez called, "you'd better come look at this."

Peyton beat Hammond to the conference room. Ramirez was looking at a GPS map of the area. A dot pulsated on the screen.

"I know where that is," Peyton said. "That's the Hampton Inn in Reeds."

1:30 p.m., a dirt road near Paradise Court

Nicolay climbed a ridge and crouched behind a balsam fir, where he lay the guitar case down in the snow and opened it. A red hawk circled overhead. He'd parked the rented Camry to the side of the dirt road. If it had been summer, he'd have driven it farther off the road and parked in a wooded area. But that wasn't possible with four-foot snow piles lining the dirt road. He had binoculars around his neck and wore a black knit cap, black gloves, a dark hoodie, and Gore-Tex boots. He was prepared—and willing—to spend a long time outside, if it came to that.

A slight breeze tickled the treetops, and light snow drifted down. He could see his breath in the afternoon air, but the sun was bright and warm on his back. The case, although shaped like a guitar, was foam lined and contained a 9mm handgun and a 12-gauge as well as ammunition for each. No one in Boston knew Victor was dead yet, and Victor had done a guy a favor in Europe once, so the case and its contents had been free.

Nicolay used binoculars to look at the house. What was going on? The email that led him here said Marfa was meeting Pyotr, but Pyotr was nowhere in sight. What he did see were three others—two men nearly fifty and one teenager. What the hell was going on?

He wanted to speak to Marfa alone, to tell her what she would do, and to explain how she would do it: the funds were to be moved directly to his account. But the additional men complicated things. If they were working with her, they might very well have to go. The thought made him wish he'd requested a long rifle with a scope; a shotgun would do little from the ridge.

He hated it when a part of his plan needed to change.

When he'd been younger, his confidence never wavered. Who had written the line, "You have youth, confidence, and a job. You have everything"? Hemingway? Nicolay knew, at sixty, he was no longer the man Hemingway described. But he had something Hemingway hadn't considered: anger. Marfa had taken two things from him—his best friend and a great deal of money that he rightfully deserved.

He would get even for Victor.

And he would get what he had coming.

He jacked a round into the chamber of the 12-gauge, tucked the 9mm into his waistband, and started moving tree to tree, edging closer to the house.

1:45 p.m., the Hampton Inn, Reeds

Hammond, Hann, and Ramirez along with Hewitt, Jimenez, and Peyton arrived in one black Suburban and one Border Patrol Expedition. No flashing lights. No sirens. To passersby, they could've been arriving for a late lunch meeting. Except, behind the tinted windows of the Suburban, Ramirez was in the back with his laptop open.

When the Suburban stopped, Hewitt hit the brakes on the green-and-white Expedition. He got out and walked to the FBI vehicle, talked to Hammond for a few minutes, then returned.

"I'm going to the front desk to show some photos," Hewitt said.

"Will the StingRay lead us to the phone?" Peyton said.

"Not to the exact location." Hewitt turned and went into the hotel lobby.

Jimenez watched Hewitt walk away. "Are we going room to room?"

"I don't know," Peyton said, "but if the desk people don't recognize the pictures, there won't be much choice." She could see Hewitt talking to a blond woman at the front desk.

Jimenez looked at the four-story hotel. "Doable, but it'll take a while."

Peyton got out of the Expedition and walked to the Suburban. She opened the back door and slid in.

Ramirez looked surprised to see her. "What's up?"

"You tell me," she said.

"I got a hit on Aleksei Vann's phone."

"Just that one?"

"So far."

"And it's here?"

"Somewhere."

"If we go room to room, it could take forever," Hann said. She took her glasses off and squeezed the bridge of her nose.

Peyton got out of the Suburban and stood thinking.

———

"So where does this leave us?" Peyton said.

Hewitt and Hammond had their people huddled between the vehicles. The sun reflected off the wet street and icy snow, and Peyton wore sunglasses and a ski cap.

"What's bothering you, Peyton?" Hewitt said. "You look impatient."

"This feels like a setup. Only one cell phone? And it's Aleksei's, the expendable one."

"What are you saying?" Hammond said.

"I'm saying, I bet the phone is in one of these garbage cans." She pointed to the receptacles around the parking lot. "They have something to move. It makes sense to draw some of us here."

"I'm getting three phones now," Ramirez said.

"That changes things," Hewitt said. "Sounds like a meeting."

"Let's spread out and go floor by floor, room to room," Hammond said. "Someone stay out here."

"Excuse me."

They turned to see the blond woman from the front desk.

"Agent, may I have a word?"

Hewitt walked to her. She spoke. He nodded, looked at Peyton, and said, "Yes, I'd like to see it." He followed her inside and returned holding a plastic garbage bag.

2:35 p.m., Garrett Station
"Are they legit?" Hewitt asked Ramirez.

Ramirez, Hann, Hammond, Peyton, and Hewitt were in the break room. Three cell phones were on the picnic table.

"Are they actual phones owned by Marfa Tankov, Aleksei Vann, and Ted Donovan? Yes, they appear to be."

"And they didn't lead us to anything," Hewitt said. He was looking at Peyton. "What tipped you off?"

She shrugged. "Just a feeling."

"If you're right," Hann said, "it means they're still in the area."

"You didn't find Michael Donovan's phone?" Peyton asked.

Ramirez shook his head. "And I haven't picked it up yet, either."

"Nicolay Fyodorov's phone?" Hammond asked.

"No," Ramirez said.

Peyton picked up the phones. "Which one is Marfa Tankov's?"

Ramirez pointed.

Peyton tried to access the phone; it was password protected. "Can you open it?" she asked.

Ramirez took it. "Probably. Why? If she planted it for us to find, I'm sure she wiped it."

"Most likely," Peyton said. "But let's leave no stone unturned."

"I get it," Ramirez said. "Give me some time."

3:10 p.m., 12 Higgins Drive
Peyton waved to Margaret Jones, Tommy's bus driver.

"Hi, Peyton," Margaret said through the open driver's side window. "I saw you on CNN this afternoon. You were walking around the Hampton Inn."

Peyton couldn't remember seeing a CNN van, which made sense; the reporter would've flown into Reeds and rented a car. Regardless, a CNN reporter obviously followed them from Garrett Station to Reeds.

"It's finally feeling like spring," Peyton said.

Margaret had been Tommy's bus driver for as long as Peyton could remember. Her husband Bill was his Little League coach.

"Can't talk about it?"

"Not unless you have information for me."

"Wish I did."

"Thanks for driving my son. Tell Bill I say hi."

"You got it," Margaret said and pulled the narrow driver's-side window closed before driving off.

Tommy wore his backpack and a Patriots sweatshirt as they started up the driveway.

"Where's your coat?"

"In my bag." He smiled.

She reached down and squeezed his knee. He jumped and laughed.

"Tickle point," she said. "I know them all. And I'm deadly with them. Where'd you get the sweatshirt?"

"Stone. When I spent the night, it was cold. He gave it to me, said to keep it."

"The other night?" she said. "When we went to his cabin?"

"Yeah. It's pretty cool. I wish we bought a cabin on the lake."

"We'd have to give up the house," she said, "and then you probably wouldn't have your own bathroom. But there are plenty of places for sale."

"Mom, what's wrong?"

She stopped walking and stood stock-still in the center of the driveway, then pulled out her phone. She dialed her real estate agent Kathy St. Pierre.

"Mom, tell me what's wrong."

"Nothing, sweetie. It's just that there are *too many* places for sale."

Kathy answered, and Peyton heard the eagerness in the agent's voice. Unfortunately for her, Peyton wasn't looking for a home to buy.

She was looking for a desperate seller.

———

Fifteen minutes later, she thanked Kathy St. Pierre and turned to Tommy, who was doing homework at the kitchen table.

"I hate to do this again, Tommy."

"I know what you're going to say: Gram is on her way to stay with me."

Her stomach sank. This day, she'd spent time with a seventeen-year-old with only months to live. And here she was leaving her own son— whom she'd seen for all of an hour in the past twenty-four—to go back to work. Worse, he could predict her abandonment.

"That's right, pal. I'm very sorry." She turned and stared out the window over the sink at the snow-covered back lawn.

"It's okay, Mom. I know you work hard. And I know you do it for me."

"Wow, thank you, Tommy. I wasn't expecting that."

"Stone told me some stuff."

She heard the single horn honk in the driveway: her mother Lois's cue that she'd arrived.

"I want to hear about that later, okay?" she said and dashed out the door.

4:15, dirt road near Paradise Court

"You're sure this is it?" Hewitt said, climbing out of the Expedition.

They'd parked at the end of the dirt road and gathered at the back of the huge Ford vehicle. Hewitt took a 12-gauge and pumped a round into the chamber. Peyton felt for her .40 on her right hip. She also took a 12-gauge.

"No," Peyton said. She closed the passenger door quietly. "I'm not sure of anything. But Kathy St. Pierre is the region's busiest realtor, and she rented this house to a man with a Russian accent just a few days ago. And he rented it for only one month."

Using the toe of his boot, Ramirez crushed an ice ball. "Who would rent someone a house for only a month?"

"Someone who's been trying to sell since the damn feds closed the military base and took half the region's population with it."

"I do believe I struck a nerve," Ramirez said.

"When the Cold War ended, Washington closed Loring Air Force Base. The region's economy hasn't been the same since."

Ramirez shook his head. "That was a long time ago."

"My point exactly."

"This political debate is fascinating," Hewitt said, "but I'd like to see if the painting is in the house. Put your earpieces in. We don't know much about these people, so proceed with caution."

"They're Russian mob," Ramirez said.

"They're art thieves," Hewitt said.

"I don't want the painting damaged," Hammond said. "Take it slowly."

They started to walk toward the house. Peyton and Hewitt were on the north side of the road walking up a ridge, Ramirez and Hann were in the woods on the opposite side of the road, and Hammond was walking on the side of the dirt road.

"There's a Camry with Massachusetts plates on it," Hammond said. He felt the hood. "Hood's cold."

"We've got something," Peyton said. "Empty guitar case. It's lined with foam and looks like it held a long gun and a pistol. Tracks lead to the house."

"Wait for us," Ramirez said. "Hann and I are crossing the street."

"This is a road, city boy," Hammond said. "Not a street."

They huddled at the top of the ridge.

Hewitt examined the guitar case. "Foam cutouts are certainly shaped for guns. Whoever was here went tree to tree until they reached the house."

"Looks like they went in the front door," Peyton said and handed the binoculars to Hammond. The sun was dropping, and a late-winter breeze was kicking up.

"Maybe someone got wind of the sale," Hammond said, "and wanted to get the painting before it went underground again."

"Can you see any movement inside the house?" Hewitt asked.

"No," Hammond said. "We need to be closer."

4:17 p.m., Paradise Court

For the first time, Michael was really scared.

The guy had simply appeared at the top of the stairs, holding a shotgun. And when Uncle Ted stood, the guy with the Santa Claus beard just knocked him down—one punch, while keeping the gun leveled on the room. He'd taken the pretty woman's purse and pulled a small handgun from it. Then he sat them in a semicircle in the living room: Dariya and Ted on the sofa, Michael and the woman like bookends in leather chairs.

Michael didn't know who the man was or what he was saying in Russian. But he sensed the tension among the adults, and he could feel sweat on his brow.

"Where's Pyotr?" Nicolay asked Marfa and glanced over his shoulder, guarding against an ambush.

"With my father, if what you say is true, and since you're here I assume it is."

Ted rubbed his jaw. "What's going on, Sonya?"

The big man shook his head. "*Sonya?*" he said in English. Then to Marfa in Russian: "They don't even know your name."

"What's going on?" Dariya said.

"What *is* going on, Nicolay?" Marfa asked.

"You know why I'm here."

"The money?"

"First, the money, yes. You're going to transfer what is owed to me."

"And then?"

"Then I go. And you do whatever you were going to do to these poor ..." He searched for a word, couldn't find it, settled for a headshake. "*Sonya?*" he said again. "That's what the gun in your purse was for, wasn't it?" He turned to Ted and spoke in English again: "She's killed two already—her father and husband. You're next."

"No," Ted said, eyes on Marfa.

"I don't know what you're talking about," she said.

"Pyotr and now these three? And a boy?" He shook his head in disgust. "A boy? You didn't get that from your father."

They were speaking English now, and Michael started to cry.

"No?" Marfa said. "My father never killed anyone? If that's true, we both know who did it all for him."

"You're wrong about all of it."

"And you're a liar."

"No time for this. Where's your computer?"

"I don't have it, Nicolay. I didn't bring it."

"It's on the table over there. I see the red sticker on the front. That's yours. I'm going to bring it to you, and you're going to transfer the money. I have someone watching my account. When he gives me the signal, I leave." He walked backward slowly, the shotgun still leveled at the room. Michael saw the big man glance at the window and do a double take.

"*Nyet! Nyet!*" Nicolay said.

"What's going on?" Ted shouted.

Nicolay ignored him. "I came for two things," he said to Marfa. "One is lost now."

"What?" she asked. "Who is out there?"

Michael could see the rage in the big man's eyes as he took three steps into the center of the room.

"I might lose out, but your father won't," he said and pointed the 12-gauge at the pretty woman.

Michael saw the realization on the woman's face, watched as she desperately pressed herself up and backward, as if trying to scamper over the back of the leather chair.

"*Nyet*," the man said for a third time, this time softly as he shrugged and pulled the trigger.

Peyton heard the blast and sprinted. Hewitt paused to call for backup. Hammond went to the right. Ramirez went straight at the house and reached it first. He went up the front stairs and kicked the door in. A shotgun's blast reverberated, and Peyton saw Ramirez leap to the side of the door and off the stairs.

"Motherfucker!" Ramirez shouted.

"*Are you hit?*" It was Hammond's voice in Peyton's earpiece.

"*No, I'm fucking pissed!*"

"*Assess the situation, Ramirez,*" Hammond said. "*Stand down and assess.*"

Peyton kept running, circling to the rear of the house. The basement door was open. She entered and went to the stairwell. She reached for the wall switch and killed the stairwell light. She crouched as she started up the stairs, the 12-gauge leveled in front of her. It was a pump-action. She wished she had a semiautomatic.

"*I see someone in the window!*" It was Ramirez's voice. "*I'm taking the shot!*"

"*How many guns are there?*" Hewitt said. "*Do you have a visual?*"

"*I see someone,*" Ramirez said. "*I'm taking the shot.*"

"*Assess the situation, Ramirez!*" Hammond said.

Peyton heard breaking glass and a shotgun's boom, then a scream from inside the house. She thought the voice was Ted Donovan's.

"*Hold your fire unless fired upon!*" Hewitt said.

Peyton was halfway up the stairs when the door flew open. Nicolay Fyodorov took two steps, his head down to see where he was going in the dark, the shotgun at his side. He looked up and froze.

"Drop it!" Peyton yelled, her 12-gauge leveled at his chest.

"I lose," he said quietly.

"Drop it!" she yelled again.

"No prison for me." He smiled and raised his shotgun.

She pulled the trigger.

In the confined area, the blast shook the house as if struck by a car. Nicolay ran backward before landing on his back at the top of the steps. His shotgun clattered down the stairs, landing on the basement floor.

Peyton took three more steps toward the open door.

"*Freeze!*" The voice was Sally Hann's. "*I said, Freeze!*"

A second figure appeared in the doorway.

Peyton pointed the shotgun at the figure. Ted Donovan stopped short.

Dariya peered over Ted's shoulder. "Run!" he said and shoved Ted. Then he saw Peyton and turned back.

"On your knees!" Hann said. "There's nowhere to go and too much bloodshed already. Get down!"

Peyton watched Dariya crouch. At the top of the stairs, she looked around the room. The woman in the photo Hewitt had shown her was no longer recognizable. Part of her face was missing; there was blood and brain matter on the wall behind the leather chair. Dariya was on his hands and knees, vomiting, and speaking rapidly in Russian.

"He's saying something about a sick wife, about using his son." Hann pulled him onto his knees and cuffed him. "He says he wants to die."

Across the room, Hammond was talking to Steven Ramirez near an overturned loveseat beneath a broken window. Hammond was whispering but waving his hands. Ramirez's face was red. Peyton saw Adidas sneakers and blue jeans protruding from behind the loveseat.

"Who's that?" she asked and moved closer.

"Is he ...?" Ted said. He forgot he was supposed to kneel. He stood and moved closer to his nephew. "Is he dead?"

As Ted shuffled toward the overturned loveseat, Hewitt was next to him all the time, his. 40 drawn, an arm on his forearm.

Ted got to the loveseat, peered around it, and immediately vomited.

"He was just trying to jump out the window!" Ted shrieked. *"You fucking killed him! He had no gun! Now he's gone!"*

Peyton heard Ramirez say, "The window broke, and he started out. I thought he was going to shoot. It was a good shooting."

"He never cleared the window," Peyton said. "Mike asked for your visual."

"It was a good shooting," Ramirez said again.

Hammond looked at Ted. "Where's the artwork?"

"We don't have it. Michael took it. We don't know where."

"There is no weapon near him," Peyton said. "The boy was unarmed."

Ramirez looked at Hammond. "It was a good fucking shooting, right Frank?"

Peyton looked from Hewitt to Hammond. They locked eyes. Then she walked outside.

9:30 p.m., Garrett Station

This time only Hewitt, Hammond, Hann, and Peyton were at the break room table. Steven Ramirez was meeting with state police officials, including Stone, to discuss the shooting of Michael Donovan.

"So what are we left with?" Hewitt asked.

The whiteboard had changed. "Dariya" and "Ted" had lines through them. "Michael," "Marfa," and "Nicolay" each had the letter D next to their names.

"Those two"—Hammond pointed at the names *Ted* and *Dariya* on the board—"are facing federal charges, and everyone else is dead."

"Nicolay wanted to die," Peyton said. Her interview with state police officials had lasted thirty minutes. "I've never been forced to ..." She couldn't find the words.

"Help someone kill themselves?" Hewitt finished her sentence.

"Yes," she said. "He said he wasn't going to prison. And then he smiled."

Hammond shook his head. "There are no winners here."

"Is Ramirez coming back?" Hann asked.

"He might be facing a murder charge," Hammond said.

"Everybody loses," Peyton said, "and we don't have the painting to show for it."

Hammond nodded. "We don't have any of the missing pieces." He was drinking Diet Pepsi. "The Gardner Museum called for an update. Both Ted and Dariya say the same thing: Michael took one painting and hid it. They don't know where. And I had to tell the museum the other works might be lost."

"Ted told me that same story in the truck on the way here," Peyton said. "I believe him."

"If he had the painting," Hewitt said, "now would be the time for him to use it."

"These guys don't have it," Hammond said.

Sally Hann rubbed her eyes. Then she pointed to the board. "So three people are dead and two others are going away for a long time.

And the painting stays lost, after coming this close? We've spent twenty-five years looking and it stays lost?"

"Maybe that's its destiny," Hewitt said. "Maybe it's just fate."

Peyton didn't say anything.

"Why would Michael take it from the uncle?" Hewitt said.

"No one knows, but it's part of some tough conversations I'm having with the boy's parents," said Hammond.

"Dear God," Peyton said. "I can only imagine. Who broke the news to them about their son?"

"Stone," Hewitt said.

"That's shitty," she said.

"The worst part of being a state cop."

"What happens to Aleksei," Peyton asked, "if his father is in prison?"

"Dariya's son?" Hammond shook his head. "That's way beyond my pay grade."

"I think Bill Hillsdale will be very involved in that decision," Hewitt said.

"The kids were pawns in all this," Peyton said. "One is planted here by his father, that father goes to prison, and now the boy probably gets sent home to care for his ill mother. And, for whatever reason, Michael tried to prevent the sale of the painting and ended up dead."

The room fell silent.

"Nothing more is happening tonight," Hammond said. "Go home, everyone. Get some rest."

Hewitt was nodding.

"I can't thank you all enough, especially you guys." Hammond pointed at Peyton and Hewitt. "You sort of fell into this shit storm, and it produced two arrests and not much else."

Peyton stood. At the door, she said, "Mike, can I ask a favor?"

"Sure. What?"

"I haven't been much of a mother the past few days. Is anyone using the snowmobile tomorrow?"

THIRTEEN

Saturday, March 15, near the Canadian border, 8 a.m.

SHE HADN'T SLEPT WELL. She woke once from a dream about a ship in a storm. Aleksei and Michael were sleeping in the center of the ship as waves crashed over the sides. The men aboard the ship stood at the sides of the deck watching the waves. Now she was on the back of the Arctic Cat while Tommy drove them down the trail.

"Not too fast, Tommy," she said, trying to sound relaxed.

He laughed.

The speedometer was bouncing near forty.

"Okay," she said, "turn up here. Let's head back toward town."

Tourist season in Aroostook County, Maine, fell during the winter, when the region's 2,300 miles of snowmobile trails were used. It wasn't uncommon to find the parking lots at the Hampton Inn and the Reeds Inn and Convention Center full of out-of-state licence plates.

Tommy turned and passed a sign that read MCCLUSKEY'S POTATO PROCESSING. SNOWMOBILE AT YOUR OWN RISK. Kyle McCluskey, she thought, what a guy—*use my land, but if you get hurt on it, I don't want to know.*

"Mom, can we stop?"

"Sure. You okay?"

"Too much hot chocolate," he said.

"Find a straightaway," she said, "and pull off the trail."

He did. They were a mile or so from McCluskey's Processing Plant.

"Never stop on the trail," she said. "Too many people go too fast and can't stop or turn."

She'd seen enough accidents where someone traveling sixty miles an hour had hit something on a trail—a snowmobile or even a moose. The worst accident scene she'd been to had involved two snowmobiles colliding head-on.

"Pick a tree," she said.

She watched him walk around in the snow, glad they had the day together. She couldn't help but think about Davey Bolstridge— seven years older than Tommy and already at the end of his life. She'd interviewed hundreds, maybe even thousands of people over the years. But his interview would stay with her a long, long time.

"Someone might see me," he said. "Can we walk deeper into the woods?"

"Okay, Mr. Modest. Follow me."

"What's that sound?" Tommy said.

It wasn't a snowmobile; she knew that much. She knew where they were.

"Hold on," she said, thinking of her conversation with Davey Bolstridge. "Wait a minute. Tommy, follow me."

"Where are we going?"

"There's a hidden building out here. The generator was supposed to be off. And I just had a thought."

"What do you mean?" Tommy struggled to walk through the snow. "What's it hidden for? What's in it?"

"Nothing that would interest you. But maybe something else."

"What are you talking about?" Tommy said.

Peyton looked down at a large track that packed the snow. It looked like a toboggan track but was much wider. It stopped at the door of the shack.

"I think we just—" She didn't finish her sentence.

She heard the generator running inside. Tommy walked to the back of the structure. She followed him.

"Privacy, Mom."

"I changed your diapers."

"That was a long time ago."

She reached up and tugged the rope, releasing the front door.

"What's that?"

"Just do your business," she said, and walked to the front door.

Inside, she saw the generator running and tracks on the plywood floor where someone had entered. She saw a chair with dried footprints on it. Then she spotted the dried tracks crossing the floor, and stopping at the edge of the ceiling loft. Someone had stood on the chair.

"Holy shit," she said aloud.

"Mom, I heard that!"

"Sorry, Tommy."

She pulled the chair to the edge of the loft, thinking about her visit to Davey Bolstridge's house.

Is there any place he might go?

Not really, just the shack in the woods. But you know all about that.

"What are you doing on that chair?" Tommy asked. "What's up there?"

"You're not going to believe it," she said and took out her cell phone to call Hewitt and Hammond.

EPILOGUE

Thursday, June 19, 3:10 p.m., 12 Higgins Drive

PEYTON WAS WEARING SHORTS and a blouse and new sandals she'd ordered online.

"Tough day?" Stone said.

They were standing at the end of the driveway.

"Memorials are always bad," she said.

Stone took her hand in his own. "They're worse when it's a kid. How were the Donovans?"

"I stood in the back. I don't think they wanted to see me."

"Ramirez goes to trial early next year."

"He should. I spoke to Aleksei, though."

"I thought he was going home," Stone said.

"No, Bohana talked about adopting him. It's in the works."

"What about Aleksei's mother?"

"We didn't get that far," Peyton said. "Maybe I can check in on him sometime."

"I think Bohana will realize you had nothing to do with her son's death."

"You're not a mother. I'd blame everyone and everything if I was in that situation."

"I don't think you would."

"You're not a mother," she said again.

It was seventy-seven degrees. She was looking at the driveway. Sand and salt had been left from the winter. "One of us needs to sweep the sand off the driveway."

"I specialize in back rubs," Stone said, "not sweeping."

"*Specialize?*" she said. "I've had your back rubs. Not sure I'd say they're special."

"Ouch." He smiled. "Here comes the bus."

Tommy got off the bus and tossed his backpack in the air. "Last day of school!"

"Now what?" Stone said.

"Fun stuff," Tommy said.

"Like what?" Peyton picked up his backpack.

Tommy took her hand and walked between them as they started up the driveway. "I don't know. I was hoping Stone could be with us a lot this summer."

"I'm sure he will be," Peyton said.

"I was thinking," Tommy said, "maybe he could spend the weekend."

"I'd like that," Stone said.

Inside, Tommy ran up to his room.

Stone turned to Peyton, "The weekend? It's a step."

"It's a big step," Peyton said. Then she moved closer and kissed him hard on the mouth. "Now about those overrated back rubs."

ABOUT THE AUTHOR

D.A. Keeley (United States) has published widely in the crime-fiction genre and is the author of eight other novels, as well as short stories and essays. In addition to being a teacher and department chair at a boarding school and a member of the Mystery Writers of America, Keeley writes a biweekly post for the blog *Type M for Murder*. You can learn more about the author and the series via Twitter @DAKeeleyAuthor or at www.amazon.com/author/dakeeley.